crossing
the
line

lauren baratz-logsted

crossing the line

the line

RED DRESS INK
™

First edition July 2004

CROSSING THE LINE

A Red Dress Ink novel

ISBN 0-373-25062-2

www.RedDressInk.com

Printed in U.S.A.

In memory of Douglas DelVecchio,
cousin, teacher and friend

ACKNOWLEDGMENTS

Acknowledgments for second novels should be briefer than those for first novels (which are written with the kitchen-sink sense that you'll never get another such chance again). In keeping with that, then...

Thanks to my editor, Margaret O'Neill Marbury, who is as bright as she is beautiful and tall; to the entire RDI team, and especially Tania Charzewski, for patience above and beyond; and to my agent, Don Maass, who is equal measures of brilliant and kind.

Special thanks to those who helped me get right whatever I got right: Nicki and Phil Thomas, for making sure my British English was British enough (any inaccuracies that still stand are wholly my own fault); Jim Wallace, for knowing a lot more about Halloween than I did; and Randall Liss, for knowing far more than I will ever know about history.

Thanks, as always, to family and friends, for patience and for not killing me.

And thanks, also as always, to everyone who has been naughty and everyone who has been nice. Somehow, it all helps.

Still December

"Tolkien," I said, "I have something to tell you."

Yes, this is where we had all left off: me, Jane Taylor, assistant editor in a publishing firm, having just faked nine months of pregnancy, just in case you need to know that about me, standing on the doorstep of the man I was in love with and who I'd recently rejected for the second time—Tolkien Donald, Scotland Yard, C.I.D. (medium build, medium height, dirty-blond, slightly receding hair, slightly darker mustache)—with my fake baby (all cloth) still strapped underneath my clothes and a real baby (which I'd just found abandoned on a church doorstep) in my arms.

I don't know about you, but my own suspicions were high that this was going to be a sticky situation to get out of.

"You have a baby," said Tolkien, awe in his eyes.

"Yes," I said, joyfully.

"Here," he said, taking my arm. "Come inside. It's too cold for you and the baby to just stand out there on the doorstep."

He led us into what passed for a living room in his life. Even though it had been months since I'd been there, nothing had changed—meaning that there was little evidence of anyone really doing any *living* there, meaning that the room was still just as "bachelor-y" as Tolkien had once upon a time warned me it would be: no discernible design scheme, only some serious stereo equipment. As a decorative concession to the holiday swirling all around us in the city, he had a half-empty bottle of holiday ale on his utilitarian wooden coffee table. From the CD player, I could hear Bing Crosby softly crooning about the white Christmas we had in fact achieved that year.

I looked at the clock on the wall, a glass-and-chrome time-piece that was so nondecorative it could have been in a tube station: not even 3:00 a.m. on Christmas Eve. I'd left my flat at 2:00 a.m. and in less than an hour's time I'd found a baby and was now visiting the love of my former life.

"You have a baby," he said again, still awed.

"Yes," I said, still joyful.

"But you're still pregnant."

Now we were getting to the less joyful part.

"No, not really," I said.

"You mean to tell me… What, Jane? What exactly *do* you mean to tell me?"

"This baby is mine," I said.

Well, the baby *was* technically mine; finders keepers and all that.

I held out the bundle in my arms, so that he could take a closer look, which he did.

He made some of those cooing noises people always make at new babies, but I must say, coming from him, they sounded genuine.

Still smiling down at the baby, he said, "I don't think so, Jane."

"Whyever not?"

"Well, for starters, this baby is black."

Well, there was that.

"Tolkien," I said, "I have something to tell you."

"Excuse me for being a stickler, but didn't we just do that part already?"

"Fine." I sighed. "Fine, fine, fine."

I handed him the baby, then I lifted the skirt of my long dress and did one of those squidgying-around moves that schoolgirls in the locker room make when trying to remove their bras without taking off their clothes, but instead I was taking off my cloth baby. I doubt I looked the coolest thing, I'll grant you, dress hiked up over my hips, bent slightly forward to undo the clasp at my waist.

There!

Tolkien tore his eyes away from the baby—well, who could blame him for his reluctance? She was beautiful—in time to see the skirt of my dress resettle itself over my now slim frame. I thought of how I must look to him: my spiky short black hair even more disheveled than usual from the night's adventures; my brown eyes hoping for a forgiveness that would probably never come.

"Only you, Jane," he said softly.

"How's that?" I asked.

"Only you could figure out a way to both have a baby and get your figure back when exactly nine months are up."

I shrugged. "I'm a bit of a Houdini, aren't I?"

"It's not funny."

"No. I suspect not."

We spoke in the same instant.

Him: "Are you going to tell me…?"

Me: "Do you want to know…?"

"I'm not sure," he said, and I could see he wasn't. This man who was the living embodiment of steadiness was shaken.

"I'm scared," I said, and I realized that I was. While my shenanigans—well, okay, my *slightly sociopathic behavior,* if you will—of the past nine months might be observed with humor by those observing from afar, to those up close and personal, to those I loved best in the world, my behavior had been quite harmful.

Once upon a time—about nine months or so ago, if you want to be technical—I'd briefly believed myself to be pregnant. In my overly enthusiastic state, I'd told everybody about it—my best friend; my family; the people I worked with at Churchill & Stewart, a London publishing firm where I was Assistant Editor; and Trevor, the man I lived with and who I believed to be the father of my baby. Then, as quickly as you can say, "This baby needs a nappy change," I'd discovered I wasn't pregnant at all. Me, being me, I couldn't tell everybody I'd made a mistake. Since Trevor hadn't been too upset about the pregnancy, and since I'd fallen in love with the idea of being pregnant, I endeavored to get pregnant. But when that didn't work, one thing led to another—some of the things rather rational, like a book contract to tell the story of my fake-pregnancy adventures; some of the things irrational, like me being me—and before I knew it, nine months of impersonating being a pregnant person had flown by.

And then I'd found this baby. I'd actually seen a huddled figure abandon the baby on the steps of a stone church, although I hadn't realized that was what I was seeing in the moment I was seeing it.

But in the meantime, in the nine months between thinking I was pregnant and finding the baby, I'd lied to everybody who'd ever cared about me and everybody who didn't. I'd even told Tolkien, who I'd met and fallen in love with after lying to and losing Trevor, that I couldn't marry him when he'd asked me, because I hadn't wanted to give up my charade.

Who knew what deep and lasting damage I had done? Even I could see that it might be irreparable.

Then Tolkien did the bravest thing. Tentatively, baby still cradled in the crook of his arm, neck perfectly supported as if he at least knew what he was doing, he reached out, took my hand in his.

"I'll listen, Jane," he said. "I can't promise you anything. I may never be able to promise you anything ever again. But I will listen."

So I explained everything to him, all the little details. About how I'd originally thought I was pregnant, while still living with Trevor, and how I'd told everybody and then wasn't. About how I'd figured I could just fake it in the beginning, you know, until the real thing came along, and how it didn't. About how I'd made up an obstetrician, but made the mistake of selecting a real and well-known obstetrician, and had to replace him with a made-up midwife/tarot-card reader. About how my best friend David, an ex-Israeli fighter pilot turned bistro owner, and his partner to whom he was now married, Christopher, had basically egged me on (okay, they didn't really). About how, on the same night I met him, the night I knew that I had met the man of my dreams, my other lifelong dream came true—an editor at a rival publishing firm, Alice Simms from Quartet Books Limited, had upon learning of my scheme to impersonate a pregnant woman for nine months, offered me a contract to write my accounting of the events in a book (*The Cloth Baby,* due out in about ten months, but I suppose I shouldn't be plugging my book right at this exact moment), fulfilling my dream of being a published writer. About how ultimately even that alone would not have kept me from saying "yes" when he'd asked me to marry him. About how it had all been because of…

"Dodo."

"Dodo?"

"Dodo," I said again, referring to my beautiful, older and terminally unmarried boss, who'd been born Lana Lane.

"I've never met her," he pointed out.

"True."

"I've never met anyone in your life."

"You haven't missed much," I said, thinking specifically of my mother and sister and most of the people from work.

"Well, except for David and Christopher—"

"Aren't they great?"

"—who I only met because they were the only two people besides me who were allowed to see you skinny, apparently."

"Er, right."

"And, uh—" he squinched his eyes together, thumb and forefinger going to bridge of nose in a combined gesture that made me suspect that I was giving him a headache "—I believe you were about to tell me, yes, how it was somehow Dodo's fault that you were unable to come clean with me and tell the truth so that maybe we'd have some insane chance at a future?"

"Well, yes, of course, you see—"

Just then, the baby woke up. And, no, I didn't pinch her to wake her up right when I needed a distraction.

Thankfully, whoever abandoned her had thought to leave a single bottle filled with formula in the basket, plus a spare can and a few nappies. We'd need to stock up again before long, but at least the bottle I'd put in her mouth bought us a few minutes.

It was a her, by the way. I'd finally sussed that fact out.

I sat down on a bare-bones sofa that would have been perfectly at home in a university dorm, rather than the flat of a man in his thirties, and felt Tolkien sit down next to me.

I watched the baby take the bottle between her perfect lips. She was so beautiful. It was easier to look at her and talk than to look at Tolkien and talk. When I looked at her, it was impossible not to smile, no matter how sad the thought of the pain I must be causing him might make me.

"It wouldn't be fair for me to say that it was Dodo's *fault,* per se. Rather, it was that I knew how much she'd always wanted a baby, how certain she was that she'd never have one of her own, how her relationships with other women have always been so strained because of her beauty, meaning that it was unlikely that anyone else would ever share a pregnancy with her, and she came so *alive* with my pregnancy, she was so supportive of me, so excited about it, so thrilled to be a part, that I just couldn't—"

"—break her heart," he finished softly.

I met his eyes, smiling through the sadness of all of my spectacular losses and the bitter knowledge that whatever had been lost had been my fault.

I bit my lip. "Do you understand?" I asked.

He shook his head: No. "I'm trying, Jane," he said, "God knows, I'm trying—"

This time it was me, reaching my hand out for his, twining my own fingers around those fingers that I loved best in the world. "It's okay, really," I said, "because I *do* understand. How could you still want or love me after all that's happened?"

He didn't answer that.

"So," he asked instead, "what are you going to do now?"

His question took me by surprise.

"Why, I'm going to keep her, of course. You?"

His answer took me by surprise.

"Well, I suppose that, somehow, I'll have to help you."

"You…?"

"I'm guessing you've already got a name picked out."

"Emma."

"Of course."

January (finally!), New Year's Day, afternoon

The only way to come clean with everyone you've lied to, and if you've lied to nearly everyone in your life, is to come clean all at once.

So what did I do?

I threw a party, a New Year's Day party, to launch my new life.

There was method to my party planning, of course. The way I figured it, the odds were that my guests would be too hungover from the night before to give me too much of a hard time about the finer details.

I sent out invitations, announcing Emma's arrival in the world, to family and friends.

It was going to be a lot of people to have in my living/dining area, which was technically two rooms but really only one, so people were going to have to eat their snacks buffet and if everyone wanted to sit at once, some would have to sit on the floor. The green party ware and napkins I'd laid out were good enough to complement the leaf-green, peach and mauve that predominated my living space, but the red I'd laid out with it kind of clashed. Still, I was hoping a leftover holiday spirit would help, and as I set things on the table, I caught sight of my wilting single-person's Christmas tree in the corner. Oh, well, I shrugged. Hopefully, the Christmas trimmings would make my guests feel more benevolently Christian and that would keep them from feeding me to the lions.

The "nearly everyone" I'd lied to included my mother and my sister Sophie, my relationships with neither ever having been what one might term "good"; Dodo; Louise, the assistant editor of Dodo's greatest rival at the firm; Constance, our tiny former receptionist, now Dodo's assistant what with me on leave, who was possessed of an overenthusiasm for what she now called New New Age (old New Age in her mind being too much your mother's brand of Zen); Minerva from Publicity, with her harlequin eyeglasses and her yellow-red beehive hairdo that was only ever going to move if one day France attacked; and Stan from Accounting (who really did deserve to be lied to). I wasn't going to worry about explaining things to my downstairs neighbors, the Marcuses. They already thought I was nuts, so who cared what false assumptions they might make? One night I'd gone out nine months pregnant, the next time they saw me I had a baby: done.

As for David and Christopher, they had enjoyed their Greek honeymoon so much two months previous, that I'd arrived home Christmas morning, after finding the baby and seeing Tolkien, to a note from David saying that they'd impulsively closed the restaurant to return there for a week and wouldn't be back until somewhere around January 2. This worked in my favor because I wasn't ready right away that first week to share Emma or deal with questions and it would have been hard to hide a new baby from my best friend, particularly since my best friend lived upstairs. Still, I'd dropped them a line to say that I had "big news" for them when they got back—although they would need to come back soon, if they wanted the hoi that had been polloi-ing their Covent Garden bistro, Meat! *Meat!! MEAT!!!,* to remember to keep polloi-ing.

So, my cast of characters was set.

The only problem, as they each arrived, was:

From Mother, patting champagne coif: "I *don't* think this could be Trevor's baby," referring to my long-gone ex-fiancé.

From sister Sophie, fingering straight blond hair to prove her point: "She doesn't really look like anybody from *our* side of the family."

And from the smashingly beautiful blond woman who had good cause to be called Dodo: "You do realize your daughter is black, Jane…don't you?"

"Yes, Dodo," I said, "I did know that. But thanks for pointing it out just in case."

"Do you think you all might give Jane and Emma some room, please?"

And just where did that voice come from?

Why, Tolkien, of course.

For I had indeed invited one other person not previously mentioned on my guest list; well, technically he *wasn't* a guest, having helped me out so much of late, sleeping over every night to help me with Emma.

True, there were probably better times—really, any single one would do—when it would have been more appropriate for him to meet my friends and family for the first time. But I just couldn't face this group all on my own, and David and Christopher were unavailable.

They were all so stunned by Emma. She was like the elephant in the corner that no one would talk about, so they began talking about anything but.

Stan from Accounting said, adjusting his steel glasses, "Did everyone read the new Smythe? *God,* it's a dog if I've ever seen one."

"Well," said Constance, winding her finger around a strand of short red hair, "you know, dog is God spelled backwards, so maybe it's a good omen?"

"We'll just throw a ton of money at it," said Minerva from Publicity, settling herself into the sofa. "That'll fix it."

"Not my money," said Stan from Accounting.

"We'll just spin it as the latest thing," said Minerva. "We'll say it's a cross between John Grisham and Sophie Kinsella, but set in Paraguay. That ought to do it. People'll get so confused they won't know what the hell they're reading."

"But it's not like any of those things you just mentioned," objected Dodo.

"Well, now, that's the beauty of it, isn't it, luv?" said Minerva. "If it *was* that, who the hell would ever buy it?"

"Then why will they buy it if we *say* it's that?" demanded Louise, whom I happened to know trimmed her blond hair with a Sabatier kitchen knife.

"Because they'll get curious, won't they?" said Minerva.

"Is it still called Paraguay?" asked Constance, a confused frown furrowing her pierced eyebrow.

"'Course it is." Minerva again.

"But are you quite certain of that?" insisted Constance. "You know, they do keep changing the countries' names over there all the time."

"No, they don't," said Minerva.

"Yes, they do," said Constance.

"No, Constance, they really don't," said Minerva. "You're confusing it with Africa."

"You mean Paraguay's not in Africa?" asked Constance.

"Nope," said Minerva. "Last time I checked, it was still in South America."

"Ah," said Constance, with great understanding. Then: "Are you sure about that?"

I ticked off hair color around me, not counting Tolkien and Stan from Accounting, because men don't count: blond, blond, blond, blond, yellow-red, red. Hey, didn't Constance used to have black hair? Once upon a time, dark hair color was considered the most common, although I'll admit my own raven was an extreme shade of dark. But still, now, everywhere I looked— except in the mirror—it was all light, light, light. Was everyone else coloring theirs?

Meanwhile, my mother was asking Sophie, "Where's Baby Jack today?"

She was referring to Sophie's own baby, now nearly four months old and never far from her side.

"I left him with Tony," said Sophie, referring to her husband. "I don't know. When Jane called us all here, I just had this funny feeling..."

"What kind of funny feeling?" asked my mother.

"Oh, you know," said Sophie, "the kind of funny feeling I get whenever Jane's involved in something. I was pretty certain that, whatever it was, it wouldn't be something I'd want to be exposing Baby Jack to."

"You know," said Constance, tapping her lower lip, "it might be an original idea if, instead of throwing money at the bad Smythe, if we instead tried promoting something good for a change."

"You're joking, right?" Louise raised her eyebrows.

"Actually," I said, disbelieving all the while that I was actually about to agree for once with something Constance had said, "Constance might just have—"

"Jane!" shouted my mother, suddenly. "Are you ever going to tell us just what the bloody hell is going on here?"

"I asked you all to keep it down, please," said Tolkien.

In a whisper, my mother said, "And who the bloody hell are you?"

I was about to answer, "He's…" but then I stopped. What could I say? The explanation of who he was—the man I'd been in love with, still was in love with, the man who had been in love with me once and who I hoped would one day be in love with me again, but whom I'd mistakenly let slip away in favor of pursuing my own previous mad scheme—well, to tell that would feel like putting the cart before the horse, since they still didn't know where Emma came from or about the fake pregnancy.

But before I could stumble any further, Tolkien saved me.

"I'm her great good friend," said Tolkien, "that's who I am."

"And your name is…?" asked my mother.

"Tolkien Donald," he said, "at your service."

"Hah," said my mother. "Pull the other."

Tolkien smiled. "If you like."

"And if you were going to pull the other," said my mother, "what would you say?"

"Well, now," said Tolkien, "I'd add Scotland Yard, C.I.D., of course."

"Of course," said my mother, with a smile that showed she was convinced he was a loon.

"Just for fun," said Tolkien. He pulled out his ID, flashed it for her.

"Huh," she sniffed, embarrassed.

"Huh," he sniffed, smiling.

"But that doesn't answer the central question here," she said.

"Which is…?" he prompted.

She looked over his shoulder at me. "This really isn't Trevor's baby, is it?"

"Er, no," I said.

She chewed on that for a long bit.

Meanwhile, everyone watched her chew.

Finally: "Is it your baby, at least?" she asked me tentatively, as if my answer might be to slap her.

"Er, no," I said, reluctantly, feeling as though I *were* slapping her, as though I were slapping them all.

Naturally, people wanted to know where Emma had come from.

"I found her on a church doorstep," I said.

"Well, now, that's convenient," snorted Stan from Accounting. "It's real *deus ex machina,* if you ask me."

"It's a real baby who needed care, if you ask me," I countered, nettled.

"If only she'd have been white," Stan mused, "you could have gone on fooling us indefinitely, eh?"

"I don't know what I'd have done if she were white," I answered honestly.

"Let me get this straight," said Dodo, genuine sadness in her eyes. "You were never pregnant in the first place?"

I shook my head.

"Ohh, *crap!*" said Constance. "Don't tell me there's no Madame Zora!"

"I'm afraid not."

Constance is nothing, if not resilient. She brightened, nearly as bright as her day's selection of contact lenses, which on this particular occasion were somewhere in the metallic pink range. "But he-e-e-e-y! It really would be brilliant if there were such a thing as a tarot-card reading midwife, wouldn't it? Why, such a person would really rake in a fortune, don't you think?"

"No and no," said Minerva from Publicity, helping herself to more of the noxious cheese straw thingies I'd put out because, well, I did know this crowd.

"I'll second that," said Louise, "and I'd also like to add that, no, I don't think you think at all."

"Straight-haired slut," said Constance. Apparently, being Dodo's new assistant, which put her on the same Churchill & Stewart ladder rung as Louise, had gone to Constance's tiny little head.

"Weird-eyed illiterate," countered Louise. Then Louise did a horse-shaking-off-gnats gesture that caused me to empathize with her for once (Constance does have that effect on people) and said, "But that's not the point!"

"The point being…?" I asked, still empathizing and thus wanting to be helpful.

"The point is *you!*" Louise j'accused me. "The point is *you* and this wool-over-our-eyes thing you did to all of us these past nine months. Please, tell us all, Jane, what was *that* all about?"

No longer feeling at all empathetic, I was tempted to call her a "straight-haired slut" myself, but it wasn't the time. Everyone in the room had closed in on me, save Tolkien rocking Emma in the corner, and they all wanted answers.

Well, could I really blame them?

"It all started with me really thinking that I *was* pregnant…" I began.

And, to reverse what they usually say, I went on as I should have begun so long ago: I told the truth. True, it was *my* truth, but do we have to quibble on everything?

"…So you see," I wound down, after telling them about the false-alarm pregnancy, the attempted pregnancy, the false-through-and-through pregnancy, and everything else—well, except for the book contract and who Tolkien really was, not wanting to be judged on the first and not wanting to have the sanctity spoiled around the second, although God knows I'd done my own share of sanctity-spoiling, "you really could say that it all began with a tiny mistake—"

"*A mistake?*" fishwifed my mother.

"Yes, a mistake," I said.

Everyone else seemed at a loss, confused really.

"A mistake?" questioned Sophie.

I realized that I had to think of something quick. Unable to think of anything better, I spoke the first thing I thought of:

"Okay, I had a bad day."

Well, isn't that the source of over half the world's problems? Someone somewhere has a bad day, and before you know it, some country's at war or there's cyanide in your painkiller or Tom Cruise is doing another running scene in a new movie. I mean, it's nearly always about *someone's* bad day.

Leave it to Louise, however, to adopt the bitch approach. "You. Had. A. Bad. *Day???*"

I actually cringe-winced. "You make it sound so…unlikely."

It may not have sounded like much of an alibi, it may not have satisfied the crowd I was working, but to my way of thinking, it was a sight better than explaining what a small-minded person I'd been. The kind of person who wants something more because everyone else is doing it than the thing itself.

Back to...Christmas Day, early-ish

Nobody ever tells you how hard it will be to bring a new baby home.

In the early hours of Christmas Day, still dark out, Tolkien and I had brought Emma back to my flat.

First, of course, we made a stop. Using the same Scotland Yard C.I.D. ID he would later flash at my mother, he did his Scotland Yard thing to get a very tired and cranky shopkeeper to open up just long enough for us to get what we'd need for Emma's immediate comfort: bottles, formula and what seemed to me like a ridiculous amount of nappies.

"Will she use these in a lifetime?" I asked.

"She'll use them in *a day,*" Tolkien answered.

Tolkien's answer made me recognize how little I knew about what I was getting myself into.

I've always felt that there are certain names that should be permanently retired—Adolf, Jesus, certainly—names that have served the world sufficiently in one shot, for good or ill. Even though Tolkien, to my knowledge, had never been used as a first name before, I would have said that it was a name, so unique, that it should be retired as well. Well, *I* hadn't given him the name. Apparently, though, Tolkien's parents had not been of similar mind. Former hippies who had jumped on the groovy bandwagon late in life, they'd renamed Tolkien when he was small, from his original name of Donald John to Tolkien Donald, in homage to the man they credited with turning them on to a more psychedelic life; don't ask why they then made what had been his first name his last name. Of course, since they were no longer into doing 'shrooms or lighting incense themselves, Tolkien's parents were more conventional now. But by the time they were ready to trade in love beads for matching Gucci watches, having traded in being hippies for being in the bond market, he was used to it and had never changed it back.

At any rate, when we got Emma back to my place, I finally asked the question that I should have asked hours ago, the question I was afraid to ask.

"Tolkien, if I were a normal person, what would I be doing right now?"

He smiled gently. "If you were a normal law-abiding citizen, you'd be required to bring her to a police station."

"Oh."

"But, speaking in the most barely technical sense, you've already done that. You brought her to me."

"What would happen then?"

"She'd be taken to a hospital to get checked over."

"Shouldn't we do that? We should do what's right by her."

He took her from my arms, gently laid her on the sofa, undid the blanket, examined her.

"Ten fingers and toes, no signs of harm whatsoever, fabulous color—she's fine."

"That's a relief. And then? What would happen to her next?"

"Social Services would need to be called. They're responsible for abandoned children as soon as they become aware of them. They'd place her in foster care, under the assumption that the mother might eventually show up."

"I see."

He moved to the phone, dialed.

"What are you doing?" I asked, alarmed.

"Shh," he said, "it's ringing…. Hello, this is Tolkien Donald here, Scotland Yard, C.I.D. I've got a situation here with an abandoned baby."

"Tolkien!"

He went on, ignoring me. "Anyway, I'm glad that Mr. Triplecorn is on call 'til after Boxing Day, but he doesn't appear to be picking up. The baby's doing perfectly fine, as it happens, so why don't we leave this one on hold until everyone has had a chance to enjoy their Christmas hols? I don't mind taking care of her until then and I'll get back with you in a few days. Merry Christmas."

He rang off.

"I was talking to a machine," he said, and I felt my heart rate begin its return to normal. "The main office is closed for the holidays. They have someone on call, but…"

I looked at him. He really was the most amazing man.

"Are you going to get into a massive amount of trouble for this?" I asked.

"Probably." He shrugged.

"Then why are you doing it?"

"Partly, I'm doing it for you."

"And the other part?"

"For Emma, of course. Things would go exactly as I said—police station, hospital, the Social, foster care. She'd be getting juddered around from place to place over a forty-eight-hour period. Sure, people would be friendly enough, maybe they'd even rock her occasionally, give her a moment of love here and there. But she'd be getting processed, a problem to be solved. It wouldn't be like this. And she deserves this, not bureaucracy."

I carried her around for the longest time, whispering to her.

"This is where I sit when I'm writing," I said. "I'm a funny lady, you know, don't always get credit for that, but I'm a funny writer, too. This is the window I look out of when I'm thinking. That's another thing people don't think I do much of, but I can assure you I do think. This is where I cook. Well, I don't really ever cook here and you don't really need me to cook just yet. But, someday, when you do, I'll learn how. I promise."

"I hate to interrupt," interrupted Tolkien, "but you may not

really cook, and God knows women these days never eat anything anymore, but I am getting a bit hungry. Do you think we
might—"

"Oh!" I could feel myself reddening in embarrassment. Here,
he'd been kindly helping me for hours and I hadn't even thought
to offer him a slice of stale bread. I started going through cup-
boards, Emma cradled in my arm.

"That's okay," he said. "I can look for myself. I just didn't
want to be going through your drawers without permission first,
that's all."

Once upon a time, I would have given anything to have
Tolkien go through my drawers—would still give anything.

"Ah!" he said, finding a half-finished jar of peanut butter.
"Success!"

He opened the twist on a loaf of bread, quickly discovering
what I already knew: it was stale.

"No matter," he said, unscrewing the jar and having at it with
a spoon. "Would you care for some dinner?" he offered, sitting
down at the table.

I shook my head and watched him dig in.

"Is this really all you have to eat in the house?"

"Well—" I tried to smile, sitting down to at least join him "—
my personal shopper hasn't been by yet this week."

"You should fire her then. It's a holiday. What were you
going to do, survive on wine and a half jar of peanut butter for
two days?"

"Beats starving," I said.

"You've gotten skinny," he observed, licking the spoon.

I shrugged.

"Women love hearing that," I said.

"Well, men don't particularly like seeing it. I'd rather see you
healthy."

It amazed me how much care he still had for my well-being.

"Don't make such a big deal out of it." I was beginning to
feel really uncomfortable. Of all of the things wrong with
me—and God knows there were a lot!—one of them has never
been an eating disorder. "I just haven't been feeling that interested in food the past few months. I've had a lot on my mind."

"Yes," he said, the dryness of his response coming from far more than peanut butter, "I know what you mean."

I wondered whether the details of the "lot" that was on his mind included our relationship.

During the sixth month of my fake pregnancy, not knowing that I was faking a pregnancy elsewhere in my world, Tolkien had asked me to marry him and I'd declined, not wanting to give up the fake pregnancy, which the merging of my two worlds would have forced me to do. Then, in my eighth month, he'd come across me while I was out having tea, my cloth baby strapped on beneath my clothes. He'd naturally assumed the fake baby was real and that it had somehow resulted in our breakup. Now he knew that pregnancy was fake and yet he was helping me to care for this baby I had found.

A part of me longed to find out what he'd been going through for the past few months, what he was going through right this minute. But that part of me was a braver part of me than the person I mostly was.

Besides, he was a man. How in touch with his feelings did I expect him to be? How up-front, how articulate?

Heh. A damned sight more in touch, up-front and articulate than me, which was why I was scared to death to ask the questions that needed asking, to hear the answers he needed to give. It was damned selfish of me, and I knew it, but I just wasn't ready.

"Yes, well," I said, rising, unable to meet his eyes, "it's been a tough season for everybody."

I continued taking Emma on the tour I'd begun earlier.

"This is the bathroom, but I don't suppose you'll be needing that just yet either. Still, I guess you'll be due for a bath eventually. I wonder how…? Oh, don't you worry, I'm sure we'll work it out. And this is my bedroom. Now, then…"

I stopped.

"Tolkien?"

"Yes?"

"Where's she going to sleep? I don't have a cot or anything."

"We'll get a cradle later on today. Babies don't like big cots. They get lost in there."

"But where will we get a cradle on Christmas Day? No one will be open."

He smiled, flashed his Scotland Yard C.I.D. ID my way. "Someone will open," he said.

"Of course."

I looked around my bedroom. "I know!" I said, opening a dresser drawer.

"Uh, no," Tolkien said, gently taking Emma from me.

"But…?"

"Emma's not sleeping her first official sleep here in a dresser drawer."

"Then where?"

"She'll sleep with us, of course," he said, settling down on the edge of the bed.

"You mean you'll stay?"

"Right now? Of course. I wouldn't leave you alone on your first day."

"Because you don't trust me to know what I'm doing? Because I might put her in the drawer?"

"Because you'd get scared. And lonely."

He was right, as usual.

We lay down on the bed, Emma between us.

I would have thought we'd both fall asleep in a second, given that we'd been up nearly twenty-four hours at that point.

But we didn't sleep, *couldn't* sleep.

We were both too scared that if we did, we'd roll over on her.

"What if we fell asleep and she cried and we didn't hear her?" I whispered.

"We'd hear her," he whispered back. "We're right here."

"What if she cries and I don't know what she wants? You know, she and I don't speak the same language, at least not yet."

"You'll learn. Check if she's wet, check if she's hungry. If it's neither, just hold her close so she can feel your heart beat."

"What if she grows up to hate me?"

"Well, of course she'll do that. They all do. The big question is always— When will it start and how long will it last? But you don't have to worry about that for at least another ten years."

"What if she doesn't like it here?"

"Are you kidding me?"

"No."

"She's going to *love* it here."

"Oh, right," I said. Then, "*Why* will she love it?"

"Because you're a lunatic."

Well, there was that. At least he smiled when he said it.

And one last question, the question that had been on my mind since I'd found her and instantly fell in love with her.

"What if they won't let me keep her?"

New Year's Day, night

Bam! Bam! Bam!

I'd fallen asleep on the sofa, but I woke to the pounding on my door. Looking at my watch, I saw that it was still just 7:00 p.m., New Year's Day.

Bam! Bam! Bam! The pounding came again. And then a familiar voice: "Jane!" David yelled. "Open up!"

I unlocked the door to find David and Christopher there, suitcases at their feet.

David's never been very tall, but just now he looked like he could take on Goliath and win. His Israeli skin was even darker after the time in Greece, his black hair just as curly as ever. As for Christopher, it still surprised me after all this time that he wasn't a blonde. He was *such* a blonde, in personality at least. And yet he wasn't. He was like a second David, which was not a bad thing but always startling.

During David's first months with Christopher, there had been some territorial prickliness between us; my fault, really. But as I'd come to realize just how much my best friend was in love with this *new person* who had come on the scene, I'd eventually learned to develop a healthy, if still sometimes grudging, respect for his position in our world. As for David himself, he'd always not only been my best friend, he'd been my best family too, my best supporter, and certainly my best conscience.

Apparently, David and Christopher hadn't even taken a moment to drop their things upstairs first.

"What are you doing back a day early?" I asked, holding the door open as David rushed in, looking worried, a bit frantic. Christopher, as usual, moved at a less hurried pace, sauntering in behind.

"What do you mean, what am I doing back early?" David asked. "You sent a message that you had big news."

"Yes, but you're supposed to still be in Greece. Didn't you like it this time?"

"Oh, you know Greece," he said. "It was soooo *Greece.*"

"What was wrong with it?" I asked. "Too much pita for your culinary taste?"

"The streets were literally paved with the stuff," he scowled. "It was like negotiating a minefield made out of dough."

"He's exaggerating, of course," yawned Christopher, plopping down on the sofa where I'd recently been snoring. "It was absolutely heaven. But once your message arrived…"

"…saying you had big news," put in David.

"…he could no longer relax," continued Christopher.

"So here we are!" said David.

"I really could have used another day at the beach," Christopher said.

"There will be other times. So—" David turned to me, all Israeli overenergy "—what is your big news, Jane?"

"*Waa!*" came the tiny cry from my bedroom.

That tiny, well-timed cry even roused Christopher from his lethargy. There were four eyebrows raised in that living room, none of which were mine.

"Do you think you might keep it down to a less-than-shout?" I whispered, myself remembering Emma for the first time. Well, it really does take time to adjust to a new baby if you've never had one in the house before, even if it does seem as though they take over every instant of your very being, which would make you think you'd by necessity get used to it faster but you don't.

"Wha—?" asked David.

The crying had already stopped. Emma would do that some-times: cry for the briefest of moments, as if she'd been awak-ened for a second and instantly wondered, "Just how the hell did I wind up with *her?*" But then she would fall right back to sleep again.

"Come on," I said, still whispering, gesturing for them to fol-low me into the bedroom.

I didn't turn on the light, allowing the light from the room be-yond to be sufficient.

We all looked down at her, sleeping in the blue and white fine-print floral cradle that had been all I'd been able to find on in-stant you-have-a-baby-on-Christmas-Day notice.

After a long moment, David spoke, still gazing on that sleep-ing face, tiny cap on her head to keep her warm. But unlike everyone else, he didn't ask me where I'd found her or what I planned to do. "She's beautiful," he said, awed by her.

"That's not what everyone else says," I said.

David looked at me abruptly. "How could they not?" He looked back at her. "It is so patent-leather obviously true."

"The first thing everyone else says," I said, "is 'she's black.'"

"Details," said David.

"Details," echoed Christopher, speaking for the first time since he'd seen her.

"Where did she come from, Jane?" David asked, reaching out one strong finger and gently touching her cheek.

I explained about finding her abandoned on the steps of the stone church.

"What do you plan on doing with her?" Christopher asked, practical. And who could blame him?

"I'm going to try to keep her, of course," I said, unable to keep a defensive, defiant note from creeping into my voice, expecting a fight.

"Of course," David agreed, finger still touching her cheek.

"Oh, *well,*" said Christopher. "I suppose if you two are agreed…"

"Exactly," said David.

"But aren't you worried?" Apparently, Christopher wasn't

finished. "Don't you think someone might come forward at some point—the mother changing her mind or someone who knows the mother realizing what's happened—who has a prior claim and wants her back?"

He was voicing my greatest fear.

"Yes," I conceded, "I do realize that could happen. But right now, she needs a home, and someone who will love her and care for her."

"And you think that person is you?" Christopher asked.

I looked at him closely, expecting an accusing or derisory look. But it wasn't like that at all. He looked sincerely curious.

"Yes," I said, feeling uncharacteristically sincere myself, "I do."

"You know, Jane," said David, derailing my sincerity, "she looks a bit like you."

"You're kidding!"

"No, I'm not. Look at her: she has your hair color—" true, we both had black hair, although mine was straight and spiky "—and your mouth. That is one hell of a determined mouth for a little baby to have—beautiful too. No one would ever dream of messing with someone with a mouth like that."

"Not if we can help it," Christopher added.

"No," echoed David, "not if we can help it."

"What are you two saying?" I asked, unable to dare believe that I was hearing what I thought I was hearing, least of all the strength of conviction in Christopher's voice.

"Remember, Jane," said David, "one time when you said, 'Just my luck. Instead of one fairy godmother…'"

"'…I have to wind up with two,'" finished Christopher.

"Yes," I said, "I do remember saying that."

"Well," said David, "now your baby has two fairy godmothers as well."

Christmas Day, later-ish

W hat with the holiday and all, and Social Services being closed for the day, or the man who was supposed to be on call not answering, Tolkien figured we'd been granted a reprieve.

"You do realize, Jane," he said, after we'd woken from the briefest of naps, Emma still safe between us, "eventually we'll need to go through the proper channels. It's not like you can go on with this indefinitely, without reporting the finding of Emma to the proper authorities."

"But—" I started to object.

"But we don't need to do it right this minute," he soothed. "Sure, they might be angry later that we didn't wake the whole country on Christmas Eve just to do things the proper way—"

"Will you get in a great deal of trouble over this?" I asked again, the thought sinking in for the first time. It was one thing to hang for my own self-involvement, quite another to pull him down with me.

"Shh," he said. "Don't worry about that now. We'll deal with that when we get to it."

What he didn't say, what hung in the air as a harsh reality, was that once the responsible organizations were called into the situation, I might not be allowed to keep her.

But we weren't going to deal with that just yet, so we spent the day getting to know what Emma was like.

What Emma was like was a great big sleeper. And a great big pee-er and pooper. And a great big eater; or drinker, I should say.

She must have been at the bottle a dozen times that first day. After a bit, though, I began to realize that every time she cried, she wasn't necessarily looking for food. For, whenever we lay down together, she'd somehow root her way around until she was at my breast. And somehow, that just didn't seem to be all about food.

One time, when we were lying down, I happened to have my top off, having just finally showered and feeling too tired to dress yet. Emma latched on to my breast and began sucking.

Some people might think that icky—something about a baby suckling a nonlactating breast somehow being icky in a way that suckling a genuinely lactating one was not—but the way I figured it, it was Emma's first full day in her new world. If she needed to do that to feel at home, I certainly wasn't about to stop her. It wasn't like she'd be doing it every day until she turned twenty or something; hell, it wasn't even like she was going to be doing it more than just this one time. But if that's what it took to make her feel comfortable in the moment, then it was fine with me until the moment passed and there was time to search for a suitable substitute.

"Not going to find anything there, I'm afraid, old girl," I said. Then I called to Tolkien: "Could you look in my writing table for *What to Expect When You're Expecting?* It should be in the second drawer, right-hand side."

He was in the doorway in a moment, book in hand. He stopped there. "You two look beautiful, you know," he said.

I blushed. It had been several months since he'd seen me with my top off.

"Crap," I said, reaching for the book. "It's just the Madonna effect."

Back during my fake-pregnancy days, I'd bought this prego bible so I'd know what I was talking about. Now I flipped to the section on breastfeeding.

Reading the section now made me feel hugely guilty.

"Do you realize," I asked Tolkien, "that breastfeeding invests kids with all kinds of antibodies that help prevent illness? And get this! Breastfed kids have IQs that are *eight points* higher than those who aren't! What the hell can I be thinking of? I can't deprive Emma of those eight points! What if they're the only difference between her being a genius and being something else?"

"It's not like it's something you can help, Jane. You didn't give birth to her, didn't plan it this way."

"No, I guess not. Still…"

"Besides, there's lots more important things to pass on to kids."

"Such as?"

"Warmth."

"I can do that. Sometimes."

"Good citizenship."

"Could be a problem."

"Humor."

"Got that."

"Anyway, don't you think that everyone worries too much about doing what's *right,* only within the greater context of what everyone else will think?"

"I'm not sure what you mean."

"I'm not sure exactly either. It's just that everything seems to be some sort of contest these days, with the sole criteria of winning being who's following things most closely to the book."

"Well, you don't have to ever worry about that with me," I said. "Even when I try doing things by the book, I somehow end up with a whole different story entirely."

Pounce! "Meow!"

It was Kick the Cat, the white-and-gray puffball I'd gotten to replace Trevor's detested Punch the Cat after he'd moved out. I'd forgotten all about Kick.

"Where did you come from?" I asked. "And where have you been?"

"Meow!"

"Ah, I see," said Tolkien, "he's been to London to visit the Queen."

"We are in London."

"True."

"Did you have a good time, Kick?"

"Meow!"

"Are you hungry? This is Emma, by the way. She'll be staying with us for a bit."

As Tolkien went to get Kick some food, Kick inched her way towards the baby at my breast.

"Be gentle, Kick," I said. "She's still smaller than you."

When Tolkien returned, I asked, "Do you think it will be a problem, having Kick here with Emma?"

He thought about it. "Nah," he said. "People have cats with babies all the time. Besides, Kick's not a violent cat. Just keep your eye out, that's all."

"Ouch!" I cried.

"What's wrong?"

"I think she *bit* me!"

"Kick?"

"No, the baby!"

"She doesn't have teeth yet, Jane. She can't bite you."

"Well, it certainly felt like it."

"Maybe she's just sucking too hard or sucking too long on one side?"

I switched her to the other, meanwhile flipping through my book, where I learned that the sucking reflex is incredibly powerful in newborns. So, after the other breast got tired (me having concluded that women who took breastfeeding on for more than one night deserved some kind of medal or something) and after she drank so much formula that she couldn't seem to hold any more—or at least not for another hour or two—I offered her the clean knuckle of my pinkie. She took to it like it was the greatest thing in the world.

"Huh," I thought, "imagine that? Imagine if the only thing standing between a human being and sheer contentment was a knuckle."

It was time for me to be a braver person than I was accustomed to being.

"What has it been like for you…" I asked Tolkien, non sequitur-ing my way along to something more serious, "…these past few months?"

He took in a deep breath, let it out softly, spoke softly. I could only guess that this was as hard for him as it was for me.

"It's been hell, Jane," he said, "sheer hell. You?"

"The same," I said simply. "A different kind of hell, I expect, but the same."

I could have gone into detail, the details I knew so painfully well, about how losing him had been the hardest thing that had ever happened to me, how it had been as though the most essential part of myself had been cut out. But it wouldn't have been fair; nothing that smacked of self-pity, however true, would have been fair. I had brought it on myself. I had no right to cry injury.

"I never stopped loving you, never stopped wanting you." He spoke as if reluctant to make those admissions. "I couldn't really understand why, even if you were pregnant with another man's child, we couldn't be together. After all, I knew you loved me."

"I did," I said. *I still do,* I thought.

"And now, to realize that what I thought was keeping us apart was something that needn't keep us apart…"

"You feel betrayed," I said.

Almost imperceptibly, he nodded.

"And you hate me now."

There was surprise in his eyes. Then, with a sad smile, he shook his head.

"I almost wish I could hate you," he said. "It would make things easier."

As much as those words hurt, I thought I understood them.

"What do you feel for me now, then?" I asked.

He looked at Emma. She was sleeping. He could say whatever he wanted.

His voice was a whisper. "I have no fucking idea."

Quiet as his voice had been, I felt as though I'd been slapped.

"Oh." I looked down. "I see."

Then I felt his fingers, soft, beneath my chin.

"I do know this," he said, sounding stronger than he had in a while. "I do know that this baby needs to be properly taken care of. I do know I don't want her processed through the system, sent off to a home where she may or may not be well off. I do know you're taking good care of her. I do know that you love her. I do know that I want to help you, if helping you means helping Emma."

Once upon a time, he had believed in me. Maybe, one day, he would again. I would have to re-earn his trust; it was that simple.

I let myself relax for just a moment, leaning into the strength of that hand as he moved it to the side of my face. I felt that hand I knew so well, wanting more, so much more. But for now, this had to be enough.

January, really and truly the first month

In television programs of all kinds, whenever a baby comes into the picture, it's like the kiss of death. Ironic, isn't it, that new life would have that effect? And yet it always comes across as an act of desperation on the part of the writers: "Well, there's nothing new we can do with these characters. Might as well throw a baby at them. We'll at least get one more season out of it." Of course, it doesn't solve anything. Either the audience never sees the baby afterwards, because the writers have realized what a mistake they've made, and are left wondering, "Did they really *have* a baby? Or did the country just mass-hallucinate that one? Ah, well. Pass the crisps." Or every episode centers around the baby, with the main characters seeming to recede into a brain-dead zone of sickly niceness.

Well, I for one wasn't about to become Mary-fucking-Poppins, I can tell you that.

In Martin Amis's nonfiction book *Experience,* he passes a remark something to the effect that—paraphrasing here—the instant you become a parent, you immediately forgive your own parents everything. I can remember thinking, "Huh. What a way he has with human nature, not to mention, words," because he makes these comments that are so stunningly self-assured, the reader starts thinking he *must* be right. I can also remember thinking, about a half second later, *Bollocks.*

Just because I now had a baby, sort of, it didn't mean that I was going to begin to see the world through rose-colored glasses. I would see Emma through them to a certain extent, naturally. But the dysfunctional relationships that predated her would continue on as such, the people who made me feel like life was one long, jagged scraping of Cher's nails down an endless chalkboard...

Which leads us, as all roads seem to lead in one way or another, to...drumroll, please:

My. Mother.

I was waiting for her at a table at Meat! *Meat!! MEAT!!!*

She'd called earlier in the morning. "Jane, I really think we need to talk about...*that baby.* I'm getting my hair done at eleven and my nails at one—damned shop was too booked to do it all back-to-back."

Well, now, how could I refuse an offer like that?

"Meet me at David's place," she'd added.

Hard to believe but my mother, who'd never liked any of the few friends I had in life, had taken a shine to David.

"He's just, oh, I don't know," she said, "so many things at once. The man is a real conversation piece."

Good thing she didn't know what he had to say about her.

She bustled into the restaurant, all champagne-helmeted hair, wielding a handbag that could have doubled as a weapon, and parked herself next to me at one of the many square tables, all of which were covered with butcher's paper.

"Your nails look awful," I said, hoping to start on the offensive, rather than the defensive she'd undoubtedly soon put me on.

"You have a formula stain on your blouse," she said.

"I think they did your hair too tight this time," I said.

"Your skirt's too short," she said. "Are you turning tricks on the side now?"

"What do you have in that purse," I asked, "an MP?"

"Some people shouldn't be allowed to breed," she said.

"And how," I said.

"Ready to order?" chippered Christopher, who David had

originally met when Christopher was the architect behind Meat! *Meat!! MEAT!!!,* and who helped David in every way now, including waiting tables.

"I'll have a big steak and an even bigger glass of wine," said my mother.

"I'll have the fish," I said.

"Nobody orders fish here," said my mother.

"I just did."

"Right," said Christopher, escaping.

"Speaking of babies…" said my mother.

"Were we?" I asked.

"I'm pretty sure we were," she said. "Where's…*that baby?*"

"Emma's in the kitchen. David's watching her. I figured that whatever we might have to say to one another might get, um, heated."

"You left that baby *in the kitchen?*"

"Yes, and she's perfectly safe there," I said. "David's just gaga over her. He can barely look at anything else when she's in the room. The only people at risk here are us. David might forget to put our meals in the oven, in which case we'll be eating raw."

Christopher brought our drinks and hurried away.

My mother sipped hers in that prissy way she has. I do realize you have to purse your lips to drink, but on her, her lips always looked *so* pursed.

"You know you can't keep her, Jane."

"Whyever not?"

"Because it wouldn't be fair."

"To whom?"

"To her, of course."

"I know I'm going to hate myself in the morning for asking this, but why do you say that?"

"Isn't it obvious? You don't know the first thing about being black."

"I know how to love her," I said. "I can do that pretty damned good."

"Oh. Love," she said. "Do you really think that's all there is to it?"

"I think it helps if it's at least there," I said pointedly, but she obviously missed the point.

"There's a lot more to being a mother than just love," she said.

"Such as?"

"Why, there's a tradition that mothers pass down. What sort of tradition will you have to pass on to her?"

I thought of the Taylor family tradition that had been passed down to me. Well, that certainly wouldn't do.

"I'll make a tradition for her," I said. "We'll make our own tradition together."

Our meals arrived. They were cooked, at least, so David must have torn his eyes off Emma for at least thirty seconds, but the veg was arranged in such a haphazard fashion, I suspected he hadn't been looking when he'd done that part.

"And you know," my mother said, lowering her voice, "they talk differently than we do."

"Who?"

"Black people."

"Only when they're born in different countries, Mother."

"And they, oh, I don't know, use different hair products than we do."

"Now there's a good reason for giving up on a child."

"It's just that—and I'm really, really *not* trying to be mean here—I simply don't think that you can handle it. It's not fair to the baby. You should give her up, because you can't be black. I'm sorry, but it's true, Jane, you just can't."

I laid my fork down and looked her in the eye.

"Oh. Yes. I. Can."

Of course, I hadn't a clue as to what I was talking about.

And here was something really weird: Even though my mother, when calling this meeting, had said she wanted to discuss the baby, and we had in fact discussed just that, I got the feeling that there was something else she wanted to talk to me about. I don't know what tipped me off. An evasive look in her eyes, perhaps? The way, whenever I tried to turn the discussion to her, she turned it back to me? Apparently, though, she'd changed her mind about telling me whatever it was. Because, try as I might to worm it out of her—my worm-ing performing two functions, since it deflected any more nonsense she might have to say about Emma—I couldn't get her to tell me what it was. Mum was keeping mum.

Considering that there were no sounds of complaints out of Emma coming from the kitchen, and that I no longer wanted to discuss Emma with my mother and my mother didn't want to discuss *whatever* with me, you could say the whole place went mum after that.

I was still on "maternity leave" and I had to be grateful that Churchill & Stewart was willing to let me remain on that status; after all, they could have sacked me for being a pathological liar. I still hadn't decided yet if I was going back. I'd delivered *The Cloth Baby* to Alice Simms, who thought it was going to be a huge success, so much so that the publisher was interested in having me write another book, but there was no immediate rush to decide on what.

So I had time on my hands, what little time wasn't taken up by Emma, but time enough to come to at least one startling realization.

I realized that my mother—God, how I hate to say these words!—was right. Oh, of course she'd said everything, as usual, in a completely wrongheaded fashion, and she was most definitely wrong about Emma not belonging with me, but she was right in her implications that Emma was going to need to grow up with a sense of heritage. I realized that I was going to need to find a way to meet some black people, for Emma's sake.

I hadn't known many black people in my life, but what few I'd known, I'd liked. I realize that sounds like one of those backhanded compliments, like when someone says, "Some of my best friends are Jewish"—which really is true in my case, but only in the singular, since my only best friend is David and he is Jewish. (At least, I'm pretty sure he is; he never really talks about it.) And, anyway, what would be better, to say that some of my enemies are Jewish or that the few black people I'd known I'd hated? Neither of which would be true, of course. As a white Christian, my random sampling of other races and religions was just too limited to make any kind of meaningful generalizations. All of this said, if anyone else ever comes up with a way to say, "I'm not a racist" without people automatically knee-jerking to "Ah, she's a racist" or "I've liked what few black people I've known" without sounding like some kind of insufferable prig, please drop me a line.

Here's one last interesting part on that subject: I can say "I haven't known many black people in my life, but what few I've known, I've liked" and fully realize that there will be someone who will find the remark offensive. And yet, any observation I make about the white people I've known would have to be more offensive, the truth being that having known a ton of white people in my life, there have been precious few I've genuinely liked. So there.

As I say, though, having come from a white family, having gone to school in situations where the majority was overwhelmingly white, having previously lived with a man whose own work circle was unicolor with a pale bias and working myself in a publishing firm that was lily-white, I've had little opportunity to develop deep friendships with people of color. And, to be fair to myself, it wasn't exactly as though the black community was knocking down my door, begging me to come on over and liven things up for them. As if they needed me.

But now things were going to have to be different. Now, instead of waiting on the vagaries of chance and personal circumstance to populate my inner circle for me in a more culturally diverse way, I was going to have to make a conscious effort to live my life on a broader canvas.

I had no illusions. Not that I expected people to throw rocks at me or even be mean or anything like that. But I also wasn't expecting people to be eager to get to know me. To be fair, sometimes *I* didn't feel so eager to get to know me.

But where to start?

A funeral seemed like the right place to start. After all, I couldn't very well go door-to-door looking for new friends and you can't crash a wedding in the same way you can crash a funeral. I mean, in the case of a wedding, the guests of honor are there, all alive and everything and able to point the finger at you as being someone who neither had put on their list. Go through the receiving line at a wedding you've not been invited to, and you're basically screwed. At a funeral, on the other hand, the guest of honor…

"I'm so sorry for your loss."

Before setting out on this particular errand, I'd checked out the obits in the paper, hoping to come up with a likely prospect. I sat at the dining-room table, my own half-eaten lunch of microwave pizza—I was officially A Mother! I cooked things now!—pushed to one side, burping Emma after her own repast of formula, as I studied the page. I spoke aloud to Emma as I studied, because, well, they do say you should talk to your baby as much as possible and this was the subject on offer at the moment.

"Pakistani, Pakistani, Pakistani," I muttered. "Rupert Hampstead-Hyde. Well, he's obviously white," I said to Em.

Then one leaped out at me.

I could tell the deceased must be black because of the neighborhood where the church was located and the particular church (plus, there was a picture): "Mary Johnson," I read the obit to Emma, "63, died peacefully in her sleep on Jan 10. An employee of U.K. Housecleaning for the past thirty years, Mary is survived by five children—John, Luke, Paul, Matthew and Mary Jr.—and twelve grandchildren. Services to be held at Shakespeare Baptist Revival Church. In lieu of flowers, the family requests donations be sent to War Child."

I was a little taken aback by that at first, thinking it would be more usual to ask that donations be sent to some disease-oriented organization, or her church. But then it occurred to me that maybe that was my own prejudices talking. Why wouldn't black people be socially conscious? After all, Mary Johnson had died in her sleep peacefully, if relatively young, so why give it to a disease when they could give it to needy children in other parts of the world?

I held Em up, touched my forehead to hers.

"Is Mummy a racist sometimes without realizing it? Can you help me out with that?"

Coo.

I scribbled out a check for fifty pounds to expiate in advance any guilt I might later feel and called a cab.

If I'd wanted to soak up some local color, or find out how the other half lives—to the extent of finding out what it's like to be a minority—I'd certainly come to the right place. Being the only white person at Mary Johnson's funeral, I was in a minority of exactly one.

The church looked just about the same as any other church I'd ever been in, save for that there were side-by-side pictures of Shakespeare and Jesus in the entryway, which seemed about right to me.

I'm not sure what I was hoping to achieve. I guess that, like several months earlier, when I'd gone trawling at a pregnancy clinic for ideas of authentic proof of pregnancy to offer nosy parkers at work, I was once again looking for ideas without knowing what ideas I was looking for.

It was a lovely service. The reverend—minister, maybe? Whatever it is Baptists have—spoke of Mary Johnson so highly, it made me wish I *had* actually known her.

As I came through the receiving line afterwards, I readjusted Emma in my arms in order to shake hands.

There were four men, who could only be John, Luke, Paul and Matthew, ranging in ages from late thirties to mid-forties—so Mary Johnson must have been very young when she had her first—with a woman I couldn't see very well at the end of the line.

I reached to take the first man's hand, planning to murmur, "So sorry," but before I could offer my condolences, he took one look at Emma in my arms and gave a little backward jump.

He held up his hands in a defensive gesture. "Whoa!" he said. "Is that your baby?"

This was something I hadn't counted on: that showing up at an all-black funeral with a black baby, and me being white, it would look as though I'd come here to accuse someone of something. It wasn't as though I thought there must be black men all over the city fathering babies and then failing to take responsibility for them. But I was the only white person in the room, holding a black baby in my arms, no escort anywhere in sight. Plus, I'm sure I looked like A Woman With A Purpose, which I was, but not a purpose anyone could readily guess.

I tried to ignore him, moving on to brother number two, only to be greeted with that same falling-away jump, hands up as if I were holding a loaded pistol. "Whoa! Is that your baby?"

And brother number three: "Whoa! Is that your baby?"

And four: "Whoa! Is that your baby?"

I felt like I'd just knocked over a line of dominos.

"Would you please stop that?" I said. "I'm not here to look for a father for my child. I'm here to pay my respects to *your* mother!"

No, I do know that shouting in the middle of a post-funeral service in a Baptist church was not my most stellar moment, but it was infuriating. Couldn't anyone see that I meant no harm?

Just as I was getting ready to skulk off—what was the use?—the woman at the end of the line came forward. While I couldn't figure out which brother was which apostle, I knew this could only be Mary Jr. She was very pretty, with chocolate-colored skin and cheekbones the envy of just about anybody, despite the ill-fitting cut of her suit, which was all loose in the stomach area, as though designed for a much larger person. As she came to me, one hand out to take mine, I saw two things: 1) she was substantially younger than her brothers, maybe around my age, making her Mary Sr.'s surprise baby; and 2) she had her own young baby cradled in the other arm. Ah! A lightbulb went off in my dim brain. Maybe the suit was from her recent pregnancy.

"I'm Mary Jr.," she said, softly, warmly. "And you are…?"

I took her hand, returned the warmth; it was easy to do that with Mary Jr.

"Jane Taylor," I said. "And this is Emma."

"Whoa!" Mary Jr. gave a soft laugh, imitating her brothers. "Is that your baby?"

"Yes." I smiled back. "This is Emma."

"This is Martha," she said, showing me her own baby, unable to keep the happy pride from her voice, even though it was clear from her eyes she'd done her share of crying that day.

We cooed at each other's babies for a minute.

"Well, all I can say is," said Mary Jr., "you must have loved Mum an awful lot to come here today."

"Oh, I did," I said, "I really did."

"I'm afraid we've put this off long enough," Tolkien said later that same day. He'd come along just as I was returning from the funeral, meaning he caught me in my mourning black.

"Did someone die, Jane?" he asked, looking concerned.

"Don't people always die?" I waved him off. "No," I said, not wanting to say, "nobody that I know died." I certainly wasn't about to tell Tolkien what I'd just been doing. No matter how good I thought my own intentions were, I just couldn't see him endorsing any plans involving unknown corpses.

"Then why…?"

"I dunno, do I," I said, looking down at my clothes. "Maybe I'm just feeling postpartum-y."

I put Emma down for a nap, kissed her on the top of the head and moved to put the kettle on, not wanting to answer any more wardrobe questions.

"You were saying something before," I said, "about putting something off long enough?"

"Right." He cleared his throat. "We're going to have to go to the authorities."

"Why now?" I asked, alarmed.

"Because not everyone in your world can be trusted. Who knows which one of them might suddenly develop a wrong-headed sense of conscience, decide to turn you in? It's better if you do it on your own steam."

"What will happen?" I asked.

He ran his fingers through his hair. "They'll assign her to a foster home, probably yell their heads off at you first for not coming in sooner."

"But I found her. And I want her."

"That won't have any meaning to them. They'll have to go by the book, they'll have to consult their lists. Emma will go, at least temporarily, to the next foster home in line."

"Isn't there anything else we can do?"

"I don't know." He thought about it for a moment. "I don't

suppose you happen to know anyone with the technological know-how of a master spy?"

As I made my way through the offices of Churchill & Stewart with Emma, I felt more self-consciously guilty than I had in all the nine months of my fake pregnancy, what with all the hard stares we were getting from people like Louise. Actually, it was just Louise that was making me feel that way, but she was staring at us so hard that it felt as though a roomful of haters were doing it.

I knocked on the door that I'd never knocked on willingly before, the door of one of whom I considered to be my most hated enemies.

"Come in if you have to!" yelled Stan from Accounting.

Amazing what I'd sunk to, but where I was a tech-not, Stan was a tech-all: if he couldn't help me, nobody could. And since Tolkien had made a date for us to see Mr. Triplecorn at Social Services right after this, Stan was going to have to help me fast.

"Jane!" he said, surprised.

And there he was in all his suspenders-straight, hair-trimmed-every-day, clean-steel-glasses anal glory. What was I thinking?

"Stan, I need your help."

Stan's office was decorated just as anally, meaning there were no decorations and that everything in it was utilitarian, save for the photo of Stan's mother, his army of sisters and all their female offspring smiling from their position on Stan's desk.

"Why should I help you?" he asked. "And while we're at it, what's in it for me?"

See what I mean?

"I want to keep Emma."

"You're not exactly what I'd consider mother material, Jane," he snorted.

Just then, Emma cooed at me. It was a sound that never failed to melt my formerly hard heart, but I saw Stan visibly steel himself against it.

"Emma needs me, Stan. If I have to turn her over to the Social, they'll likely place her in a home where she won't be properly loved, certainly not the way I can love her."

"Oh, I'm sure that's exactly what she needs, a slightly socio-pathic mother with a tendency toward faking pregnancies."

Emma cooed again. Stan stiffened again, took a step backwards.

"Stan, I haven't got time for that right now! I need your help! In another hour, I'm due at their offices. And if we don't do something soon, the Social will take her from me."

Emma cooed yet again. But this time, Stan took a tiny step towards us. Tentatively, he put a finger under her chin. "She's a cute little bugger, isn't she?"

"Yes, she is," I said, "and she deserves a chance at something better."

"Hah!" He drew back again. "And you think *you're* something better?"

I knew it was useless, but I stood my ground. Emma was at stake.

"Yes, I am."

Just then, Emma cooed once more, only this time, she turned her tiny head into the crook of my shoulder and released a puffy little sigh of air as though she were the most contented little creature in the world, before settling in for a snooze.

"My God!" Stan whispered in awe. "The little bugger *likes* you!"

"She loves me, Stan," I said simply. "She's, oh, I don't know, *imprinted* on me somehow, like all those ducklings. Believe it or not, I think she believes I'm her mother."

Stan stared at us for one more minute, then he looked at me for the very first time in our acquaintanceship as if I might actually be a human being. More, he looked at me as though he might be one, too.

"What do you need me to do?" he asked.

I quickly explained to him the situation with Emma and Stephen Triplecorn at Social Services, and Tolkien's cryptic suggestion that someone with superior technological know-how could somehow help me out. I'd honestly had no idea what Tolkien specifically meant, but apparently Stan did.

"You need me to hack into the system at Social Services," he said.

"Okay," I said.

"You need me to somehow get you on the list they have of potential foster homes that are waiting for a child."

"Okay." I shrugged. "If you say so."

He moved to his desk, quicker than I'd ever seen him move before. He started tapping at the keys.

"You're going to do it?"

"Just don't ever tell anybody that I did something nice for you or I'll turn you in myself."

"You *can* do it?" I asked.

He looked up briefly, glint of fluorescent lights off steel.

"Are you kidding?" he asked. "I could hack into *God's* system if I wanted to. It's just that nobody's ever asked before. Now, go on. By the time you get there, you'll be all set."

"Thanks, Stan." I hesitated, then, awkwardly, I crossed the room and kissed him on that anally straight hair.

He blushed.

"Go!" he ordered again, returning to the screen.

Nobody had to tell me and my baby more than twice.

Emma and I went.

Mr. Triplecorn—Mr. Stephen Triplecorn, to be exact—was the most beautiful man I'd ever seen in my life.

You expect a woman to be running your local branch office of the Social, you really do, an overworked, frenzied middle-aged lady with her glasses on a chain around her neck. What you don't expect is black hair, seriously blue eyes, a gym-hardened body and a bulge in his pants as he rose from his desk—the bulge presumably "in a state of rest," yet clearly discernible, packaged as it was in his tight jeans, with which he wore a striped shirt and tie.

He was so perfect, I was certain he must be gay, until Tolkien introduced himself, leaned forward to shake hands, and immediately the level of competing as opposed to complementary testosterone present in the room ratcheted itself up about a thousand notches.

"You!" Stephen Triplecorn said.

Stephen Triplecorn was also the grumpiest man I'd ever met in my life.

Wanting to look anywhere but at those angry blue eyes, I glanced around the office. God! What a dump! No wonder he was so crabby; if I had to work in such a mean little sterile place, I'd hate the world too.

"You!" he said again to Tolkien. "I've been waiting to hear from *you* for over a week now! First, you leave that message on the machine saying you've found *a baby*. And then, when I try to ring you back, some toff at the Yard tells me you're—" and here he did a mincing-face thing "'—working undercover, can't be reached.'"

"I couldn't," Tolkien said evenly.

"Apparently," Stephen Triplecorn snorted. Then, he did a chin nod at Emma in my arms. "That the baby?"

"Yes," I said, straightening.

"Right," he said, coming round the desk. He moved to take her from me.

"You can't take her!" I said.

"Well, you can't keep her! And, by the way, who the hell are you?"

"This is Jane Taylor," Tolkien said. "She found Emma."

"Named her already, did you? No guaranteeing that'll stick. I don't suppose she came with a birth certificate?"

"No," I said, and I proceeded to tell him how I'd found Emma, having seen a figure abandon her on the church steps. I neglected to mention the part about me being in the last month of my own fake pregnancy at the time.

"And you think you can just keep her," he said when I'd finished, "like you would if you'd found a stray cat without a collar or something?"

"No," I said, getting confused, "I'm not saying it's the same thing as that—"

"Look," Tolkien interrupted me, "we know you'll need to try to locate the birth mother—"

"We *do?*" I half shrieked.

"—but in the meantime, can't Ms. Taylor take care of the baby? You know, you may never find the mother."

Stephen Triplecorn gaped at Tolkien as if he were bonkers.

"*No.* No, we can't just let Ms. Taylor take care of the baby.

Are you insane? There are procedures to be followed. Don't you Yard boys ever follow procedures, or is the work you do too important for due process?"

"Name-calling probably won't help here," said Tolkien.

"Name…? Look," said Stephen Triplecorn in more restrained tones, "surely, even you two must realize that the proper channels must be followed. Do you have any idea how many babies this office is responsible for placing over the course of the year? The Queen may be getting twelve billion, but who do you think is doing all the work?"

And, oh God, it hit me right then, because of course it hadn't made any sense before: after all, why would this brilliantly beautiful man be working in such a job in such a place? It was because he was A. Man. With. A. Mission.

"The proper channels…" he was droning on again.

Oh, *fuck!* He wasn't just A Man With A Mission; he was Inspector *fucking* Javert!

"Okay," said Tolkien, holding up his hand, "I get it. But Jane *is* part of the proper channels."

"She is?"

"I am?"

"Yes," he looked at me meaningfully. "You're on the list of foster homes waiting for children."

I'd gotten so caught up in the anxiety Stephen Triplecorn was causing to stir in me, I'd forgotten about that.

On the way over, I'd filled Tolkien in on what Stan was up to. But being here before this person who was the embodiment of everything standing between me and my happily ever after, I'd grown so rattled that I'd forgotten that technology had come down for once on my side.

"Yes," I said, chin going up, "yes, I am."

"You're…" he sputtered. "No, you're not. I'd remember if you were."

"Overworked, underpaid," sympathized Tolkien. "You can't be expected to be hands-on with everything yourself. You're only human."

"Look, I'll show you," Stephen Triplecorn said. Seating himself at his desk once again, he pulled up a page on the computer screen that said in bold letters at the top: Waiting Homes—Approved. He ran his finger down the list. "See?" he asked, although we couldn't from where we were standing. "No Jane Taylor on my list."

I rushed around the desk, Emma in my arms, Tolkien right there with me.

"It has to be there!" I said, looking at the screen.

But it wasn't.

Oh, fucking *Stan!* He'd promised! This is what I got for putting my future with Emma in the hands of an accountant. *Fucking* Stan!

"It must be a mistake!" I said.

Stephen Triplecorn swiveled in his chair to face me. "It's no mistake," he said. "I told you before that your name wasn't familiar to me."

"Well," I said, stalling for time, although why, I didn't know, "you can't be expected to know every single name of every single person in the city of London."

"Perhaps not," he said. "But I know my list. And since your name simply isn't there and since merely finding the baby gives you no priority whatsoever—"

The screen behind him flashed, just the briefest of brightenings and there it was.

"Look!" I pointed, jumping up and down, Emma in my arms. "There it is!"

"What the—"

I swiveled him around in his chair so he was facing the screen.

"See!" I exulted. "Jane Taylor! Knightsbridge! That's me!" I'd been able to afford Knightsbridge when I lived with Trevor, who made a lot of money. Then, after he left me, I'd been offered a big advance for *The Cloth Baby,* making it possible for me to stay.

He was clearly flustered. "But…but…that wasn't there a second ago!"

"Eyestrain too." Tolkien tut-tutted. "Don't they ever let you people go on holiday? It's a disgrace to push such hard workers so hard."

"But that wasn't there before!" he still protested.

"Well, it is now," said Tolkien, "so why don't Ms. Taylor and I just—"

"Wait!" Stephen Triplecorn's bellow stopped us mid-tiptoe to the door.

"Wait for what?" we asked at the same time.

"Just because her name's suddenly on the list, it changes nothing. All it means is that she's in line for *a* baby. But she's not first in line, so she has no right to *this* baby."

Oh, God. It was like all the air went out of the room. Why hadn't I thought of that? Why hadn't I thought to have Stan put me first?

I looked down at Emma. I couldn't believe we'd made it this far, only to lose her.

I suppose I could have made a dash for it, taken our chances living life on the run, but I wanted what was best for her. And while I was certain that "best for her" involved being with me somewhere in the equation, I didn't think it could be achieved by leapfrogging to Turkey for safety.

She was so beautiful. I'd only known her for a couple of weeks, and already I loved her so much.

Then I heard Tolkien talk.

"You've got the chance to do something really wonderful here, Mr. Triplecorn. You've got a chance to do what your job is supposed to be about—finding a loving home for a baby who desperately needs one. Look at them. Look at how happy Emma is with Jane. Do you really think it's in Emma's best interests to take her from the only mother she's known so far, a good mother, and put her with someone else who might not love her quite so much?"

"But the list…"

"So what? Are you really going to let Jane's placement on the list interfere with doing what's right?"

"I—"

"Tell you what," Tolkien's voice silkened, sweetening the pot, "isn't there anything we can do to make your life easier?"

Stephen Triplecorn reddened, then he yanked open the drawer of his desk and pulled out a massive sheaf of small papers, each one a separate parking ticket.

"Can you do anything about this?" He waved them at Tolkien.

Tolkien smiled, then snatched them from his hand. "Done," he said.

This time we were at the door, we were really going to make it this time, when I heard Stephen Triplecorn level one last warning at us.

"Just remember," he said. "We'll be looking for the birth mother *and* we'll be keeping an eye on you. However you think this is going to turn out, you're probably wrong."

Bam! Bam! Bam! I pounded on David and Christopher's door, having left Emma downstairs for the moment with Tolkien.

The door opened and they both stood there, cautiously expectant expressions on their faces.

"How did it go?" David finally dared to ask.

"I need your help," I said, all seriousness.

"Anything, Jane," said David.

"I need for you to go to W.H. Smith and pick me up a copy of *What to Expect the First Year.*"

It was like the sun bursting through the clouds, which may be trite, but there was no other phrase for it.

"Really?" David smiled.

"Yes." I smiled back. "Really." Then I hurled myself into my best friend's arms. "We've got a baby to raise!"

According to the book, by the end of the first month—now!— my baby should be able to lift her head briefly while on her stomach on a flat surface (she could do that!) and focus on a face (she could definitely do that). I flat-out loved the way she looked at me as though I were the greatest thing since silicone nipples, and I don't even think it was so much an ego thing as it was nice to have some sort of concrete validation that I was doing my job properly.

Under the list of things she would probably be able to do, she could respond to a bell and under the list of things she might be able to do, she could vocalize in ways other than crying, for example by cooing (she was a great cooer!) and she could smile in response to my smile (I became another person when she did that). Finally, under the super-child list of things she might even be able to do, while she couldn't lift her head ninety degrees or hold it steady when upright, and whenever I tried to get her to follow an arc about six inches above her face for 180 degrees she just stared at me, she could bring both hands together, smile spontaneously, laugh out loud and squeal with delight.

So, from a pure happiness standpoint, Emma and I were doing just great.

February, the second month

"So, are you and Tolkien back to being a romantic couple?"

The speaker was David, and the place was his apartment, where he and Christopher and I had just finished Sunday dinner together, Emma asleep in her carrier.

Like Tolkien, the centerpiece of their living space was a CD player, plus a huge collection of CDs. Unlike Tolkien, however, there was warmth to where they lived.

David had always been more of a nester than I was; even before Christopher, his flat had been more like a home. Then, with the advent of Christopher, the atmosphere had grown more so. Now, even though they'd only been married a couple of months, the place had the look of one they'd shared for years. The ecru velvet sofa begged to be read on, lounged on, loved on; the eclectic selection of prints on the walls—Chagall, Orpen, a soothing Frankenthaler—were all obviously things they loved rather than just things to take up space; the dining-room table, where we were seated now, was always set nicely, with real napkins rather than paper (which I supposed was easier for some when those some owned a restaurant business), the over-all feel being that this was a place where real conversations were had, where greater things transpired than the mere passing of butter.

But getting back to the point about me and Tolkien…

"No, why do you ask?" I asked, busying myself with clearing the table.

"Because he's at your place nearly all the time now," said David.

"Because he sleeps there at night," said Christopher.

"Although he's not there now," said David.

"That's probably just because he's working at the moment," said Christopher.

"Yes, he is working right now," I said. "And no, we're not a romantic couple."

"It certainly seems that shoe fits to me," said David.

"Well, it doesn't fit Tolkien," I said.

"Whyever not?" he asked.

"Because I've hurt him so much?" I asked-answered. "Because he doesn't know if he can trust me not to hurt him again?" I shook it off. "Besides, haven't you two been paying attention? It was last month that he stayed over every night, and I think that was mostly because he was worried I might do something stupid with Emma, like toss her up in the air or try to feed her a steak or something."

"And now?" asked David.

And now…

I remembered the first night I'd been all alone with her. Tolkien, with no warning, had announced, "It's time, Jane."

"But—"

"You'll do fine," he said. "You're Emma's mother."

"But what about you?"

"Well, I'm not Emma's father," he smiled ruefully.

"I think she thinks you are," I said.

"Yes, well…"

"I thought we might…"

"What?" he asked. "Get back together again?"

I didn't say anything. Of course, for me to think that was foolish.

"I'll be honest, Jane, I don't know what I feel for you anymore. The way you deceived me and everyone else…"

I still didn't say anything.

"But now I see you with Emma and..."

"Yes?"

He shook his head. "I just don't know." Then he grabbed his bag. Apparently, he'd done his packing when I wasn't looking.

"It'll be okay, Jane," he said. "I'll still be your friend, I'll still help you out, no matter what. But she is *your* baby. To give her the idea that I'll always be here, for the rest of her life, would just be wrong."

And then he was gone.

That first night, I was terrified. It was far worse than that first scary night we'd brought her home together, when I was worried we would crush her, when I was worried that if I fell asleep even for a second she would cease to be.

But, somehow, she and I got through it together. For such a tiny thing, there was great strength in her. Look what she had survived already! I took her strength as my own model, put one foot in front of the other, and moved on.

"And now we're friends," I at last answered David and Christopher, thinking that with all I'd put Tolkien through, all the lies I'd told, it was no wonder he was reluctant to resume a romantic relationship. "Like you, he's my friend."

The look they gave me said they didn't believe that one for a second, but they were gracious enough to let it drop.

"And what about work?" Christopher asked, changing the subject.

"What about work?" I asked.

"Are you ever going to do any again?" teased David.

"Raising a baby is full-time work," I said. "You two ought to try it sometime."

"I'm serious, Jane," said David, laying out dessert.

I tucked in to the chocolate mud cake. If I had enough sugar, maybe I'd go into some kind of food-clot fugue state where I wouldn't need to make any more momentous decisions.

"This is really good!" I said, mouth full.

"Jane," David warned, full stop, as he always did whenever he felt I needed reining in.

"I *don't* know," I whined. "You decide."

"You want him to decide whether you should go back to work or not?" asked Christopher.

"Yes," I said.

"Fair enough," said Christopher. "But which job is he supposed to be deciding for you about—Churchill & Stewart or being a writer?"

"C&S, of course," I said. "Once you're a writer, you never retire from it. Whether you write again or not, you're still a writer until the day you die. It's who you are."

There. I was extraordinarily pleased with that statement, which sounded exactly to me like the kind of pronouncement one might hear Martin Amis make; in other words, provocative, labyrinthine and, yes, quite probably wrongheaded.

"I think you should go back to C&S," said David.

"But why?" I whined.

"Hey," said Christopher, "I thought you wanted someone else to decide this for you."

"I did, but—"

"You should go back because it will be good for both you and Emma," David said.

"How so?" I asked.

"Because you'll be a more well-squared person."

"Rounded," Christopher said around a mouthful of cake. "He means well-rounded."

"That's exactly what I mean, although I do think a square would do as well."

While Christopher and I tried to figure that one out, confused frowns on our faces and everything, David went on.

"You'll be better for Emma if you have more in your life than *just* Emma—"

"There's no such thing as '*just* Emma'!" I objected.

"—and Emma will be more appreciative of her time with you if she has something to weigh it against," he continued, ignoring my outburst. "Plus, she won't grow up terrified of other people or of losing you."

He made a weird kind of maternal sense for a gay guy who'd never had any kids.

"But will she still realize how much I love her if I'm not with her all the time?"

"Yes," said David, "because you love her so much whenever you *are* with her."

"But how will I work the childcare thing? I *won't* leave her with a stranger!"

I will admit here, by the way, that whenever I wasn't feeling totally serene because of Emma, being a new mother was bringing out the more strident sides of my personality. It felt like my life was full of exclamation points all of a sudden.

"You'll leave her with us," said David.

"Of course," said Christopher.

"But you both work! You have the restaurant!" There were those exclamation points again.

"So what?" David shrugged. "We could let George," he added, referring to the sous chef, "run lunch so we don't have to go in until five."

"Or we could just play around with our hours a bit," said Christopher.

"You mean work different shifts from one another?" David asked.

"Sure. Why not? That way, one of us can be here for Emma all the time," said Christopher, evading David's gaze, which was odd for him.

"You think that will be good for our relationship?" asked David.

"Yes," said Christopher, still evading. "Like with Jane and Emma. Too much togetherness can be a negative thing. It's best if you can always find ways to keep an old thing new."

"True," David admitted.

"Besides," said Christopher, looking at me now, "tons of people telecommute for at least part of the workweek now. I'd think that, with your book coming out and its undoubted success, it would add a little cachet to old C&S to keep you on staff, even part-time."

They'd thought of everything.

I exhaled. "Well it looks like you two have made up my mind for me."

"Looks like," they said.

"Now, then, the next question… Will Churchill & Stewart *want* me back?"

Even though it had been months since I'd been over there, Dodo's apartment was unchanged. It was still the *Architectural Digest* retreat of a sad lonely princess: beautiful and sterile, untouched. All it needed was a man, or any kind of mate really, to make it come alive, but none was forthcoming.

A mate is not the answer to life for every woman, but it would have been for Dodo. Despite the soft lighting, the chenille throws and carpet, the presence of much-loved books encased in beautiful cherry wood barrister's shelves, where David's and Christopher's place soothed "warmth," Dodo's place averred "cold." I dunno. Maybe it was just the glass coffee table that was putting me off.

I sat on Dodo's plush moss-colored velvet sofa much as I had those months before, only this time, I didn't have a fake baby wrapped around my belly.

When I'd rung Dodo up, asking if I could come over for a chat, I'd said I wanted to bring Emma with me. I'll admit it: I was scared to face Dodo alone. I had, in a sense, let her down more than anybody—she had invested more interest and more sheer goodness in my "pregnancy" than anybody, and I was using my beautiful baby as armor. If a train were to come barreling down the tracks one day, I'd do what any self-respecting parent would do: I'd push my baby out of the way and take the hit. But take the brunt from a wounded Dodo?

I made sure Emma was between us at all times.

"So you feel as though you're ready to return to work," she said, pouring tea.

"You did say before I went on maternity leave that whenever I was ready to come back, a job would be waiting for me."

"I also said you'd be returning to a new job as an editor in your own right, since Constance is now my assistant."

"You did say that." I tread carefully, not wanting to rock her boat.

"Of course—" she stirred her tea "—that was before I learned that *your* maternity leave was not your typical run-of-the-mill maternity leave."

"I realize that, Dodo, but I thought I explained already—"

"What? That somehow the reason you continued with your charade of a fake pregnancy was somehow for my benefit?"

"For your benefit? No, I guess not. But because I didn't want to hurt you by having you learn the truth after how you'd helped me so? In a very real sense, yes, Dodo."

"But I found out anyway."

"Yes."

"And I'm hurt anyway."

"I'm sorry."

"And now you want to come back to work with me anyway."

"Yes."

Coo. Emma, of course.

"And—" Dodo tried to continue.

Coo. Emma, again.

"And—"

Coo.

"And, my *God,* but she's the most beautiful baby who ever lived, isn't she?"

"Yes, she is, Dodo, she really is!"

"Can I hold her?"

"Of course. Here, let me help you."

Dodo carefully took her from me, beaming at her all the while.

"Just be sure to support her neck," I said. "That's really the big thing you need to worry about."

"She really is beautiful, Jane."

"Thanks." I blushed, feeling inordinately proud, even though I had nothing to do with the making of her. "David says she has my mouth."

Dodo looked at me sharply.

"David's right," she said.

Then her gaze returned to Emma and she caressed her cheek with a finger, cooing back at her.

"Are you sure you know what you're doing?" Dodo asked.

"How so?"

"Don't you think she deserves to be raised by her real mother, or at least her own people?"

"Oh, no! Not you too!"

She looked up. "Who else has said this to you?"

"My mother."

"Oh." She was silent for a minute, clearly flummoxed by that news. "Oh," she finally said again. "Well, I'm not sure that's a category I want to find myself in."

"Then don't!" I implored her.

"But what other choice do I have? Because the truth is, I firmly believe a child is better off growing up in the culture he or she comes from."

"Whoever gave birth to Emma was able to just walk away from her, Dodo. However painful it might have been—and I can't imagine it being anything but—the woman was able to walk away from her."

"Yes, but—"

"And. I. Love. Her."

"Yes, but—"

"Don't help the world to hurt her more, Dodo. Help *me* to help *her.*"

"How?"

"By, oh, I don't know, instead of telling me what I don't know, helping me learn what I should know."

"For example?"

"Food, music—whatever might have been in Emma's background that I might not know about."

"But what music, what food?"

"I'm thinking Caribbean, specifically Trinidad. That's where I think Emma's ancestors came from."

"Why?"

"I dunno…hunch? Statistics, at any rate."

I was pretty sure I had read that somewhere.

"So you want me to research Caribbean food and music, and you think that will somehow help Emma?"

"It will certainly add richness to the life I can give her, yes. What else is there to life, besides food and music and love?"

"Language?" she suggested.

"I'll get that for her somehow. Just watch me."

"I'm good at research," she said.

"I know that."

"And you'll probably want me to sit for her sometimes, right? I mean, after all, I will be the one who will know all about the food and music."

"Emma and I wouldn't have it any other way."

"When do you want to come back to work?" she asked.

"You mean you'll have me back?" I asked, not daring to believe it.

"Well," she said, "you did discover Mona Shakespeare, after all," Mona Shakespeare being the crazy but brilliant American author I'd discovered about halfway through my fake-pregnancy days.

"In that case, I'd like to come back next month," I said, caressing Emma's other cheek and thinking about what a truly fine woman Dodo was. "I'm in no rush to leave her just yet."

Then we talked for a moment about the practical details, about David's and Christopher's idea that I could work from home part of the time, which she agreed with.

Just then, Emma spit up a bit, but Dodo blithely smiled as she gently wiped Emma's mouth before dabbing at her own expensive blouse.

"Of course, you'll need an assistant," she said.

"I will?"

"Of course. All editors need an assistant."

Dodo had decided to throw me a shower.

True, I'd already had one shower, given by my mother as a matter of shocking fact. Not to sound like an ingrate, but it had hardly been a treat. When I tried to object to the notion of a second shower, Dodo objected, "But that was during the fake pregnancy! Now you have a real baby here! We *must* do something to mark the occasion!"

Perhaps her new role in Emma's life, as cultural ambassador, had gone to her pretty little well-meaning head? Regardless, she must have realized that my mother, feeling as she did about Emma, wasn't likely to throw a second shower. As for Soph, what few times she and Dodo were in the same room together, there was always some kind of Battle of the Blondes thing going on that led me to believe each found the other in some way intimidating, so I supposed Dodo didn't feel she could prod her into doing it.

Dodo, being Dodo, wanted to do things in a genteel way. So she'd rented out a tearoom not far from her place. Extreme? You may well wonder. But the way I looked at it, Dodo was probably reckoning that she'd rather pay for what breakage and spitting up a small herd of people plus a baby or two might cause in a public place, than seeing her own designer flat ill-used.

Realizing that it would be best not to surprise me, she'd even consulted me on the guest list.

"Who do you want to have from work?" she asked, and I could almost see her bright eyes through the phone line, see her as she excitedly drew up her list.

"You?" I offered.

"Oh," she laughed, "you're being silly. I'm sure you'll want to have Constance and Louise and Minerva—"

"And Stan from Accounting, of course."

"Really?" she said, surprised.

No, not really, I thought. I didn't want to have any of them. But she was trying *so* hard, she was being *so* nice...

"Yeah, sure," I said, "why not?"

"Okay," she replied, I'd bet anything scribbling Stan's name down while shaking her head, "it's your party."

"Thanks."

"David, Christopher, Tolkien—"

"Of course," I said, liking that she'd figured out on her own how important Tolkien was to me, despite the fact that I'd still not told everyone just exactly who he was to me, perhaps because I was no longer sure myself.

She paused for a moment and I was pretty sure she was chewing the end of her pen in thought, squinting her eyes.

"How about those women I met at your first shower—"

"God no!" I knew she was referring to Sophie's six-pack of friends from her parentcraft class who'd been in attendance.

"That's kind of a strong reaction," Dodo said, taken aback.

"Well, they're a strong group, and I'd just as soon enjoy my moment with Emma, thanks, rather than be judged and hanged."

"I thought they seemed nice."

"You think everyone seems nice. You probably thought Margaret Thatcher seemed *nice*."

She continued her list-making. "And your mother and Sophie and Baby Jack and Sophie's Tony if he can get away."

"Do we have to?"

"I'm afraid so," Dodo said. "If they found out about it later on, they'd be hurt."

"I suppose."

"Okay, then, let's see… We've got, including us, seven women, five men and two babies, provided everybody comes. Why, it'll be a Jack and Jill party!"

"Sounds great," I said, trying to muster enthusiasm. After all, she meant well.

The day of the party, we all met at Wilson's Tearoom. Something with padded walls might've worked better with this group, but the flower arrangements were nice and the sandwiches looked good.

"Didn't we do this for you once already?" My mother seethed ill humor as she walked in.

"Yes," Dodo said, stepping in and seeking to divert unpleasantness while at the same time making a stand, "and you did a lovely job by Jane. But I thought that, oh, you know, maybe she'd like to have another shower, only this time, with people she actually likes."

"Ooh, good one!" smirked Stan from Accounting, squeezing past my mother and tossing a poorly wrapped package with no card attached on the present table. He leaned over from behind me and whispered in my ear, "It's a furry quilt with a cow pattern on it and pink satin trim. My nieces are all gaga over them, but don't tell anyone it's from me." Then, louder, hitching up his pants and strutting as he moved into the room: "Is there any beer in this place?—" and after no response "—what kind of party is this, then?"

Then David and Christopher came in: "We got her little lamb pajamas!"

And Tolkien: "A Pooh bear mobile for over the cradle."

And Minerva: "A collection of Madeline books for when she's older."

And Constance, a long earring dangling from her eyebrow piercing as she hauled something rather large onto the table: "A month's supply of nappies for whenever she, oh, you know."

And Louise: "Socks."

Dodo chippered her way over, I suspect hoping to deflect the nakedness of that single-word utterance "socks," and picked up a beautifully wrapped package all done up in cows jumping over the moon that had already been on the table when I arrived. "And I got you a Pooh quilt to match Tolkien's mobile!" she enthused. "We worked on this together!"

I was getting infuriated. "Don't you people have any patience? Couldn't you all maybe have restrained yourselves and waited for me to open the presents, rather than telling me what's inside them?"

Just then, Sophie entered for the first time, pushing past me without so much as a hello. Behind her, Tony carried Baby Jack. The former readjusted the latter in his arms so he could extract a crumpled envelope from his pocket, which he added to the table. He shrugged uncomfortably, looking embarrassed as he said, "From your mother and Soph. They said that, since that was all you gave your sister…"

I suppose I might have been annoyed, and maybe I was for a second, but I did realize that they had a point there. At Sophie's shower, not realizing what such things were about, I'd given her a gift certificate to some breastfeeding store. It was the kind of fits-in-an-envelope present that screeches "Impersonal!" when coming from a sister; a fine enough thing if it came from someone you didn't know well or a man like Stan from Accounting who could be depended upon not to know better (but who apparently did), not from a sister. At the time, I hadn't understood that these kinds of things actually meant something to people, and not because of the gifts so much as because of the feeling of community support.

Even after my poor showing for Sophie, my mother had still had that shower for me at her place that Sophie and her friends had attended. They'd been very nice to me that day—as nice as my family gets—but I suppose the wounds had rankled, that this second shower had brought them back to the surface. I looked at that impersonal envelope on the table. This was now finally payback time. It was a bitch.

It occurred to me that I shouldn't always wait for others to come to me to set things right. If I wanted something fixed, I should try to do it myself.

Cautiously, I made my way over to Sophie, where she was eating cucumber sandwiches one after another, as though they might actually be good.

"Breastfeeding," she mumbled around a full mouth. "It gives you one hell of an appetite."

"I wouldn't know. Soph, can we talk?"

"You're kidding, right?"

"No, not really."

"What in the world would we talk about?"

"I don't know." And I didn't. "Us? Our relationship?"

"You're kidding, right?"

"No, not really."

I asked myself why I was doing this, when she was making it so difficult. What was the point in attempting to mend fences with her when I could be over there talking with Tolkien, Christopher and David about whatever was making them all laugh so hard, probably something to do with folding napkins into swans or collaring criminals? Or talking shop in an unpleasant way with Louise, a confounding way with Constance or a challenging way with Minerva? Or even talking football with Tony or thanking Dodo for her incredible largesse or finding something to say to, of all people, my mother?

Suddenly, Sophie leaned toward me, eyes all a-glitter.

"There *is* something I've been wanting to talk to you about, Jane."

"Hmm…?"

"I think Mother is having an affair!"

Once upon a time, I'd turned to David in moments of crisis, however great or small.

But times had changed.

My best friend was married now, after all, and Tolkien *had* said to call whenever I was worried about anything….

Answer the phone, I thought. *Come on, answer the phone.*

"Yes?"

"Apgar Scores!"

"What?" he asked, perhaps understandably.

"Apgar Scores! I've been looking over *What to Expect the First Year* and in the section on 'Your Newborn Baby' it has a subheading called 'Apgar Test.' It says it's the first test most babies are given. But when you checked her over on Christmas Day—remember when you did that?—I know you didn't say anything about checking her Apgar."

"What's an Apgar, Jane?"

"It's a baby test."

"What kind of a baby test?"

"Well, I don't know yet. I didn't read past the first line, where it says it's the first test."

"Perhaps you could do that now?"

I read quickly. "It says the scores reflect the newborn's general condition in five categories and are based on observations. It says that babies who score between 7 and 10 are in good to excellent condition and just need routine care, 4 to 6 is fair and may need help, under 4 is poor and needs immediate lifesaving efforts. And we didn't check this!"

"But you didn't have Emma yet at that point."

"I can't believe the things we missed!"

"Jane."

"How could we have been so stupid?"

"Jane!"

"Hmm?"

"Go look at Emma now."

I went. I looked.

There she was in the blue and white cradle Tolkien and I had got for her. We'd been so desperate to get something for her quickly—I was scared to have her in bed with us more than the one time—that we'd grabbed the first thing we'd seen. It turned out to be used, and must have previously belonged to an American family living abroad, because it had a very large warning, printed in several languages, on a patch of cloth that was stitched to the inside wall of the cradle, something along the lines of: WARNING! Misuse of this product may result in DEATH! Every night, when I put Emma down, she always turned her head towards the side with the warning patch. When Tolkien had been sleeping here nights, we'd look at each other fondly: "There's Em, looking at her security warning." Now I just thought it fondly to myself.

Yes, there she was, all curled up, head turned toward her security warning, asleep with her fist near her mouth. She was so beautiful.

"Jane?"

I loved that thing she did with her tiny fist. It was so vulnerable and strong all at the same time.

"Jane?"

I could just look at her all day…

"Jane!"

"Hmm?"

"How does she look?"

"She looks perfect."

"What's her color like?"

I looked at that tiny brown face, all scrunched up in sleep.

"Her color's perfect," I said.

"See?" he said. "She's fine. So whatever we might have missed before, she's fine now."

We might have missed something else?

I tore myself away from staring at Emma, picked up my new bible again.

"There's also something here," I said, "about checking her reflexes, which we also didn't do."

"Jane?"

"Do you know what a Moro reflex is?"

"Jane?"

"Or a Babinski reflex?"

"Jane!"

"Hmm?"

"Perhaps you should confine yourself to reading that book in small doses?"

That was a sound suggestion. Not that I was likely to take it.

I've got a good one:

What's the difference between Jane Taylor asking her sister Sophie to accompany her on her first visit to the pediatrician—Can you come with me to the pediatrician, Sophie?—and a masochist?

Answer: twenty-eight letters.

Okay*okayOKAY!* Yes, I do realize that it was sheer madness on my part, what with the history Soph and I shared, to ask her to go with me in my hour of need, but I ask you: What choice did I have?

Is it too late for me to say that I'm scared to death of doctors? Put it another way: Have you ever heard me talk about going to see a doctor when I wasn't making the entire doctor up?

But now I had Emma. And Emma was just a baby. And babies need, certainly in the first year of life, to be seen regularly by doctors. I'd already missed the first month's checkup, what with Tolkien going over her for me at home. And while from the looks of things, she was as healthy as a baby could be—knock on all the wood you can find—I wasn't about to take any chances with her health; certainly not when no one I knew could tell me what the hell a Babinski reflex was. True, I could have looked up Babinski in the dictionary or Googled it on the Internet, as any smart editor or writer would have done, but that would have been too easy.

The problem was, with nearly everyone I felt close to—Tolkien, David, Dodo—they all had to work for a living. True, if I confessed my fear of doctors, I knew that one of them would take time off to take me and Em, but there was only so much I felt I could impose.

God! Was that *me* talking? What the *hell* was happening to me?

At any rate, if, for whatever *insane* reason, I was reluctant to impose one step further on the three people I was closest to, that only left the choice of: 1) my mother (Can you say "over my dead body"?) and 2) Soph.

And Soph was only too glad of the chance to be superior.

Of course, I'd also been hoping to learn from her just exactly what she'd meant about Mother "having an affair," since we'd been interrupted right after she'd dropped that bombshell on me at the shower. But on the phone she'd been too busy being superior for me to squeeze a word in edgewise, and now that we were face-to-face…

"Did you remember to bring the baby?" Sophie joked as I met up with her on the pavement outside Dr. Khouri's office.

"Very funny," I said, adjusting Emma's hat against the cold. "Do you want to freeze out here or go inside?"

She held the glass door for us, her blond hair as knife-straight as a schoolgirl's over her green plaid coat.

"Thanks," I said. "Where's Baby Jack?"

She gave one of those sniffs that on Sophie translates to "shows how much you know." Well, at least she saves on excess talking.

"Pediatricians' offices are the worst places to bring babies if you don't have to," she said.

"They are?"

"Yes. They're all just big germ factories. Oh, sure, they have a separate waiting room for the sick kids, to keep them from infecting the ones there for well visits, but the so-called separate room is right smack in the middle of the regular waiting room and it doesn't even have a proper door on it, just a doorway. Believe me, doctors' offices are no place for healthy people."

I looked at her as I signed us in at the nurses' station. "Can you tell me why I asked you to come with me?" I asked.

"Don't be silly," she laughed, and it was a rather sunny laugh coming from Soph, giving my arm a reassuring pat. "You asked me to come for support."

There were times I thought her name should be Sybil.

As we waited among the presumably healthy, I felt myself growing anxious; okay, *more* anxious.

"What'll they do to her?" I asked.

"For her two-month visit?" asked The Expert, eyeing Em. The Expert must have deduced that, Emma being a newborn when I found her and two months having passed and two-month visits being something you did with babies—it must be time for that particular visit. "Everything."

"Everything?"

"Everything. They'll ask you about eating, sleeping, general progress. They'll want to know what her childcare situation is, what it's going to be for the near future. They'll measure all sorts of things—pfft!" she let out a little explosion of serious-thinker's breath "—weight, length, head circumference—"

"*Head* circumference?"

"Oh, yes. They're very big on that. The idea is that all those things are supposed to keep growing. Then of course they'll want to use those numbers to plot her progress since birth."

"But I don't know what her head circumference was at birth! Tolkien and I never—"

"Emma Taylor?" the nurse called into the waiting room.

It was the first time I'd ever heard anyone speak her full name like that out loud. True, she might not legally be mine—yet—but it wasn't like there was anything else to call her. I was still awestruck at the sound of it, "Emma Taylor," when I heard Sophie hiss at me:

"Just make some numbers up for head size and all the rest. After all, you're good at making things up, aren't you?"

I resented that remark, however true it might be.

Dr. Khouri, a petite Indonesian woman, asked and did all the things Sophie said she would.

When she asked me about height and weight, I estimated based on things I'd heard Sophie and others say when their own children were born. But when she asked me that one about head circumference, I really was stumped. Well, I figured, one hundred always represented a perfect mark on exams…

Not wanting to boast, then, I blurted, "Ninety-two!"

Dr. Khouri stared at me. "Ninety-two? You're saying Emma was born with a head ninety-two centimeters in circumference? I don't think so."

"If that were true," sniggered Sophie, "she'd be walking around with a beach ball on her shoulders."

"Um…five!" I blurted, erring in the other direction.

Dr. Khouri looked for help to Sophie, who returned the look with a shrug that seemed to say, "See what Jane's like?"

"You don't seem to know very much about your baby's medical history," Dr. Khouri said.

I thought of the checkup Tolkien had given Emma. "She was born Christmas Eve." I shrugged. "You know—everyone was pretty busy."

Then Dr. Khouri did some more things.

"What are you doing with her head?" I asked, alarmed.

"She's testing Emma's head control," Sophie informed me, as if I were the stupidest woman who ever lived. Then Sophie turned to Dr. Khouri. "It's not like anyone in the family ever said Jane was mother material."

See what I mean? My sister was fucking Sybil! Whatever happened to the supportive Soph of the arm pat?

Then Dr. Khouri, with Sophie translating for idiot me, checked Em's hand use, vision and hearing.

"How is Emma's social interaction?" Dr. Khouri asked.

"She's delightful!" Sophie enthused, before I could answer. "Which is really amazing, considering who's raising her."

I wasn't sure who the doctor found more odd: me or Soph.

The doctor readied a needle.

"Is that necessary?" I asked, holding Em closer as if to shield her.

"Second month," said Soph, The Expert, squidgying her nose in thought, "so she's going to get polio and DTaP."

"DTaP? What's that?"

"Diphtheria, Tetanus and something-I-can-never-remember Pertussis. The last is for whooping cough, even if I can't remember the first part of it."

"Acellular," Dr. Khouri provided.

"That's right!" Sophie smiled, giving the doctor at least an A. "Anyway, Jane, you wouldn't want Em catching any of those things, would you? And you certainly wouldn't want her passing them on to anyone else."

"No," I said reluctantly, "I suppose—"

"OWWWWW!!!"

Of all the different cries I'd heard Emma make—the hungry cry, the sleepy cry, the I-need-to-be-loved-*right-now* cry—I'd never heard her make a sound like that before. I also never knew before that I could feel so much distress at an obvious pain not my own.

It took all eleven verses I knew of "Twinkle, Twinkle, Little Star" to settle her back down again.

By the time I got to the end of verse eleven—"What a special star you are!"—Sophie had calmly discussed with Dr. Khouri supplementation and any of the questions I myself would normally have asked about immunization: what reactions to expect, how to treat them, when to call the doctor.

"Any more questions?" asked Dr. Khouri, as Emma at last fell asleep in my arms, bottle in mouth, a tiny frown of remembered pain still creasing her brow. "Are you having any issues with anything you'd care to discuss? Any family-adjustment problems?"

Sophie nearly choked on that last. "You're kidding, right?"

Dr. Khouri looked perplexed.

"With Jane," said Sophie, hustling me out of the office, "the family's been adjusting for nearly thirty years."

"That wasn't very nice, Soph," I said, after I'd made an appointment for Emma's fourth-month visit and once we were out on the cold pavement again.

"Oh, don't be so serious." Sophie smiled serenely, just like the cat who'd swallowed the Prozac. "You're always so serious all the time."

"But what if I'd wanted to ask the doctor some more questions?"

"Emma's fine, Jane. She's fine!"

"Well, then, can I ask you something?"

"Hmm?"

"What's with the mood swings? One minute, you're Sybil—"

"Sybil?"

"—and the next, you're like…like…"

"Like what, Jane?"

"Like a real sister."

"Oh, that," she smiled.

"Yes," I said, dead serious, "that."

"It's the breastfeeding. It's worse than pregnancy that way. Plays bloody fuck-all with your hormones, it does. Taxi!"

I knew one thing for certain, as my ears tried to recover from Sophie's screech: When it came time for Emma's fourth-month visit, I was going to just have to bite the rattle and go with her on my own.

I'd asked Dodo if she would take me shopping on her lunch hour. She was very flattered.

"Me?" she asked, hand going modestly to chest. "You want *my* fashion advice?"

It was hard to understand why she was so surprised. As an editor, as a member of the female race, Dodo had the most impeccable taste.

"What do you need help with?" she gushed, as we exited the office building that housed Churchill & Stewart, our bags slung firmly over our shoulders in the serious-shoppers stance that all women recognize. "New furniture for your living room? Things for the kitchen?"

I stopped in my tracks on the sidewalk, shoulder bag in midswing.

"What do you mean?" I demanded. "What's wrong with my living room? What's wrong with my kitchen?"

"Oops," Dodo said quietly, "sorry." Then she linked her arm with mine to jolly me along. "Come on, then," she said. "So, what did you say we were looking for?"

"Clothes for Emma." I explained how, even though I'd been given a lot of things for the baby at both showers, there had been a paucity of clothing. "And babies just keep growing!" I expressed the awe I constantly felt at how much Emma continued to change from one day to the next.

"Oh, good!" enthused Dodo, hailing a cab. "I know just the place."

Just the place turned out to be a store I hadn't set foot in since…

"Harrod's???" I demanded-asked, standing on the pavement as I looked up at the familiar green sign.

The last time I'd been in Harrod's had been during the fifth month of my pregnancy charade. I'd come to try on maternity clothes, just to see what I looked like, and wound up stealing what I had come to think of as "The Cloth Baby," hence the title of my book, one of those fabric-stuffed wrap-around-the-waist contraptions that they keep in maternity dressing rooms so that women who are not very far along can get an idea of how the clothing will look when they are. My theft had earned me the distrust of the Security Department and I hadn't hazarded a return trip since.

"I can't go in there!" I objected. "They probably have my picture on a wanted poster!"

"Of course, you can," Dodo soothed, gently tugging on my arm. "It's been months. Besides which, you won't be going to the same department. No one will recognize you in the baby department."

"But," I tried one last objection, "*Harrod's?* It'll cost me a fortune. I said I wanted to pick up a few baby clothes, not spend the equivalent of a down payment on a yacht."

"It'll be fine," Dodo said, leading me through the store. "You did say you didn't want to get Emma just the usual kind of boring baby clothes..."

True, I had said that, in the cab on the way over. I'd told Dodo that I didn't want Emma looking like one of those boringly silly babies, always dressed in too-cute things; I wanted her to be a cool baby. Of course, I did realize that last made me sound like a silly woman.

I'd been right to ask Dodo's advice, I realized, as I stood there in the baby department, arms stretched out as though I were a mannequin as Dodo piled items on top.

I didn't care how silly it made me sound: "Dodo!" I squealed, me never having been much of a squealer before. "These are sooo cool!"

And they were.

No Peter Pan collars for Em. No bloomers with tight elastic bands that would hurt as they cut into chubby little baby thighs. No endless sea of pink. Some pink, of course, but no sea.

Instead, my baby was going to be decked out in *cool* colors, like aqua and red and yellow and even a black long-sleeved T-shirt with a tiny pumpkin on it that Dodo found on the very back of the rack that was sized just right for Emma to wear the following autumn, provided she kept growing at the same rate. There were *cool* denim overalls. There were *cool* one-piece playsuits that looked so comfortable I wouldn't have minded having some myself. There was even a *cool* lime-colored hat.

"I know Emma will wear that with great élan," Dodo said, tossing that last on my pile.

"This is all sooo…*cool*," I said again, not daring to look at the total as the sales clerk ran my credit card through.

"I'm so glad I was able to help," Dodo smiled. "If that's everything, I should get back to work."

"Actually there was one other thing I was hoping you could help me with."

Okay, so maybe I'd had an ulterior motive when I'd asked Dodo to help me pick out Emma's wardrobe. Did that necessarily make me a bad person?

"Oh?" asked Dodo.

"What kind of clothes would you wear—" how best to put this "—if you wanted to seduce a man's interest without obviously seducing him?"

She looked at me shrewdly.

"Is the man in question Tolkien?" she asked.

After the shower she'd thrown me, I'd found myself fielding a string of questions from family and the people at C&S concerning Tolkien's real place in my life. The combination of him having been there New Year's Day coupled with his presence at the shower had telegraphed the fact that he was something more than just the simple "great good friend" he'd claimed to be. So I'd confessed, told everyone—even Stan from Accounting—about our romantic past, our tentative present, our uncertain future. It seemed scary, almost unbearably vulnerable, having so many people know about something that meant so much to me, but sometimes the truth hunts you down like a dog and there's just no escaping it.

I rolled my eyes at Dodo's question, trying to mask the importance of this all to me. "Well, duh, Dodo."

"Just a suggestion," she said, "but I'm much more likely to help you if you're nice to me than if you're not."

"Sorry."

I do realize that some might question my wisdom: asking

man-challenged Dodo for fashion suggestions that would catch a man. But I wasn't crazy. Dodo had never had any problem attracting men. No, her problem was that they always managed to slip off the hook, the slippage having nothing to do with how she looked. Hell, if I were a man I'd...

"Jane?"

"Hmm?"

"Stop looking at me like that. You're making me damned uncomfortable."

"Sorry."

Feeling somewhat chastened, I behaved myself as, toting my bags of stuff for Emma, Dodo led me to the women's department.

Dodo, in typical fashion, found what she was looking for in no time.

"A black turtleneck?" I scoffed as she held up the offending object. "I'm not planning on robbing a bank!"

"It's not just any black turtleneck," she said, eyes glittering, holding the shirt against me to size it up. "On you, it'll be a tight black turtleneck."

"Great," I said. "I'll spend the whole time in it worrying if I'm getting any back fat and if he can see it."

She ignored my surliness.

"And the perfect thing to pair it with," she said, holding up a red plaid miniskirt, "is this!"

"I'll look like a schoolgirl," I objected.

"Exactly!" she said.

"But Tolkien's not one of those kind." I was offended. "He doesn't like little girls."

"Of course not, Jane." She looked exasperated, as though it was just too much, dealing with a woman who didn't know her Armani from a hole in the ground, which I didn't. "So you'll wear the ensemble with sheer black stockings and high-high heels."

"And men like that sort of thing?" I asked, skeptical.

"Men *love* that sort of thing," she insisted. "On you it'll look..." And here, she began looking at me in a way that I recognized as being the same sort of look I'd given her back in the baby department.

"Cut it out," I said, taking the items from her. "You're making me damned uncomfortable."

"Sorry."

Even though I'd tried to tell myself that I should be patient, that I should wait until Tolkien was ready for us to get closer, I couldn't help myself. Feeling anxious that progress wasn't being made quickly enough, I decided to take matters into my own hands by visiting the proper authorities. Thus, leaving Emma in the capable care of David, having first verified with Tolkien that he was working in the office all day, I embarked on a visit to Scotland Yard.

I'd never seen where he worked before. Oh, sure, I'd passed by it a thousand times, but, never having been arrested for anything major, I'd never once been inside.

Not having thought things through completely, I hadn't counted on being stopped at the door, having my purpose there questioned, having the picnic basket I'd brought with me thoroughly examined for explosive devices.

"Do I look dangerous to you?" I asked the guard with some asperity.

He gave me a rather long once-over, taking in my red plaid miniskirt, my tight black turtleneck, my black sheer stockings and high-high heels.

"Actually," he said, "you look very dangerous to me."

"There's only Tuscan sandwiches in there," I said, as he tossed through my basket.

"And chocolate mousse," he said, holding up a covered china bowl.

"People need to eat." I shrugged.

"Nice cutlery," he said, inspecting one of the silver spoons I'd put in for the mousse.

"Thanks, I cleaned it myself."

"And you say Inspector Donald is expecting you?" he asked, replacing the fork and tucking everything up again nicely.

"No, I never said—"

"Best call up to make sure," he cut me off.

He lifted his phone, pushed some buttons.

"Inspector Donald, there's a Jane Taylor here says she's got an appointment with you, but she's not on my list…uh-huh…uh-huh…okay, right."

He hung up.

"He says you *don't* have an appointment with him—"

"I never said—"

"—but he'll see you all the same."

Feeling there was no point in my objecting yet again to what he was saying I'd said but had never said, I accepted his directions to Tolkien's office, thanked him for his help, and tried to ignore the feeling that he was watching my legs as I walked away.

Tolkien's office, if anything, was even less personal than his home, meaning that there wasn't even a CD player here to show that the occupant had anything other than business interests: no personal photos of him getting knighted by the Queen or shaking hands with Tony Blair (okay, I knew that nothing like that was likely to have happened in his life, but it *should* have happened), no metronoming silver-ball thingy on his desk for contemplative moments, no tiny fake putting green to brush up on a game he didn't play; just a big map of the city on the wall with some stickpins in it that meant nothing to me but hopefully something to him and a large computer on a desk that was buried under the papers covering every inch.

"Jane," he said, half-rising, "you should never have told the guard you had an appointment with me when you didn't."

He looked heart-stoppingly handsome in his dark suit, something I'd never seen him in before. You wouldn't think a suit could stop a heart, but his did mine. On some men—men like Stan from Accounting, for instance—a suit is no more than the natural extension of an anal personality. But on a certain other kind of man, it becomes the most shockingly attractive accessory. If I weren't so insanely in love with him already, that moment would have been for me like the moment when Elizabeth Bennett first glimpsed Mr. Darcy's estate.

"But I never said that," I protested, snapping myself out of my own eye feast and getting angry now. I was beginning to wish I had given that guard grief for ogling me. "All I said was that I was here to see you. It was that guard who decided—"

"It doesn't matter," he said. "What's up?"

I raised my basket, half-expecting him to toss me out.

"Lunch?" I said timidly.

"You know," he said, his actual words indicating that his tone should be harsh and yet it wasn't, "I am working here."

"But you still have to eat," said I, "and you did say that you were going to be chained to your desk all day doing paperwork, so I only thought to save you the trouble of having to go out and, oh, you know, forage for something and—"

"It's all right," he said, mercifully stopping me in mid-frantic stride, coming around the desk and relieving me of my basket. "I was beginning to get hungry. So, what have you got in here?"

I pulled out the Tuscan sandwiches, tried on a smile.

"I thought maybe you'd like a change from turkey and cheese?"

"How did you know that's what I eat every day?"

"Because you don't look like a ham person?" I guessed. "Now, then, where should we…?"

I looked over at his desk. Well, that was out. If I were to become responsible for messing up whatever system of order was going on over there, it wasn't likely to make him feel more warmly towards me.

Seeing my confusion, he went to a closet, pulled out a navy fleece blanket that looked like the kind of thing you'd offer to a victim in shock at a crime scene.

"I know it's not the most picnic-y blanket in the world," he said, spreading it out on the floor, "no red-and-white checks, but it'll do. I keep it on hand for those nights I find myself sleeping in the office because I've worked so late."

I settled myself down on the blanket, feeling closer to him somehow as I pictured him sleeping under it. As I laid out the sandwiches, I thought that even if that old blue blanket weren't the most romantic thing in the world, I'd give anything to be sleeping under it with him.

He took a large bite of sandwich, chewed in that manly way men have—yes, I do know I'm a bit gaga over this guy—and swallowed.

"So," he said, "what did you want to talk to me about?"

Talk to him about? I had to have a reason?

"You didn't come out here just to bring me lunch."

"Actually, I did."

"Come on. There must be something you want to discuss."

Oh, great, I thought. I'd imagined this impromptu lunch thing was such a good idea, an end in and of itself, but now, apparently, I was going to have to make some kind of purposeful conversation, too.

I tucked my legs to one side, thinking, thinking…

"Your parents!" I finally blurted out.

"My *parents?*"

"Yes, your parents. Don't look so surprised. You and I have been back in touch for—what?—nearly two months now and you've never once mentioned how they're doing."

"Fine," he shrugged, looking somewhat bewildered, "same as always."

"Yes, but how did they react to our breakup?" I asked, and I realized suddenly that I *was* curious about these things. "What do you think about what's been going on?"

"Well," he said, swallowing with a bit more difficulty it seemed, "of course I told them when we stopped seeing each other and of course they were distressed, said something about you being the most fun girl I'd ever brought home."

I nearly smiled—that seemed like a fine honor to win from his quirky parents—but then I realized the conversation was causing him discomfort.

"Naturally, I never told them the reason for the breakup."

"Whyever not?"

"I'm not sure really. I think I didn't want it to reflect badly on you."

He took my breath away. After everything that had happened, he was still so protective of me.

I thought back to all the boys, all the men I'd dated in my life, right up to and including Trevor. Every single one would have jumped at the chance to tell a story that reflected badly on me, if it meant saving face with their mates and kin. And who could blame them, really? Most people, when faced with the short end of the stick of romantic loss, are all about saving face.

"Then what *did* you tell them?" I asked.

He shrugged. "I told them we just hadn't been able to work it out."

"And now," I pressed, "since the night I showed up on your doorstep with Emma?"

There was that shrug again. "I haven't even told them we're back in touch again," he said.

I had to ask it again: "Whyever not?"

"Because I don't know what the future will be. Because they had a lot invested in you, in the idea of *us*." He looked at me hard. "They *liked* you, Jane. I don't want to get them started thinking that there might be an ending to the story that just may not be possible."

I didn't know what to say to that. On one level, I knew I was hearing one of the most serious truths he'd ever spoken to me. On another level, I was aware that, despite his ambivalent feelings toward me, toward any future we might still have together, he had yet to send me away, he had yet to tell me he no longer wanted to be a part of my crazy life.

For all the seriousness of our talk, it was nice to finally be alone with him again. Much as I loved Em—was obsessed nearly every breathing moment with Em—it was nice to be talking with him about something other than baby for a change.

I finished off the last of my own sandwich and tried to put a bright face on it as I reached into the basket for the mousse. "There's no need for us to solve the entire problem of our futures right this second."

Just then, there was a knock on the door and the guard I'd encountered earlier poked his head around the door.

Seeing us as we were situated on the blanket on the floor, me on my knees as I was about to serve Tolkien dessert, he gave Tolkien an amused smile.

"Right, guv," he said, "just wanted to make sure you were doing okay in here. You know—" he nodded at me "—that one really does look dangerous."

I rang the bell, then waited with Emma in my arms. As I waited for the door to be opened, I glanced at my watch—*ten minutes early!* I was that nervous, I was actually early for an appointment.

The door swung open and there was Mary Jr., baby Martha all snuggled in her arms.

"You found it! Great!" she enthused. "Well, come on."

When I'd attended—er, *crashed*—Mary Sr.'s funeral the month before, after thanking me for coming, Mary Jr. had asked how I knew her mother, her mother whom I had claimed to love so well.

Not able to think of anything better, and remembering from the obit that Mary Sr. had been a cleaning lady, I'd said, "From my office, of course. She used to do the offices where I work. And your mother was so, well, *you* know what your mother was like, that we all just loved her so much, she was more like family than someone who cleaned up after us."

"I felt the same about her," she smiled ruefully and it took me a minute to grasp what she meant.

"Yes, I guess she would be more like family to you, because she *was* family," I said, wishing I could stop feeling as though I were putting my foot in it.

"It's strange, though," she said.

"What's strange?"

"All the people my mother did for over the years and you're the only one to show up."

"Yes, well," I said, "you know how white people are."

"Come again?" she said.

"It's just that I think some of them might feel awkward, like maybe they'd be intruding or something."

"You do realize you're white, don't you?" she asked.

"Yes, but…" I said, tilting Emma's face toward Mary Jr. so she could get another look at her.

"Where's her father?" Mary Jr. asked, seemingly out of the blue, although I suppose it could have been one of those just-trying-to-be-polite-by-making-conversation-with-the-whacko gestures.

"I don't know," I answered truthfully.

"You mean you don't know where he is at the moment, as in 'He could be doing the shopping or out with his mates' or do you mean it like 'He's gone and I don't know his whereabouts or if he's ever coming back'?"

"Both," I said.

"How so?"

"Well, since the second is most definitely true, the first fits neatly inside that, doesn't it? If I don't know where he is in London, England, the United Kingdom, Europe, planet Earth, the universe, then I don't really know if he's shopping or with his mates either, do I? I guess he could be, but there's no way for me to know that, is there?"

"Ah," was all she said, "one of those."

From there we turned to talk of our babies. Hers, Martha, was her first, and she was just a month older than Emma. Mary Jr. was also a single mother, only she'd had to return to work almost right away.

Before I got to ask about what she did, though, her brothers indicated that she should be spending time with some mourners other than me. For myself, I was surprised she'd spent so much time with me, but I supposed that maybe it was a bit of a relief, talking about something other than loss.

As she turned to go, I said, "Hang on, please!"

"Yes?"

"I don't suppose…I mean, well…that is…you see, I don't know many black people, not any in fact now that your mother is gone—"

"Well, you do know Emma's father."

"Right. But, er, as I thought we've agreed, he's nowhere to be found. Anyway, I don't want to rob Emma of her rightful cultural tradition—"

"What about the father's family?"

"His family? Um, no, I don't exactly know his family…"

"That's a real shame," she said. "The older generation always has so much to share."

I thought of my own mother and how little she had to share that I thought worth having. Mary Jr. couldn't have made that statement to a less sympathetic listener.

"Right," I said. "Anyway, I was thinking it might be good to get Emma involved in some kind of play with other kids—"

"You mean like a playgroup?" she brightened.

"Sure. I guess that's what you'd call it."

She juggled Martha, reached into her purse and extracted pen and paper, commenced scribbling on her lifted knee; it's amazing what mothers can do with one hand.

"Here you go," she said. "Ring me. I'm in a group with four other women. We meet at my place, Saturday mornings because we all work during the week. Everybody brings a bit of food and a toy to share, so it's not the same stuff all the time, but I suspect that as the babies get bigger, they won't be so satisfied with just a ball or two."

And she was gone, moving on to speak with the other funeral attendees.

It had taken me nearly a month to get over my nervousness and now here I was, at her home.

As she led me through the flat, I asked, "What did you say you do again?"

"I'm a secretary to a lawyer," she said.

I tried not to look shocked at the meager place she lived in: a single room bedsit in Brixton with kitchenette and a shared bath down the hall.

"What can I say?" she shrugged. "I never said he was a good lawyer."

On a small table by the window, there were pictures of Mary Jr.'s family, nearly all of whom I recognized from the funeral. There was one girl, however, a teenager with haunted eyes that I didn't recall having seen there.

"Who's this?" I asked.

"Oh," Mary Jr. sighed, "that's Sarah. She's one of Luke's girls. She went missing several months ago and no one's heard from her since. That was her last school picture."

Then the doorbell rang and it was time for me to meet Jade, Chantelle, Marisa and Charmaine, not to mention their babies.

Surprisingly, at least to me, they took my presence there in stride. I supposed Mary Jr. must have warned them about me, perhaps something along the lines of, "I met this weird white woman at Mum's funeral who has a black baby and wants to see if we do things any different—hope that's okay," but there was no way of knowing and no polite way to ask. What with all the comparing of babies' progress, and voiced concerns over things like cradle cap and Charmaine's personal concern that her husband's strictly Spanish language approach might put her daughter at a learning disadvantage, I quickly forgot the distances between where I was and where I lived, and just about everything else for that matter.

God, what I wouldn't give for a cigarette, I thought, leaving Mary Jr. and her friends behind me as I closed the door.

Correction, I wouldn't give Emma for a cigarette—and I wouldn't give Tolkien or David or Dodo (or Kick the Cat or Christopher on their good days)—but, well, pretty much everyone else was up for grabs.

I'd been a casual smoker since I was something like *ten,* which may be a bit of a Jane exaggeration…but not by much. I'd also been a casual drinker for nearly just as long, ever since I'd nicked some Blackberry Schnapps from Mum's liquor cabinet and got Sister Soph drunk. Even during my pretend-pregnancy days, I hadn't quit either habit, which had been David's main argument as proof that I wasn't really serious, at the time, about being a mother.

Not that I'd indulged in either all that much. If I smoked more than five cigarettes, it had to have been a pretty shitty day at work. If I smoked more than ten, it meant I'd got drunk. As for the drinking itself, it wasn't like I was an alcoholic; and yeah, I do know that all alcoholics say that, but I really wasn't. Every now and then I'd have a glass of wine with dinner, if there was a party I'd have a few with everyone else, if life really sucked I'd get drunk with David. Sounds pretty normal, right?

Of course, a lot has been made in the critical press about the drinking/smoking habits of women of a certain age: mine. Particularly when referring to books, they like to point out those habits, in addition to a propensity to shop, as being prime indicators of shallowness.

As if.

I've never been a big shopper myself, but I applaud the women who do; after all, they're the ones driving the economy, right? As for the other vices, smoking and drinking, I just could never see the need to demonize people. I mean, there're a lot worse things a person can do, right? Incest, rape and world leaders who lie being just a few things that spring readily to mind.

Of course, since I'd had Emma, my thinking had changed a bit. Oh, I don't mean I was ready to tell everyone else how to live their lives. But the day I'd brought her home, I'd tossed the remainder of a pack of cigarettes without thinking twice. Not that it was easy, mind you. But I couldn't see blowing smoke around her and, frankly, she didn't give me the time.

Hell, babies don't even give you time to masturbate.

I couldn't imagine what it was like having a new baby in the house for women who'd borne their own children, their bodies feeling tired from performing a miracle. All I'd done prior to having my baby was to spend the evening feeling sorry for myself and then I'd taken a little walk, until I found a baby on a doorstep. No need for a doula there. But imagine trying to care for a baby after, say, a sixteen-hour labor or tearing or stitches. I couldn't.

I supposed that there might come a time when Emma kept me less busy, that I might someday smoke the odd cigarette or two outside the house, since it was something I enjoyed. And I was sure I'd have wine again with friends, although I couldn't ever see getting drunk unless someone else was taking care of Emma for the night. But yes, I would drink again. After all, just because I *wouldn't* do those things right now, it didn't mean I'd ceased *wanting* to.

So, since I was no longer a smoker or a regular drinker, did this all make me A New Jane?

I looked down at Em in my arms.

"Bollocks," I said to her softly.

I was The Old Jane + Baby.

I'd just put Emma down for her nap, thinking to get a load of laundry in—again, it's amazing how little you get done with a small child in the house!—when the phone rang. I snatched it up, hoping it wouldn't wake Emma before she'd got the chance to properly start sleeping.

"Hello?" I whispered.

"Jane Taylor?"

"Yes," I replied cautiously, thinking if it was yet another person calling to offer me a new credit card or life insurance, I'd hang up.

"Stephen Triplecorn here."

Drat! I'd been wondering when his other shoe was going to drop on me. Then I went into a panic. Barely daring to breathe, I asked, "Have you found Emma's birth mother?"

"Oh, no," he said, "not that we haven't tried, but it would appear, at least for the moment, that the baby you found has no history at all. At any rate, I've been going over your file in my computer here and I've noticed something troubling."

"Yes?"

"Yes. Even though your name is on my list of approved homes, I don't seem to have a Home Study here."

"You don't?"

"No. I don't."

"I see."

"Well, I don't." He sounded exasperated.

I tried to tell myself that he was an easily exasperated man, but my guess was that it was just me.

"How can you have been approved without a Home Study?" he demanded.

"Must be one of those bureaucracy glitches you read about happening all the time."

"Well, I haven't read about them. At any rate, something will need to be done about this."

"Such as?"

"We'll have to do one now."

"And what exactly does a Home Study entail?"

"Oh, you know, looking into every corner of your life, checking all your records, financial and otherwise, interviewing your family and friends. It'll be kind of like a proctologist's visit, only without the rubber glove."

This couldn't be good.

"And who," I swallowed, "will be doing all of this looking? I assume you'll assign it to one of the women in your office."

I was pretty sure I *had* seen other people in his office when we'd been there, although I couldn't for the life of me remember any.

"Oh, no," he said, and I felt as though I could actually see his sinister smile through the phone. "I'll want to handle this case myself."

"Are you the only worker in that whole office?" I asked with some asperity.

There was that audible nasty smile again: "Sometimes it seems so, doesn't it?"

According to *What to Expect the First Year,* Emma was right on target. She could do everything she should be able to do, plus she could grasp a rattle, reach for an object she wanted and pay attention to a raisin (even though the book said "raisin or other very small object," I'd gone out especially to purchase raisins, which I despise, for this purpose). She could also say "ah-goo" and other similar vowel-consonant combinations, so she had strong verbal skills; no surprise, really, given her talkative mother.

March, the third month

My return to the offices of Churchill & Stewart, now as an editor, began rather ignominiously.

"Who the hell are you when you're at home?" said the woman who could only be the new receptionist, because of where she was sitting, as I tried to walk past her on my way to Dodo's office.

Dodo had mentioned that there was a new receptionist, and that her name was Hilda; what she'd neglected to do was couch her mention as a warning.

Hilda looked to be about the same age as Constance, meaning ridiculously young, but all similarities ended there. Having effectively stopped me in my tracks, she returned to her typing while obviously expecting an answer from me and expecting I wouldn't dare take a step farther until granted permission, her typing clipping along at something like a gazillion perfectly spelled words a minute. Clearly, the Constance days of letters typed with fyuu;tig/fd in the middle of them were over with.

Hilda also had short-cropped blond hair and must have been wearing a conical bra, the tips so pointy that they looked as though they'd impale even Colin Firth if he ever dared to come too close.

"I'm Jane Taylor at home *and* here," I said.

"Oh, right," she said not bothering to look up, "the crazy lady who used to work here and is now back again. Well, go on then. Don't keep Dodo waiting any longer."

"I wasn't—"

"Jane!" It was Dodo, coming out of her office to greet me. "Come on in!"

Seated across from her, we discussed how best to slide me back into things, particularly since I had a new position now.

Behind Dodo, on the wall, were oversized pictures of book jackets of titles she was most proud of having published. Looking at them, I longed to have my own display like that one day.

Dodo briefed me on the manuscripts C&S was currently excited about acquiring and she even asked about the progress of my own book, *The Cloth Baby.*

"You know how slowly publishing can grind," I said. "Even though I've already delivered it, it won't be out until October."

"Are you and Alice editing it now?"

"Yes, and I must say, it's a rather novel experience for me, having someone else insist that I improve on something I thought was just fine to begin with."

"You'll be getting a lot of that experience from the other side of the equation soon. Now, then, we need to talk about an assistant for you."

"Yes, you mentioned that before, when I came to visit you. I assumed you'd need to hire someone new for me."

"Oh, no," she shook her head. "I'm sorry, Jane, but it's just not in the budget. Dexter Schlager," she went on, referring to our hairless Editor-in-Chief, "was pretty adamant. He said that he hadn't expected to take on a new editor's salary this year, but that he had—yours. And please don't think he's sorry for a minute. He thinks it's great that we'll have a 'writing editor in residence,' as he put it, on staff. But as for springing for a second unexpected salary for a new assistant editor—"

Knock, knock.

"Yes?" invited Dodo.

The door swung open, apparently pushed by a sullenly nasty

toe, and there stood Louise, slouched with arms crossed against the doorway, in all her surly glory.

"Jane," announced Dodo, trying to strike a bright tone but failing miserably, "meet your new assistant!"

While waiting for Stephen Triplecorn to arrive for his first visit in regards to doing a Home Study, I did some quick research on foundlings, foster care and, my ultimate did-not-dare-to-dream-yet goal, adoption. I learned that fifty-six abandoned babies were discovered here a year, according to Home Office figures; that it was highly irregular for a black baby to be placed in a white home—which really bothered me and not just because of my situation with Emma—but that at least my unmarried status wasn't a mark against me; and that adoption, if it were even possible, would take years.

As I opened the door on Stephen Triplecorn, I saw that he was still favoring tight trousers, which he wore with a short-sleeved striped shirt and tie, and no jacket.

"I know people get excited at the prospect of spring coming," I said, "but you do realize that it's bloody freezing out today."

Wrong, wrong, wrong, Jane. I wanted to hit myself in the head with my own fist. *Do not, DO NOT alienate the man who holds your life—Emma's life—in his hands.*

"Would you like some tea?" I asked sweetly.

"No, thanks," he said. "Tea's too warm. That's why I favor the short sleeves when I can get away with it—too hot-blooded for my own good."

"I see. So where shall we…?"

"Actually, I'd like to talk to your neighbors first. You did tell me you'd tell them to be expecting my visit."

"Right."

An hour later, he was back, clipboard in hand.

"How did it go?" I asked, anxiously.

"Well," he said, "the two gay guys upstairs vouched for you completely. But we expected that, didn't we? After all, the Israeli one is your best friend, correct?"

"Yes, but that's never stopped him from speaking the truth about me before."

"Yes, well… They also said they watch the baby for you frequently while you're at work. Is that true?"

I prepared to get defensive. "Is there a problem with that?"

"No." He shook his head mildly. "No problem at all. As a matter of fact, they both seem saner than you do."

"Thanks."

"Welcome." He chewed on his pen, did a squinting thing at me. "Now, the Marcuses downstairs… Do they drink?"

I was surprised. "Why do you ask?"

"Not sure, but they both seemed somewhat dotty. They said you used to be a bit noisy sometimes, before the baby, but much less so since, and that they were surprised at the color of the baby, said they thought for sure your baby's father was white."

"Oh."

"Now, why do you think they'd say that?"

I wince-smiled. "Because they drink?"

He nodded. "That's what I was thinking. At any rate, the important thing is, at least so far, that everyone says the same thing…Emma appears to be happy in your care."

He looked over to her, as if to confirm this, and Emma obliged him with a smile.

And Emma *was* a happy baby, an *extraordinarily* happy baby. All you had to do was look at her to see that. Sure, she did her share of crying every day—like when she woke hungry or when she wanted to be changed or got frustrated or when she just wanted to be held—and sometimes that crying could get to me, but she was *so* much happier the vast majority of the time than most babies I knew about. She was a joy. She gave it. She was it.

"Yup," said Stephen Triplecorn. "There's no denying that's one happy kid."

I started to smile.

"But that doesn't mean you're in the clear," he added.

I wanted to tell him to stuff a sock in it. But, unable to avoid a glance at the bulging crotch of his trousers, it looked like he already had.

I'd been meeting with the playgroup at Mary Jr.'s house for a few weeks now. We did try for every week, but with everyone's busy lives, we weren't always all able to make it. Sometimes, like now, there was only one other woman—in this instance, Charmaine—there with us.

With fewer people, the conversation tended to be more personal.

"Excuse me for not remembering," asked Charmaine, "but how is it again that you and Mary know each other?"

"You remember," answered Mary Jr., "she came to Mum's funeral."

"Oh, right," said Charmaine. "She used to clean your office or something—was that it?"

"Yes," I said, feeling vaguely embarrassed at maintaining this lie about a woman I'd never met, or had only met in her coffin.

"Where was that again?" asked Mary Jr.

Before I had Emma, I would have found it odd, her forgetting a piece of my own personal trivia that was so essential to my identity. But since? I knew now that if you put a half dozen women plus babies together in a room, they were a lot more likely to discuss feeding concerns and sleeping habits as opposed to the fate of the euro or Middle East relations. And that's not condescension talking, by the way; for in that room, I realized that, in a sense we were doing the most essential work that allowed the rest of the world to spin blithely on.

"Churchill & Stewart," I answered.

Mary Jr. was puzzled.

"Huh," she said. "I don't remember Mum ever mentioning that place." But then her brow eased as she observed Martha doing yet another spectacular-baby thing, and she shrugged. "No matter. It's not like cleaning offices is the most exciting thing in the world. I suspect Mum must have done a lot of places she didn't bother to mention."

"Hey!" I exclaimed, hoping to deflect the subject. "Did you see what Martha just did with her feet?"

Mary Jr. glowed with pride. "Yeah, she's pretty brilliant, that one."

We were eight around my table.

We were a tight fit, I'll grant you, but we were eight.

With David and Christopher, who I'd always expected to vouch for me anyway, and the drunken Marcuses out of the way, I realized that it would only be a matter of time before Stephen Triplecorn—The Man With The Big Package—would be calling on my family and co-workers. Admittedly, the wheels of Social Services seemed to take forever to grind—believe me, I wasn't complaining!—but I needed to plan ahead. So, in the hopes of enlisting their aid, or at the very least persuading them *not* to say "Oh, Jane Taylor? Right. The pathological liar with the fake pregnancy," I called them all together for another party. Not wanting to take any chances, I had David do the cooking, so what we wound up with was a nice big salad of field greens, something bruschetta-y and a game animal nobody recognized, plus chocolate for dessert, which somehow made it all okay.

Once dessert was over, though…

"What are you up to, Jane?" my mother asked.

I'd already tried to corner my mother several times, hoping to get to the bottom of Sophie's "Mother is having an affair" assertion. But every time I'd tried to do so, she'd been practicing that safety-in-numbers thing, actually talking to others in such a way that it would have been socially awkward for me to grill her.

"'Up to?'" I asked.

"You didn't call us all here to feed us well," said sister Soph.

"Are you going to read a will?" asked Constance, gleefully. "I always wanted to be at a will-reading in a drawing room."

"This isn't a drawing room," Stan from Accounting pointed out.

"Nobody died," said Louise, through gritted teeth.

"Are we completely sure of that?" Dodo asked mildly.

"Of course we're sure of that!" I said. "Nobody *died!* Why would you even think such a thing?"

"You have to forgive Dodo her anything-is-possible stance," said Stan, "because with you, anything *is* possible."

I don't know why, but I actually suspected Stan meant that as a compliment. What was going on with him?

"He's right," agreed Minerva from Publicity. "You're just like that Corinthians verse."

"You mean the one they use at weddings? Isn't that about love, faith and hope?" Louise sneered.

"That's the one," said Minerva. "Do you have any more of this chocolate?"

"But Jane is *nothing* like that Corinthians verse!" Louise objected.

"If you like," conceded Minerva, "I'd still like some more chocolate, please."

I cut her some.

"There really isn't a dead body in this anywhere, if you must know," I said.

"We must." Louise was adamant.

"Well, there isn't," I said. "What there is…"

"Yes, Jane?" Constance leaned forward.

"Spit it *out,* Jane!" said my sweet mother.

I spoke the words in a rush. "Stephen Triplecorn, the Social Services person who's handling my case, is going to want to interview all of you to check my references."

"You already know what I think about you keeping Emma," sniffed my mother.

It never failed to amaze me. I had yet to come across a black person who expressed the belief that I had no right to keep Emma and yet my own mother still insisted on being dead-set against.

"This isn't *about* the social aspect of the case," I said, "or what your views are on cross-cultural placement. It's about whether or not I'm a fit mother for Emma."

Louise spewed wine across the table.

"You want *us* to vouch for *you?*" she laughed.

It did get better from there, but please believe me when I say: not by much.

Later on, as everyone was leaving, Stan from Accounting stopped for a moment.

"I'm just curious, Jane," he said.

"Yes?"

"Nearly a year ago, you began your fake-pregnancy scam."

"Eleven months," I corrected.

"Fine. Eleven months. But that's hardly the point."

"Which is?"

"It just seems to me, that anyone who would go to such great lengths to fake a pregnancy, must have had real ambivalence about having a real child. So, what I want to know is: What changed? What's changed in the last eleven months?"

His question surprised me.

"Why," I said, "I found Emma."

"And that's it?" he asked.

I thought about it; it seemed so important to him.

"Yes," I said, finally. "I was never ready before I found her. But I am now."

As my mother used to like to say, every year of my growing up, "Yes, even Jane's got to have a birthday. Might as well do something to mark the day."

I couldn't agree with her more. The only problem was, my day was here and there was no one for me to mark it with.

David was working; Christopher was off doing one of those ex-architect type of things he'd begun doing lately, Frisbee golf or something, (not that he and I would ever do anything alone together anyway); my mother, ever since I'd moved out of her house, had failed to mark the day; my sister, likewise; and I'd worked from home all afternoon, so it wasn't even like I could have an absolute-minimum workplace birthday with cloying cake and a five-minute break.

"Oh, well." I held Emma in my arms as I sat on the couch, legs tucked under me with Kick the Cat nuzzling against my bent knees. "Mummy is thirty today. It's easy to remember. It's March 30th and Mummy is thirty. You'd think someone might remember that, wouldn't you? No? I guess not. It's all still gibberish to you anyway, right? How about we go out for some cake and milk, just me and you? You can have the milk—"

Knock, knock.

The three of us made our way to the door.

It was Tolkien, looking a little the worse for the rain that was pelting against the windows.

Since my impromptu visit to Scotland Yard, I hadn't seen him once. Sure, we'd talked on the phone for at least a few minutes every day—he liked to keep on top of how things were going with Emma—but having made my first aggressive move, I'd decided to hang back and wait for him to make the second. That second move had been long coming, I'd started to believe it would never come, but now, apparently—I hoped!—it had arrived.

"You never ask 'Who's there,' do you?" he asked.

"Emma and I like being surprised," I said, holding the door open. "Besides, the Marcuses wouldn't let anyone pass without giving them the evil eye first."

He looked around, as though he might be expecting someone other than we three: Emma, the cat and me.

"Were you meeting someone here?" I asked, sarcastic perhaps, but that's me.

"No." He reddened. "It's just that before I knocked, I thought I heard voices."

Now it was my turn to redden. "Oh. That."

I explained how the baby-care book recommended talking to your child as much as possible, that language acquisition was easier for children who heard it a lot—I mean, duh—and that early language acquisition helped children feel less frustrated with the world.

"So I talk to her nearly all the time," I said. "Most of the time, I feel like the greatest moron who ever lived, you know, sitting here talking about the light fixtures or how to boil an egg or Chaucer to a baby who can't answer back. But the book does say it's good for her...."

He was staring at me.

"What?"

He shook his head.

"I don't know," he said. "Nothing. Something. Who knows what I was thinking? At any rate, I brought you these."

And here, he produced a bouquet of flowers.

They were nothing you'd call grand, having in fact wilted somewhat in the rain, not the proverbial dozen roses or anything exotic or out of season; it was just a small bunch of wildflowers in need of a vase.

"What's—?"

"For your birthday," he answered my not-wholly-formed question.

"But how did you know?"

"Don't you remember, when we were dating? We had those

conversations that people always have early on in a relationship, you know, where people exchange favorite colors and foods and Beatles…"

"…and flowers and birth dates," I finished for him.

"Exactly," he said, as Emma and I went to find a vase. "As a matter of fact, I did remember your favorite flowers are peonies, but when I looked, they said they were out of season." Now he really looked embarrassed. "At any rate, I rang your office, thinking you'd be there, but that new receptionist—Helga?"

"Hilda," I corrected.

"Nasty thing, isn't she? Anyway, she said today was one of your work-at-home days, so here I am."

"With flowers."

"Yes, well…"

He actually shuffled his feet.

"Do you want to sit down?" I asked. "I could get you something to drink. Emma and I were just going out for milk and cake, but we can all go."

"Oh, no," he waved his hand. "I can't intrude on that."

"But you wouldn't be—"

"You and Emma are doing just great, aren't you?"

"Yes, we are."

"I can see that." He smiled, a smile that was equal parts sad and happy. "I'm glad, Jane. Emma deserves to be happy and you seem to be doing a good job with her."

"Well, thanks, but I still don't see why you can't come with us."

"I need to get going now," he said abruptly. Then he kissed me on the top of my head, just the briefest brush of air and warmth that I wished I could capture somehow like a firefly under glass.

"Take care of her," he said to me. Then, "Take care of your mum, Em."

He kissed each of us on the cheek, quickly, and left.

Emma could now lift her head like a trouper, could follow an "object in arc" in whatever ways the book said she should or might, and could make a razzing sound.

Who would have ever thought that I'd experience so much joy from a tiny little person giving me a raspberry?

April, the fourth month

Louise was blocking me at every turn.

That day when Louise had virtually kicked open Dodo's door, and Dodo announced her as my new assistant, I'd nearly fallen off my chair. What could Dodo have been thinking of? Louise *hated* me!

After Louise had slunk off, Dodo had explained:

"The way Dexter Schlager figured it, one of the editors would have to share their assistant with you, since he wasn't about to spring for a new one. It was either her or Constance, and, well, Jane, surely, you must understand, *I* can't start sharing an assistant at this stage in my career."

So Dodo had persuaded Dexter to make Louise's boss share *her*.

"And who knows, Jane?" Dodo tried to put a bright face on it. "Maybe you'll do so many brilliant things, right out of the gate, that Dexter will find it worthwhile to get you your very own assistant."

Not bloody Rupert Murdoch likely, I thought.

"You do realize, don't you," I'd pointed out, "that Louise will despise working under me? That she'll thwart me at every turn?"

"Oh, surely, it won't be *that* bad."

But it was.

And who could blame Louise, really? Certainly not me, not when I stopped to give it any thought.

Never known for either self-awareness or great reserves of empathy, I still managed to put myself in Louise's knockoff Manolo Blahniks: What if *she,* previously on the same stratum as I once was when I started at Churchill & Stewart, were suddenly to successfully leapfrog from assistant to assistant editorship to full editorship *and* the company turned around and appointed me her assistant?

I'd swallow toner hoping for the effects of cyanide, shove blue pencils through my eyeballs, slit my wrists with Hilda's scimitar-shaped letter-opener and call it a bad day. Then, if I were still alive, I'd go look for a new job.

But, for some reason, Louise wasn't doing any of those things. She chose to stay in her newly untenable position and she chose to make my life a living hell while doing so.

When I asked her something about the Parker manuscript, she e-mailed me a memo about the Drew. When I asked her to send Drew a letter, detailing suggested changes, she worded it in such a way that I wound up spending half the afternoon on the phone with a justifiably pissed-off author.

I didn't dare let her bring me coffee, although this she repeatedly offered to do, for fear she'd poison me or put laxatives in it.

And yet…and yet…what choice did I have?

Best-case scenario? I'd persuade Dodo and Dexter Schlager that there was no way Louise and I could ever successfully work as a team. And then what? Either: 1) they'd tell me I needed to find a new editorial home, since they couldn't—*wouldn't*—afford another assistant, or 2) Dodo would be compelled to share Constance with me, which would make usually kind Dodo permanently tetchy and make me…what? *What* would having Constance as my assistant make me?

Bonkers, that's what it would make me.

There would be me, trying to be businesslike, however sociopathic some might think me; and there would be Constance, recommending a manuscript because it had made her mood ring turn the proper color.

There would be me, looking for a property that would raise the respectability level of the company's profile; and there would be Constance, pushing for a healing-crystals laden epic saga with "commercial appeal *and* great karma!"

There would be me…

The list wasn't worth continuing. It just wouldn't work. In a contest between the multicolor-eyed, overenthusiastic New New-Ager and the bitch who hated my guts but who was also at least intelligent, the bitch had it by a mile.

Surprisingly enough, it was Sophie who called to give me a heads-up that Stephen Triplecorn was paying a visit to her and my mother.

"I don't know why I'm warning you like this," she said, "since I'm not even sure how I feel about what you're doing."

Thinking back on the Sophie of my childhood—one year older, always light-years ahead of me in our mother's mind and in her own—I did also wonder why she was doing it. Old Sophie would be doing it to advance-rub my nose in what she was sure would be my own failure. Old Sophie liked the status quo of her always winding up on top just fine.

Of course, during the days of my "pregnancy," that had changed a bit: she'd grown moderately warmer, as though we might one day be breastfeeding comrades-in-arms or something, and she'd offered me advice, however heavy-handed. ("Don't do anything stupid, Jane!") But, then, she hadn't known my pregnancy was fake at the time, had she? Since the enlightenment, she'd become decidedly chilly, with the exception of the sisterly mood swings she'd evinced on the day of the visit to the pediatrician—claiming breastfeeding-induced hormonal misalliance—and that brief sorority-sister exchange at the second shower over Mum's purported affair, which she *still* hadn't elucidated upon.

Well, who could blame her for being mostly chilly? Not even me, although I'd certainly spent most of my thirty years blaming Sophie—justifiably, in my mind—for a lot.

Okay, maybe I could have made some effort too. Still, so why was she warning me now? Was it a true warning, like "get out of the way, because that cliff is falling towards you!" or was it a warning-just-for-the-sake-of-gloating warning?

I had no idea.

I did know that there wasn't much good it could do me, since I couldn't very well be on my mother's premises when Stephen Triplecorn's interview with them took place.

Apparently, though, while Sophie had said she wasn't sure how she felt about what I was doing, she felt sufficiently moved to call me back that evening to tell me what had happened.

"Mother did tell him that you were never the greatest with your dolls when you were little," she said.

"And?"

"And I pointed out that while your dolls may never have been given the usual professions by you—after all, you did have that one who you said danced the cancan for sailors at the Moulin Rouge—that you'd never abandoned any of them."

"True."

"Then mother said that you were never an easy child, that you'd never really gotten on with her, or with me for that matter."

"And?"

"And I said that had nothing to do with your ability to be a good mother now, that maybe you'd even be a better and more sensitive mother than you might have been otherwise, given the challenges you'd had to face in your own youth."

"I never thought about it that way."

"You're welcome, Jane."

"Thank you, Soph."

"Then Mother started to say something about you 'deceiving everyone' you'd ever met—"

"Oh no!"

"Which was when I kicked her and said I heard Baby Jack calling for her, which he wasn't of course, since he doesn't say 'Granny' just yet and which I'd have thought she'd hate even if he did. But *she* bought it—or at least she fell in love with the idea of him calling her and she went running."

"Phew! But, then, what did Stephen Triplecorn say?"

"Well, he asked what Mother had meant by that. Can you blame him?"

"And?"

"And I told him exactly what I thought. I said that you had indeed deceived everyone you'd ever met. You'd deceived them because, while no one would have ever pegged you as 'good mother' material, you were indeed all that."

I didn't know what to say.

Finally, "Did you really, Soph?"

"Yeah, I really did."

"But why?"

"Because it's true, Jane."

"You mean that?"

"'Course I do. All anyone has to do is see Emma with you to realize you're the best thing for her. True, I'm not sure it's the best of all worlds—whites raising blacks, or vice versa come to that—but all worlds has nothing to do with specific worlds. In Emma's specific world, you're the center. And you've earned the right to be."

Now I really didn't know what to say. But I didn't have to, because it was then that Sophie reverted to type:

"Just don't louse it up, Jane," she warned.

I actually swallowed, and took her warning to heart. After all, Emma's future happiness and life were what was at stake.

"I'll try not to, Soph."

"I believe you."

"Good. By the way, what did Stephen Triplecorn say after you said that?"

"He didn't say anything, because I didn't give him the chance. I was too worried Mother might come back and start to tar you again, so I told him it was time for Baby Jack's breastfeeding and that we'd all have to do it together, if he wanted to stay, since Mother never breastfed either of us and she always likes to watch."

"You didn't!"

"I did. And you'd be surprised how quickly he left, once I started undoing my blouse. For a man who's spent his career in Social Services, and who presumably has had much prior experience of mothers and infants, he was damned scared of my breasts. Made that big thing in his pants jump, it did."

"You noticed it too?"

"How could I miss it? The thing is a cricket bat!"

David was taking what he called a chef's holiday.

We were seated at his favorite Chinese restaurant, waiting on his Mu Shu and my Lo Mein—okay, we're boring eaters; Christopher was off, presumably doing one of those Frisbee golf-type things he did these days, only it was nighttime, so it probably wasn't that; and Dodo had Emma in care. Dodo was playing some Trinidadian music when I left them and cooking some Trinidadian dish on the back burner of the stove.

"I know she can't eat it yet," she'd said, stirring, "but she can smell it in the air. Getting culture through her nose must be good too, no?"

I'd shrugged. How do you answer that?

David rearranged his chopsticks. Even the prospect of Mu Shu wasn't pleasing him tonight.

As the waiter brought our food I asked, "Why so glum, chum?" which was what he usually asked me whenever I was down.

He was silent as he folded his crepe into a triangle, then tossed it back on the plate. "Bleagh. I could do better than this."

"I'm sure you could. You always do."

"It's Christopher," he finally sighed.

I put down my fork, which I was using because I never use chopsticks.

"What's wrong?" I asked. "Is he sick?"

God, please don't let anything be wrong with Christopher that might take him from David or that David might catch and that might take him from me.

"No, it's nothing like that. There is nothing physically wrong with anybody."

"Phew!" I settled back in my chair.

"Well, of course, there are things physically wrong with people all over the place, it's just that Christopher and I aren't part of those physically-wronged people."

I grabbed on to his gesticulating hand, stroked the hairy back of that palm I knew so well.

"What is it, David?" I asked softly. "What's happening?"

"I don't think he's happy with me, Jane," David said.

"What are you—mad? Of course he's happy with you! How could anybody not be?"

And I really meant it. In the years I'd known David, there were countless times I'd wished that we were oriented somehow differently—that either he wasn't homosexual or I was homosexual but I was a guy or *whatever* it would have taken for us to be in the romantic sweepstakes for each other's hearts. But it wasn't the way the world was, at least not our world. We loved each other almost more than we loved anyone else on the planet, the only person ever managing to outpace him with me being Emma. And Tolkien. Regardless of the fact that I couldn't and wouldn't ever be in love with David myself—not in that way—I still couldn't accept the notion that anyone he chose to pay attention to wouldn't be madly in love with him.

"No, really, Jane, I don't think that he is any longer."

"Oh, you're just going through a bad patch. Everyone has them. Why, Trevor and I used to have bad patches all the time."

"Exactly," he said pointedly. "And look what happened with you two."

True.

"Tell me, what makes you think his feelings have changed?"

"At first, I thought he agreed to us working different shifts in the restaurant because he wanted to help you out with Emma."

"That's what I thought, too."

"It turns out, he never liked working shifts with me in the first place."

"How come?"

"Said it was too much my place, me being the chef and all."

"He kind of has something there."

"Yes, but he was originally the architect. He *built* that place."

"Good point."

"What?" He looked at me. "Now you're agreeing with both of us?"

"No. Yes. Well, sort of. People get all territorial about things and they get really weird when shifting power is involved. Take where I work, for instance."

"Is this going to somehow circle back to me and my problem?" he asked.

"Yes. Why do you ask?"

"Because I've been studying up on the way you do self-involvement over the years and I think I've got it down now pitty-pat. It's okay if we talk about you so long as it's really about me—have I got that right?"

"Perfectly."

"Good. Go on."

"It's like this," I said. "The hierarchy and power dynamics at C&S have all gotten screwed up. How can we take Constance seriously as an assistant editor? How can Louise take Constance seriously as her equal? How can Louise take me seriously as her boss? How can Dodo take me seriously as a senior editor? Or Louise's other boss—how can she take me seriously?"

All of a sudden, despite the frenzied spate of chatter I'd just engaged in, I felt deflated.

"Christ, I've got it hard," I said. I took a sip of Chinese wine. "I've got it worse than Constance, having to put up with the resentments of Louise."

David used one finger to tap the top of my glass.

"Hmm?" I asked.

"And how does this relate back to me and my problem?"

"Oh, right," I said, "sorry. Well, as I say, it's all in the power dynamics. First, the restaurant was your dream. Then you hired Christopher, who was the architect. Now, your hiring him should have made him subordinate to you, because, after all, you were the one with the money, or the bank's money. But, anyway, you were the boss. Except that you can't boss an architect, can you? I mean, they're all so self-confident, all that he-man—" and here I went baritone "—'I know how to build a building' Howard Roark stuff, so it's always like they're working for themselves rather than you. Like, do you remember I. M. Pei and that whole Louvre thing?"

"Vaguely. The French wanted somewhere to stow the Mona Lisa and he gave them Egypt instead."

"Exactly! I mean, who could have stopped him?"

"I'm used to it by now," he said.

"What? Your problems with Christopher?"

"No, the Louvre. I mean, it kind of looks like all those World's Fair domes, but at least it's a triangle."

"Favorite geometric figure of yours, is it?"

"How did you ever guess?"

"Because—"

"Jane?"

"Hmm?"

"You were saying?"

"Right. So, anyway, there's you and Christopher, pre-opening of the restaurant, maintaining parallel power since back then you were both kind of the boss. But then the restaurant opens—"

"And he says he wants to help me—"

"But helping you puts him in a subordinate position—"

"Even though he was initially doing it for love—"

"Which starts to rankle after a few months—"

"Which is why he's now playing Frisbee golf at night," David finished, throwing his napkin on the table. "So, basically, what you're saying is that I've professionally emasculated my partner."

"Exactly," I said. "Except I'd never put it like that."

"No, of course not."

"You know what Christopher needs?"

"What?"

"Christopher needs to find a glass pyramid to build."

I was sitting in my office—which still had no oversized prints of book jackets on the walls, because of course I hadn't edited any yet—wondering how to drum up business.

Dodo had been a senior editor for donkey's ages, so all the agents were used to approaching her first. But I'd only been in the role of editor for a short time, so it was as though the publishing world barely knew I was there.

Since my return to work, Dodo had been generous enough to steer a couple of decent manuscripts my way. There was the Drew and that other one I could never remember the name of, but they were minor things. Neither of them was likely to make my name in the business. True, I'd been the one to originally discover Mona Shakespeare, but the real editing on that had been done by Dodo while I was out on my maternity-leave-that-wasn't. What I needed was something that I alone could acquire, something I alone could edit, so that later on, when people thought of the book, they'd say, "Ah! Jane Taylor did that one! Let's try to get Jane Taylor for this one...."

But where to look, where to look...

Since I'd always done some of my best thinking while surfing around the Web, I went online to see what I could find. If nothing else, I could clear out my e-mail inbox.

Along with the usual nonsense—offers to make my penis grow larger (as if I needed that!); interoffice e-mail from Constance with some panicked request (as if I wanted to read that!)—there was nothing of any substance, so I clicked on the daily e-mail from Market Smackerel, which posted up-to-the-minute news on the publishing business: what notable deals had been made, what film rights had been optioned, what editors had switched houses or been promoted. Huh. There hadn't been anything in Market Smackerel when I'd been promoted.

I scrolled down through all the news that the green-eyed monster part of me wished I'd been a part of. Oh, why couldn't *I* be the editor of a nominee on the short list for the Man Booker Prize?

I finally scrolled upon something that really interested me:

In an unusual move, Simon Smock, of The Simon Smock Literary Agency, has sold the rights to a novel by an unnamed British author to publishers in France, Germany, Holland and Sweden. The book, submitted without either title or author, is what Smock terms a "sexual *folie a quatre*," and is purported to be a "Rashomon-like tale involving four girlfriends and a sex crime." When asked to compare it to previously published books, Smock said, "It's not really like *any* other book I've ever read. But, if you absolutely need a slugline for it, I'd say it's a cross between *Divine Secrets of the Ya-Ya Sisterhood* and *The Story of O.*" This, quite naturally, leaves the Smackerel to wonder: If the book has already been sold in four foreign markets, but it is by a *British* author, when, pray tell, will rights be sold here?

The item ended, as always, with an e-mail contact address for the person reporting the news; in this case, The Simon Smock Literary Agency.

As quick as you can say, "I want that fucking book about fucking!," I was all over that e-mail address, typing in my request to Mr. Smock that he send a copy of the book here to me at C&S for my consideration. I mentioned how I'd been the one to originally discover Mona Shakespeare, a discovery that had been made much of in the press, even though the book wasn't due out until sometime around November or December. I suppose Mona's book, *The Rubber Slipper,* about a pregnant woman who finds herself with ten suitors fighting for paternity of her baby, had captured people's imaginations. In a world fraught with endless hardships and heartache, I suppose people just like to latch on to something whimsical and diverting whenever they can. I told Mr. Smock that I felt confident that C&S could do the same kind of big-splash launch in the U.K. for his client's book as we were planning on doing for the Shakespeare. Then I punched Send and prayed.

I sat back in my chair, wishing it were a more comfortable chair, reviewing what I knew of Simon Smock.

Simon Smock was a schmuck, of course.

Now, then. Some people will tell you that all agents are schmucks, but that isn't true. Sure, there are some hard-asses in the business, just as there are some incompetents and some substance abusers and some who ride the glory of one shining success through a thousand failures, but there are also a lot of brilliant minds in that end of the business. Why, in today's rush-rush publishing climate, the good agents really wind up functioning as the best of editors as well, not merely selling the book but also shaping the content and style even as they shape the career.

But Simon Smock wasn't one of those brilliant agents. Simon Smock was a prima donna, a fop. Having seen pictures of him

in the trades, I knew him to be a lion's-head cane-wielding, in-
digo cape-wearing, Truman Capote-esque figure. Not to mention a pain in the ass. But Simon had something I wanted, and
if I wanted to get what I wanted, then I was going to have to work
with him.

The nice thing about e-mail is that, if your timing is lucky
and you send your message when the other person is online
too, and if that other person is the type to deal with new business promptly, you can receive a response far quicker than you
ever would have had you employed snail mail or picked up
the phone, trying—and failing—to get through.

There was a new message in my inbox and it was from—Yes!
Yes! YES!!!—Simon Smock.

Dear Ms. Taylor,
I'm out of the country for another four weeks.
I'm traveling in America, talking to editors about that
book you're interested in, as it happens. Rather than send-
ing it to you now, though, I'd like to add you to my list of
British editors I'll be meeting with about it upon my return.
Perhaps Churchill & Stewart would like you to take me to
The Connaught? I like the dining room there; there's a paint-
ing there, either a Turner or something Turner-esque, that I
am fond of gazing upon, but the lounge is nice too and we
could always have a drink there in those lovely burgundy
Windsor chairs.
Please call my secretary and arrange it.
Best,
SS

What a self-important little toad!

I immediately sent a reply stating that I would gladly do as
he suggested, all the while keeping my he's-a-self-important-lit-
tle-toad thoughts to myself.

Tolkien and I were going on A DATE!!!

I'm not sure exactly what had brought it about—the past few
months of over-Emma's-cradle friendship, when he'd visited on

my birthday or the fact that he'd run into David in Marks &
Sparks, where David had given him the "Jane really is the most
amazing, if strange, girl in the world" speech—but I sure wasn't
going to argue. Whatever had brought this good fortune my way,
I was taking it this time.

When he'd first rung up to ask me out, he'd been as nervous
as if he was asking me for the first time.

"Jane?"

"Yes?"

"Will you…?"

"Yes."

"We could…"

"Yes."

"Yes?"

"Yes."

What that all translated to was:

Sunday afternoon at Round Pond, directly in front of Ken-
sington Palace, where Tolkien had laid a checkered blanket on
the grass and from which vantage point he and I and Emma
watched the kite-flyers on the grass and the little yachtsmen
sailing their boats as we picnicked on the lunch he'd provided
from home.

During the course of that nearly indiscernible asking-you-out-
on-a-date conversation we'd had, he'd insisted we bring Emma.

While having a nearly four-month-old baby with me on the
first date I'd been out on in months might impress some as sub-
romantic, he seemed to need the security—having mumbled
something along the lines of, "I need the buffer, Jane, without it
I'm worried I'll fall in love with you all over again too fast"—
and I had to admit that I was grateful for the buffer, too. It may
have been me who had broken his heart last time around, and I
may have been pushing for more by visiting him at his office and
hoping for more ever since, but I'd broken my own heart at the
same time I'd broken his as well.

With her there, we could safely talk about neutral Emma-cen-
tered topics. Maybe it wasn't the kind of talk that others would
call "romantic," but any talk between us was further progress
as far as I was concerned. If we just kept talking about periph-

eral things, one day we might just get around to talking about us again.

So I told him about the playgroup I'd been taking her to, about the other women in it, the other babies.

"However did you meet up with these women? Not that I don't think it's a great idea, which I do, of course."

How to tell him…how to tell him…how to tell him I'd met the women by pretending to know one of the women's dead mother and crashing her funeral?

The only way to do that was *not.*

"I was in line behind her at the supermarket," I said.

"And what?" he asked. "You said, 'Excuse me, but my kid's black too, do you think we can all play together?'"

"I didn't put it quite like that, but, yeah—" I nodded "—that was the general gist."

Then, before he could ask more about Mary Jr., I told him my concerns for Emma, my hopes, my dreams.

Again, I suppose another woman might have taken the chance to talk to him about her own hopes, her own dreams, even what she'd missed most…okay, what *I'd* missed most since breaking things off with him. But even I, insensitive me, could see he needed me to go cautiously, so I talked about Emma instead.

"I hope she'll want to take ballet," I said. "I always wanted to as a girl, never did, though."

"And if she's not interested?"

I looked at her, playing contentedly on the blanket.

"It won't matter a single bit," I said, and meant it.

And then he kissed me. Not much of a kiss, really, by most people's standards, just his lips softly brushing against mine for the briefest of moments.

I didn't care.

It was the kind of kiss that contained all the dreams we foolish mortals are made of.

"It's not like you're a different person," he said. "I don't think there is any such thing. It's more like you've become more of a different part of you, in a different direction."

And then he kissed me again.

Two foolish mortals dreaming, Emma on the grass.

* * *

Emma was such a superior baby, it was hard not to get caught up in the baby expectations of *What to Expect*. At the end of her fourth month, she could do all of the "may even be able to" things: she could bear some weight on her chubby little legs when held upright, sit without support (well, for about a half second), objected strongly if her favorite toy was taken away and would turn in the direction of a voice other than mine; she particularly loved the sound of Tolkien's voice.

Smart girl, eh?

May, the fifth month

Stephen Triplecorn was ready to begin his visits to Churchill & Stewart to talk to my co-workers, so that he could see what people who weren't tied to me by the bonds of either blood or best friendship would say about my character.

ACK!!!

Oops, sorry about that. Just one of those bouts of instant mass panic this whole process could induce in a person.

When he'd called on the phone to set it up, he'd explained that he'd be seeing them one at a time: Constance, Minerva from Publicity, Dodo, Stan from Accounting and Louise.

"But won't that take all day to do it like that?" I'd asked.

"All day?" he snorted. "It'll take about five months."

"Months? You can't be serious!"

He snorted again. "I'm as serious as an underbudgeted office, that's how serious I am. I simply can't pursue any one case in more than dribs and drabs at a time. There are too many cases and too few caseworkers."

"No wonder it takes so long for kids to get adopted or even placed," I'd sniffed.

"Well, if I were you," he advised, "I wouldn't be so quick to complain. The longer it takes me to process your case, the longer you have with Emma."

God, that sounded ominous.

So now here he was, in the outer office of Churchill & Stewart, being grilled by Hilda.

"If you're not an agent and you're not an author and you're not here about a book and you're not the boy to fix my copier—"

"That's quite all right, Hilda," Dodo said in her most silken editor's tone. She held out a beautiful hand. "You must be Stephen Triplecorn. Jane's told me so much about you. I'm Lana Lane."

God! I always forgot that was her real name!

Stephen took her hand; a trifle suspicious, perhaps, but he took it just the same.

That handshake was like Moses parting the Red Sea, like lightning striking the Frankenstein Castle, it was like—

Okay, so maybe it was like none of those things, but it *was* cataclysmic. I mean, how could it not be? They had to be the two most physically beautiful people in all of the U.K.—she with that blond hair and those elegant fingers, he with that black hair, blue eyes combo plus, er, big package—and here they were, in one small room. Why, it was like Godzilla meets King Kong, except that no one was ugly.

"Jane hasn't said a thing about you," he said, snapping me out of my reverie. "I thought her boss was someone named Dodo."

"I'm Dodo," said Dodo. "And Jane told me how you'd be coming here to interview us each over a period of time. Since I'm in charge here—" but she wasn't in charge! Dexter Schlager was! "—I'm afraid I wouldn't feel quite right having you interview the people who work under me unless I was there, too. Surely you understand." She indicated her office. "Won't you come in? Then we can see if Constance is ready."

As Dodo closed the door behind them, her eyes met mine and she winked.

What in the world was Dodo up to?

What Dodo was up to was something I learned an hour later, when she ushered Stephen Triplecorn out of her office with a warm wave ("See you in another month, Stephen!") and commanded me to come inside.

"What are you up to?" I asked.

"I'm trying to help you," she said. "You really think it's wise, letting harebrained people like Constance—"

"But I thought you thought she was smarter than we used to think she was and that was why you were so keen to make her your new assistant."

Dodo gave a long-suffering sigh. "Do we really need to go through this again? How many times do I have to tell you, the only reason I wanted Constance—who was showing some real, er, that is to say minor glimmerings of improvement around that time—was because you were in the midst of your eighth month in your fake pregnancy for which you'd soon be taking maternity leave, although none of us knew at the time that it was—"

"Okay," I held up my hand. "Okayokayokay."

"As I was saying," Dodo said pointedly, "do you really think it's wise, letting harebrained people like Constance and people who've always hated you like Stan speak unbuffered to a man who holds your maternal future in his hands?"

She had a point.

"At least," she went on, "with me there, I can head them off at the stupidity pass or give you a heads-up afterwards as to what you need to prepare for."

I sat myself down across from her, leaning forward in my chair. "So tell me," I said, "how did it go?"

"Oh, well," she said, suddenly going all evasive on me, "you know Constance."

"You mean she said something incredibly stupid?" I prompted.

"In a word, yes."

"What was it?" I couldn't keep the note of desperation out of my voice. Still, Stephen Triplecorn hadn't slapped the cuffs on me on his way out—not that I really thought someone from Social Services was empowered to do that, which may have explained some of his daily grumpiness—so there was at least that.

"Er," began Dodo in Hugh Grant fashion, "I believe Constance started out by saying, you know, in that just-joined-the-Moonies overly enthusiastic gaga way she has—" and here she did a credible imitation of the twit at hand "—'Jane was *brilliant* when she was pregnant, er, uh, um, I mean she's great with that black baby!'"

"She didn't!" I gasped.

"I'm afraid so," said Dodo.

"But then what did you do? What did he say?"

"Well, I got Constance the hell out of there as quickly as I could, didn't I? After all, another minute and she'd have been bringing up that tarot card-reading midwife you'd fabricated, if only because she still thinks such a creature would be a damned neat idea."

"And then?"

"And then I flashed a bit of leg—" and here she shot one perfect leg out to the side of the desk so I could see it and, damn, but that was one beautiful leg "—and told him how bonkers our Constance has always been. Said her family really had dropped her on her head when she was just a tiny crystal-sucking baby and that we'd given her a job out of pity. Said you'd always been the biggest of sisters to her here, that she looked up to you as the old woman in her shoe and that her reference to your pregnancy was merely a confused metaphor on her part, since to her you were like the Earth Mother and hence eternally preggers."

"That sounds like the biggest line of crap I've ever heard in my life."

"Well, of course it is," she said. "But do you think he noticed? He was too busy looking at my leg."

Now that I knew I'd dodged the Constance bullet, it seemed fairly safe to relax for a moment.

"Didn't you notice anything odd about Stephen Triplecorn?" I asked.

"Now that you mention it," she said, "I did."

I leaned forward again. "Isn't it the biggest—"

"He has the most amazing eyes," she interrupted. "At first, you think they're cold. But look a little harder, and they're intelligent eyes. Look harder still, and you realize he truly cares about what he's doing."

"But you lied to him," I said.

"Nah," she pooh-poohed me with a wave of the hand. "Constance has always been a nutter. I merely tinkered a bit with the particulars of her résumé."

"But getting back to Stephen," I said, "you didn't notice—"

"Notice what? That he has a crush on you?"

"What?"

"Well," she shrugged, "why else would he be stretching this out over several months?"

"He told me his office was underfunded."

"And I'm sure it is," she conceded. "But I'm also sure that there's more to this than meets your eye. I really think he likes you, Jane."

The previous year, I'd become friends—well, not really *friends,* more like barely tolerable acquaintances—with the women Sophie had become friends with (*she* really had) during her parentcraft classes. There was Peg, known only to me as Goodie Peg, for her likelihood to drown a carrot for being a witch; huffy Trudy; busy Helena; Dora, the legal assistant; cosmetics-happy Elizabeth; and Patty, the equivalent Marisa from Mary Jr.'s playgroup—practically a teenager.

When Sophie had learned about the playgroup I was in with Mary Jr. and company, she'd invited me to hers "for a change."

"What do you think might be different?" I asked.

"Oh, I don't know," she said, sounding a bit embarrassed. "Our kids are all a few months older than Emma. I suppose I was thinking it'll give you an idea of what's in store for you."

Tolkien had said something about my experiences with Emma changing me, or maybe it was that he'd said she brought something that was already in me out more strongly. Whatever the exact words, I entered Sophie's playgroup—late, because Emma'd spit up on me when we were halfway out the door—with the vague expectation that these women would now somehow be different than they had been when last we'd met. Who knew what I expected exactly? That Peg would be a little less Proctor in Salem-ish? I don't know. But whatever it was, I wasn't expecting to have them all be...

Exactly. The. Same.

I hadn't seen them in over six months and they still looked the same, still sounded the same, still all jumped on Trudy—not that Trudy didn't ask for it—and still looked at me, despite a slight warming the very last time we'd met, as though they might need a cross and garlic to keep me away from their kids.

In truth, maybe they were a bit justified with that last, given that Sophie must have explained to them that my former pregnancy had been, er, false, and that now I had a black baby I'd found and wanted to raise. I don't know what her exact words were, because she wouldn't tell me, but whatever she'd said had been persuasive enough that they'd at least been willing to grant me one-day's admission, if guarded, into their inner sanctum of breastfeeding and sleep problems.

Unlike at Mary Jr.'s place, these women all came equipped with their own copies of *What to Expect the First Year,* which they consulted regularly. I'd thought I was bad, what with how religiously I consulted the thing every night at home, but when Goodie Peg realized that I didn't keep a copy in my purse at all times, she asked, "But what will you do if—" and here she flipped pages until she arrived at the sort of thing she was looking for "—if Emma pulls on her ear?"

"Ask her to stop?" And then, when no one responded, I wince-smiled. "Wait until I get home and then look in the book?"

Apparently, that wasn't good enough.

Nor was anything else I did or didn't do.

In Mary Jr.'s group all the women breastfed as a matter of course, but none of them made me feel guilty that I didn't and none even asked *why* I didn't.

But here?

It seemed like every five minutes, one of the coven was whipping out a breast and popping a nipple into a baby's mouth, willing or no.

And every time Emma fussed, if she even made a "coo," one of them would look at me pointedly and start to say, "Why don't you just...?"; followed by, "Oh, that's right—you can't."

I thought I'd long since made peace with my inability to nurture my child in that way, but each time one of them succeeded in making me feel bad, succeeded in making me feel like I was *less,* I thought to myself, *Damn! Why should Peg's little whinger deserve to get eight free IQ points rather than Emma?*

And, needless to say, none of them thought I should be raising Emma in the first place. Not. At. All.

"It's an, um, weird situation you're in," said Patty.

"It's hard enough you're doing it alone," said Elizabeth.

"Shouldn't Emma be with her own kind?" asked Helena.

"She might be better off..." Dora trailed off.

"You do realize, don't you, that your baby is black?" Trudy pointed out.

"It's just not natural." This, from Goodie Peg, as she promptly whipped out the other breast.

"But—" I began in my own behalf, not to mention Emma's. Yet I didn't need to go any further. Sophie's "but," as it were, trumped my "but."

"But Jane is doing a good job. None of us could do better. And now I really wish we could talk about something else, please. Either that, or perhaps we should just call it a day."

Sophie??? This was my content-to-hate-my-sister-for-the-rest-of-my-life sister *Sophie???*

But, clearly, she meant it; and, amazingly enough, they backed off.

Even with them backing off, however, the rest of the play-group time felt rather strained. It was certainly not a place I would want to return to again.

While they were polite enough to me and Em, there was no real warmth there; and I don't just mean towards us, I mean towards each other and their own kids as well.

At Mary Jr.'s—and yes, I know, I know, I'm beginning to talk about Mary Jr.'s like it was some sort of Utopia, which it absolutely was not, but it was so much better than this—the babies seemed to be a part of their mothers; here, the kids seemed like an extension, like appendages. I'm not sure if the distinction would be clear to anyone who hasn't witnessed it, but it certainly was to me.

I hugged Sophie before I left because she'd stood up for me, but I knew I wouldn't be going back, at least not for playgroup.

* * *

The suspense was killing me.

It had been months since Sophie's allusion to our mother "having an affair" and I was still no closer to discovering the truth. This was in part my fault because I barely ever spoke with Sophie and I nearly never spoke with Mum, but the suspense was still killing me.

So, I did the only thing a self-respecting daughter could do: Having learned that my mother was going out on Saturday night, and having made arrangements for Emma to spend a few hours with Dodo, I decided to break into her house.

Now "breaking in" is a bit of an extreme way of putting it. Ever since I'd moved out, years before, I'd retained my key. True, I'd never once used it to gain entry, and, true, if my mother realized I still had it, she would have undoubtedly demanded I return it or changed the locks. But apparently she hadn't realized it, so all I had to do was steal up the gravel driveway and sneak up on the ancestral home (okay, it wasn't an ancestral home, just a fairly nice house outside of London) in dark of night, turn my key in the lock and…

Voilà! Time to start snooping.

I realize it was a lot of bother to go to when I could have asked my mother directly, but have you been paying any attention at all to our dysfunctional relationship? Mum and I didn't *ask* each other direct questions, we didn't *tell* each other things; we were more like two armies, forever engaged in evasive maneuvers.

From the entry hall I made my way into the living room.

The last time I'd been in this house, it had been for the shower my mother had thrown me several months before. At that time, the place had looked the same as it had for years—except for the presence of some of the more nauseating baby-shower decorations—as if time had stopped, as if when my father had died my mother had decided to freeze it all in amber.

But now everything had changed.

The blue sofa we'd had forever was now gone and in its place was a beige leather one that smelled as though it had just been delivered. Everything—the carpeting on the floor, the paintings on the walls—were all things I didn't recognize. And, on the end table, where once upon a time there had been family photos of us doing family-type things—hard to believe that Sophie and my mother and I had ever been part of a unit that did family-type things together, but there you have it—there were still school photos of me and Soph, and even some of Mum with us girls, but there were no longer any of my father. It was as though he had never been.

When I realized what was missing—him—I felt a sharp pain inside. I've never been one to give over to the sentimentalizing of kin, probably because mine were mostly so bad, but my dad had always been the bright spot in the family for me. He'd died when I was very young, so maybe I just loved him with the peculiar eyesight of time and distance, or maybe things really had been that way, but I always remembered him as being my champion in that family. And now that champion was completely gone, no longer existing even in pictures.

Not wanting to dwell on the loss of my father, either literally or now metaphorically, I made my way to the kitchen, intent on helping myself to a glass of the cheap wine I knew my mother always kept in the fridge.

But even that was different.

Instead of the oversized jug I was accustomed to, there were expensive bottles of Chianti and Bordeaux from vineyards I'd never heard of. The bottles were unopened as though waiting for a special occasion or someone to share with.

Oh, great, I thought. *I can't even pinch a single glass of wine to steady my nerves, because she'd notice it.*

Having been thwarted in the kitchen, I decided to head straight for her bedroom.

The door was closed, which seemed odd for a person living alone. But then the thought occurred to me that she must have gotten used to it like that when Sophie and I had still lived at home, each of us needing our own privacy, and she'd never changed the habit.

I slowly pushed the door open, expecting who knows what, and hit the light switch.

Oh. My. God.

Even this had changed!

I ticked the changes off on my fingers: the living room, the kitchen, the dining room. I felt like the three bears stumbling upon Goldilocks, save that my mother wasn't here and there was only one of me.

My mother's bedroom, previously a sanctum sanctorum of frilly pinkness that had made me wonder how my father had stuck it out for so long, had been transformed into the kind of room that, hell, *I* would live in.

Gone was the cabbage-rose needlepoint carpet; instead, she'd left the original and very beautiful wide floorboards exposed, polished to so high a sheen it invited you to skate across it in bare socks. Where once there had been a white-and-gold painted bed with about sixteen pillows plus a stuffed cat on it, there was now a simple oak sleigh bed with a white down comforter on it so thick it looked like a cloud. And, where once there had been a vanity table so froufrou it would've made Barbie barf, there was a writing desk, which was antique wood and had a design of trailing ivy that looked to have been handpainted on the gently curved drawers.

As I stood there lusting after that beautiful writing desk, it suddenly occurred to me: a writing desk! If my mother were likely to keep a written record of what she was up to, or anything of that nature, this was where it would be.

It took me all of two seconds to locate a datebook she had tucked away in the center drawer. I paused a moment before opening it, feeling a guilty pang that I was violating someone else's privacy. But then I thought—I *rationalized*—that if it had been anything so personal as an actual diary, I never would have looked inside. But this was a mere datebook. How private could the things here be? I'd probably just see things like "Dentist appointment, 2:00 p.m." or "Don't forget to plant the tulip bulbs" or "Do something to mark Jane's birthday..."

I riffled through the pages, working my way backwards from today. And there was a pattern, a pattern that had nothing to do with teeth or flowers or me. On every weekend, going back to the beginning of the year, there were entries that alternated "Vic here this weekend" with "Me at Vic's this weekend."

I sat down on my mother's cloud of a bed, shocked, and wondering why I was shocked. I'd known this was coming, right? I certainly hadn't *dis*believed Sophie when she'd voiced her suspicions, but somehow, I supposed I hadn't internalized it. And now I had.

My mother was having an affair…okay, maybe not an affair since my father was no longer living. My mother was having a *liaison* with someone named Vic. Every weekend, either he came here or she went there, which explained where she was tonight— at Vic's.

"Should I be raising Emma?"

The speaker was, of course, me.

My audience?

Mary Jr.'s playgroup. Or what there was of it that day, at least, as we played with our babies in a playground not far from her Brixton address.

They—Mary Jr. plus Marisa and Chantelle—didn't appear to understand my question.

"Who would raise Emma," asked Mary Jr., speaking for the group, "if not you?"

"I don't know." I thought about it. "Perhaps someone with a Trinidadian background."

Chantelle was surprised. "Why would she want that?"

"Er," quickly I sought to backpedal, realizing that—of course!—none of them knew I wasn't Emma's natural mother. "Well, I never knew what her father's background was and I just thought that I didn't want to rob her of anything. But, if say, she had a Trinidadian to raise her…"

I was losing myself.

"I don't know," I tried again, "so she could fit in with the kids she'd be playing with, I suppose, like your kids. So she'd have some sense of where she came from."

Marisa shook her head. "None of our people came from Trinidad," she said.

"They didn't?" I asked.

"No," said Mary Jr. "Tobago."

"All of you?" I asked in disbelief.

"Well, except for Charmaine's people," Marisa said. "They came here from the Dominican Republic, but that's just them."

I was stunned.

Apparently, they were too.

"Why'd you think all our people originally came from Trinidad?" asked Mary Jr.

"I dunno," I shrugged. "Statistics?"

"Statistics?"

"Yes, statistics. Don't the majority of blacks in England originally come from Trinidad?"

"Just because something's a majority," said Marisa with a very precise seriousness, "it doesn't mean every single individual."

"I mean, it's like America," Chantelle pointed out. "Everyone who comes here from America isn't from Texas."

I looked at Emma playing.

"So," I said, "like all of you, Emma's people could have come from somewhere other than Trinidad."

"Oh, yeah," said Chantelle. "Her people could have come from any of a number of places."

I thought about Dodo with her Trinidadian recipes and Trinidadian music. I closed my eyes. No way could I tell her I'd fucked up again. And what would be the point? So maybe there was no way of knowing if we were giving Emma the *right* cultural heritage, but at least we were giving her *some* cultural heritage. I mean, wasn't it a bit like the whole God thing? People all over the world were constantly arguing, sometimes even killing each other, over who knew the only way to get into heaven. The way I figured it, just so long as you could get everyone to agree on the Thou Shalt Not Murder thing—and maybe the one about honoring thy mother and thy father too, now that I was one of the former—it was all the same in the end.

So I would let Dodo go on playing the music and making the food and I'd be grateful that Emma was getting *something,* even if there might never be any way of knowing for sure if that something was right.

"God but this playground sucks," Chantelle spoke with uncharacteristic disgust, snapping me out of my self-concern.

I looked around me, at the overgrown grass that was more like a field, at the rusted equipment, at the seesaw that would only see and never saw.

"Well," I said, forcing a smile and trying to put a bright spin on it, "it is a bit—"

"Sucky," Chantelle said.

I gave up.

"Yeah," I agreed. "It is."

Churchill & Stewart had been willing to let me expense lunch at The Connaught, if it meant possibly snagging a hot book away from our competitors. And so I found myself on a bright spring day, sitting on a Queen Anne chair, trying to decide what to do with a capon, trying to help Simon Smock decide if that painting we were looking at was a real Turner or something else.

"I suppose," I suggested, hoping I was sounding diplomatic, "one of us could always go over there and glance at the signature."

"Ach," he made a German sound, even though he had no German accent, as he pooh-poohed me, "what would be the fun in that?"

"None," I agreed brightly, hoping I was coming across as being agreeable.

Simon Smock in the flesh was exactly what his pictures had promised, but shorter. He really did use a lion's-head cane he didn't need. He really did wear a purple cape that was always hitting someone in the face when he put it on. He really was Capote-ish in a rotund way, only with black Salvador Dali hair and a Zorro mustache. If the man were a book, store clerks would be at a loss as to where to shelve him.

Prior to the meeting, I'd put my head together with Dodo's more experienced one to try to figure out in advance what was going on with Simon Smock and all the mystique he was surrounding this book with.

"Isn't that weird," I'd asked Dodo, "the way he made a big deal out of selling a book written by a British author in foreign markets before attempting to sell it here?"

"Weird," she agreed, fingers steepled thoughtfully against her lips, "but not unprecedented."

"No?"

"No," she said, relaxing back. "I'll bet this is what's going on… The author, whoever she is, is probably a midlist author—some nice reviews, respectable sales, but nothing to go into a bidding war over. Now she's written something uncharacteristic, something that Simon thinks could make a lot of money. The problem is that if he tries to sell it with her name on it, no matter how hard he pushes it as her breakout book, publishers will just check the sales records through the chains and say, 'Oh, right. She's a 10,000-copy author. Thanks, but no, I don't think we'd want to do 100,000 copies of that one' and move on."

I thought I was catching on.

"So," I said, "rather than trying to sell it here first, Simon takes it elsewhere, starts all kinds of buzz going with the foreign scouts, begins all this mysterious-author stuff… Why, can't you just hear people now? 'Who's he got? Is it Joyce Carol Oates with a new personality? Has Stephen King decided to do another Richard Bachman? Is Martin Amis trying to see if people will still recognize his writing if he writes as a woman?' Before you know it, we're all falling all over ourselves to give him all the money we've got in the budget when we don't even really know what he has."

"Exactly," smiled Dodo.

"So," I asked, "will we do it?"

She stopped smiling. "Yeah. Of course we'll do it."

Now that I was face-to-face with this weird little man, still debating the damned maybe-Turner, I was wondering, *Could he really be so wily?*

Realizing one of us had to finally break the business-talk ice, "So, about this book you've got…"

"Here," he said, pulling several hundred loose pages out of a satchel I hadn't seen before. I hadn't seen the satchel previously because it had been obscured by the cape.

He thrust the pages into my hands and started to rise.

I hoped he wasn't going to whip that cape around himself again. People got hurt whenever he did that.

He whipped.

The waiter, experienced from before, dodged it.

"But," I protested, "aren't you going to have a sweet?"

"No. I'm having that with Sam Peters of Willow Press as soon as I get over there." He consulted his watch. "And I'm late. Oh, well." He patted his satchel beneath the cape. "He'll wait."

"But what…?" I half rose, shouting after him.

He waved two fingers in the air, without turning around. "Two weeks! I'm giving everybody two weeks to make offers!"

Blasted books that are always telling you what to expect!

Emma would not roll over.

Back in February, at the end of Emma's second month, I'd first seen the dreaded words appear under the May Even Be Able To list: "roll over (one way)." Two little words, plus that two-word parenthetical aside, had driven part of our playtime for the past three months. Now, here we were, May 31, the last day of her fifth month, and that blasted "roll over (one way)" directive had risen to the top of the section, where it now perched like a vulture under the "By end of this month, your baby should be able to" heading.

I tried everything over the past three months: placing her on her stomach with her head turned away from me, as I lay on the other side, singing or clapping, in the hopes that her desire to see the person that matched the voice would make her somehow turn her head hard in the right direction to tip her over. But, the smart minx, she just slowly turned her head around facedown until she saw what she wanted to see, no rolling over required. I tried lining up her stuffed animals, especially fuzzy bunny. I even enlisted Kick the Cat, but Kick got distracted while rolling over himself, which caused Emma to make raspberries of appreciation but in no way encouraged her to emulate Kick's feats.

I promised her a car and a month in Costa del Sol when she was old enough, but it was still no go. I even tried yelling, "Come on, Em! Roll, baby, roll!"

Finally, in despair, I phoned David.

"I'm working, Jane," he said, the background noise of a cleaver striking a butcher's block confirming his words.

I could picture him there, phone wedged in the crook between ear and shoulder as he eviscerated cattle.

"What's going on?" he asked.

"It's Emma."

The striking sounds stopped.

"What's wrong with Emma?" he asked, concern evident.

"She won't…she won't…"

"She won't what, Jane?"

"She won't roll over!"

"And she needs to do this because…?"

"Because the book says she should be doing it by now! It's the last day of her fifth month! If she doesn't do it by midnight, I'll need to call in a doctor!"

"Of course you won't need to do that."

"I won't?"

"No. Throw that stupid book away."

"But I can't do that! And, anyway, *why* would I do that?"

"Because these books don't know anything. My mother raised five boys—five boys, Jane—in *Israel*. Do you think she sat there with her nose in some book, saying, 'Oh, no! Benjamin hasn't picked up a raisin yet!'?"

Damn! I knew I should never have told him about the raisins.

"You have a brother named Benjamin?" I asked, trying to deflect.

"You know I do, Jane. There's Benjamin, Jacob, Seth, Moshe and me."

"Oh, right."

"And my mother didn't have any trouble raising us without any books telling her what to expect and we *still* all know how to cut up a cow."

"You're an amazing clan."

"Do us both a favor, Jane?"

"Hmm?"

"Call Tolkien right now instead."

Cleaver strike and *click!*

Although it was sort of rude on David's part to hang up, he did have a good idea: I phoned Tolkien at the Yard.

Initially, the conversation went exactly as the beginning of my conversation with David had done, save that he didn't tell me right off the bat that he was working and I don't think he was cutting up a cow. Where the script parted company was when we got to the part where I screeched "The book says she should be doing it by now!" to which he replied, "It will be fine, Jane."

"It will?" I already felt inexplicably calmer by just a smidgen; not calm, never that, but at least I'd got my smidgen.

"Oh, yes," he said. "You know, I was a late roller."

"You're kidding!"

"Oh, yes. Made my mother frantic."

"I didn't think your mother ever got frantic."

"Oh, yes," he soothed once more, "she got frantic over this."

With each "Oh, yes" he murmured, I felt myself calming by yet another smidgen.

"See, the way I figure it, new little people can only concentrate their energies on just so much at a time…."

As his voice went on, not really a drone but it was soothing, I gazed down at Emma, still happily lying on her stomach, in her blue overalls, watching Kick.

"…I mean there's so much bombarding their heads at once…"

Emma smiled at Kick.

"…Emma just has such strong verbal skills—"

"She does?"

"Oh, yes. You can tell she's going to be a huge talker. So, since she's so busy working on being the next Disraeli…"

From her belly, Emma tried to reach for Kick as he zipped by. It was kind of a facedown lunge if such a thing makes sense.

"…the fact that the physical might lag just a teensy bit behind…"

She was on her back!

One second, Emma was on her stomach doing her beetle routine and the next she was on her back!

I put my hand to my mouth; I felt that awed.

"…is really no surprise—"

"She did it!" I screamed in his ear.

"Excuse me?"

"Emma—she just rolled over!"

"Right while we were talking?"

"Yes." I scooped her up, hugged her to me. "Good girl, Em."
Then I flopped down on the sofa, my elation turning to en-

ervation. God, that book was killing me. What was I ever going to do when we got to crawling?

But Tolkien was talking to me again.

"She really did it," he asked, "right while we were talking?"

"Oh, yes," I said.

"We make a great team," he said.

Emma was progressing nicely. She could keep her head level with her body when pulled to a sitting position, would work to get a toy out of reach (she loved the fuzzy bunny), could pass a cube or other object from one hand to the other, would look for a dropped object, could rake a raisin and pick it up in her fist (amazing how much a part of my life raisins now were), and—*yes, yes, YES*—she could roll over…(one way).

She could also babble to beat the band, combining vowels and consonants.

When she combined her *M*'s and her *A*'s in particular, babbling "ma-ma-ma-ma," my heart overflowed.

June, the sixth month

I'd figured out the perfect thing for Christopher to do to get back on track. David was working and I'd brought Emma upstairs for a little friendly visit.

"You want me to design *a kiddie playground?*"

"Not just any playground," I said. I produced some snaps I'd taken of the playground near Mary Jr.'s, with just this purpose in mind. "This is where my friends and I take the babies. Look at the condition of it."

He looked, reluctantly, but he looked.

"Can you see anything you could improve upon?" I asked, hopefully.

"Well," he said, "the first thing I'd do is get someone in there to cut that grass."

"Yes," I said, "it is a bit too Amazon at present."

"And next, I don't know, I suppose I'd get rid of everything that's there already and just start fresh."

"Yes!" I said, excited. "That's exactly what I was thinking too! Why bother doing just a little bit, like adding benches and tables for the mothers with babies to sit at, while leaving the old rusty equipment there?"

"There'd be no reason to bother at all," he agreed. "But who'd pay for it? I can't imagine the area residents have any extra money to chip in. If they did, they wouldn't be living there in the first place."

"True, but I'm sure there must be some kind of city council I can appeal to. David always does say I'm a *force majeure*. I'll just apply some *majeure force* to the appropriate parties. I'm sure they'll see things my way."

"And if they don't?"

I thought of the tidy sum of money that I still had in the bank from the sale of *The Cloth Baby*.

I shrugged. "Something will come up. David always says—"

The first time I'd mentioned David's name, I thought I'd seen Christopher stiffen, but now that stiffening was so pronounced, it stopped me in my verbal tracks.

"What's wrong?" I asked.

"This whole *thing*—" he flicked at the pictures "—this somehow has to do with *him,* doesn't it?"

I was startled. I'd never before heard Christopher speak of David with anything other than love and respect. Come to that, I'd never heard anyone speak of David with anything other than love and respect, and that included my mother; well, except for my ex-fiancé, Trevor, but Trevor's opinion on such things never counted; even when he'd been my fiancé, they hadn't counted.

David had told me there were problems...

"Well," I said, trying to be as delicate as possible, "he did mention that you no longer seemed happy working at the restaurant...."

"Of course I'm not happy!" he nearly shouted, but then I could visibly see him make an effort to rein in his emotions.

"Of course I'm not happy," he said again in a quiet, a sadder tone. "Oh, it's fine, helping someone you love build their dream. But David's dream is a success now."

And it was true. Ever since Kevin Spacey had stopped off there after a night at the Old Vic, although I do believe he ordered the fish, Meat! *Meat!! MEAT!!!* had become the official dining playground for the young acting set.

"He doesn't really need me there anymore," said Christopher. "And, truth be told, I no longer want to be there."

"Of course you don't," I said.

"You're agreeing with me?"

"What's so strange about that?"

"Only the fact that you've never agreed with me about anything before, including whether *The Piano* was a good movie or not."

"That's just because you're always wrong whenever we disagree. *The Piano* was a *great* movie."

"Oh, *please!* Do I have to remind you again about Sam Neill's hair?"

"No, thank you. And you're still wrong."

"Oh, I don't think—"

"And there's something else you're wrong about. There is one other thing we agree on, outside of the fact that you shouldn't go on working for David."

"There is? What?"

"We both love David."

He looked at me.

"Yes," he finally said, softly, "we both love David."

"Which means that in order to save your relationship, we need to get you out of a situation that is only serving to build up resentment in you, and back into doing something you love."

"You're right, Jane."

I couldn't believe I'd just heard those three words, *from him,* but I wasn't about to let on by showing my shock, lest we get derailed again.

"It's time," he said, "that I got back to working on my own dream."

"Exactly."

He looked at the snaps of the decrepit playground again.

"But *a kiddie playground?*" he bemoaned. "It's not exactly like working on the Louvre, is it?"

"No." I smiled. "But it could be."

Today it was Minerva from Publicity's turn to be grilled by Stephen Triplecorn.

Thank God, Dodo was still determined to do her Witness Protection Act—or maybe that should read Jane Protection Act— because at least I'd have someone in there to look out for me.

It wasn't so much that I suspected Minerva from Publicity of having it in for me—not in the way that Louise did or Stan from Accounting, for that matter (Stan having reverted to his former out-from-under-a-rock type hard on the heels of his helping me hack into Stephen Triplecorn's computer) with the one exception being that on-the-side chat we'd had at my place after the last party. It was more that Minerva was the kind of person I thought of as being *too much* her own person, making her, in essence, like me; in other words, she was what some might term A Loose Cannon. Having no discernible side in anything, who knew which side she might come down on? One thing was certain: she would speak her mind.

What did I know about Minerva that might weigh in the balance? For, certainly, those harlequin glasses meant nothing, save that she had as peculiar a taste as Constance but in another direction. I knew that she had no overt prejudices. I knew that, for whatever Minerva-like reason, she'd turned down nearly every request I'd ever made to get more publicity for any of my authors. I knew she knew that I'd faked a pregnancy for nine months. As I say, who knew which way she might go?

According to Dodo, who told me afterwards, Minerva came down on the side of decency and common sense.

"Great," I said, "but what the hell does that mean?"

Dodo did a little swively thing in her chair because, apparently, she could hardly contain her glee. "It means that I took care of everything."

"What did you take care of?" I said with growing exasperation.

She leaned forward, going straight from Pleased With Myself mode into Girl Detectives Conferring Together mode.

"Minerva said," she whispered across the table, even though there was no one but we two in the room, "that you were the most inventive employee the company had."

I leaned towards her, playing along.

"That doesn't sound so bad."

"It wasn't," Dodo said. Then she looked over each shoulder, as though someone might yet overhear. "It wasn't so bad until she started making a list of your inventions."

"Uh-oh."

"Uh-oh is right. Minerva recalled for Stephen Triplecorn the time you'd, er, falsified an author's previous sell-through in hopes of justifying more publicity money for his new book."

"But I was only making the world the way it should be! *Talking in Your Coffin* was a book that *should* have had a greater sell-through, and the sequel—"

"I know that, Jane," she soothed, "but that's really not the issue right now. May I go on?"

I nodded.

"Then Minerva recalled for Stephen Triplecorn the time you invented a Royal Ascot Week in July that you claimed to be invited to, when what you really wanted to do was take the week off to go to Provence with Trevor, who'd received the trip as a work bonus, but you were out of your own holiday time and felt compelled to invent the ruse."

"But it was *Provence,* Dodo!"

"And we are *British,* Jane. Don't you think we could be depended upon to know that Royal Ascot Week is always in June?"

"I just thought that you'd all be so royalty-besotted that you'd be happy to let me go."

"You could have just told the truth at the time, Jane."

I rolled my eyes. "Yeah, right. You and the world keep on telling me that."

"But that really is all past history that no longer matters, because *then* Minerva said…and I quote, 'And then there was the time Jane invented a tilted uterus,' end quote."

"Oh no!"

I knew exactly what she was referring to. During my baby charade, in order to get Minerva to feel sympathy for me, hoping she'd throw some extra publicity Colin Smythe's way, I'd invented a tilted uterus. Naturally, my invented female-plumbing problems had earned me squat.

"Oh, yes," said Dodo.

"So what happened next?"

"Well, I realized I needed to call in the heavy artillery then, didn't I? So, I did this."

And here she leaned forward even farther, so that a glimpse of cleavage showed through the opening of her cream silk blouse.

She really was an impressive woman.

I shook my head, tore my gaze away.

"But I don't understand. Why would your breasts stop Minerva?"

"I didn't do it for Minerva," she said, exasperated. "I did it for Stephen Triplecorn!"

"Oh. I see. And what effect did those, um, *that* have on him?"

"He turned red, of course, like you're doing now, and went into a coughing fit."

I wasn't surprised.

Then I wondered: Did Dodo realize she'd just set women back about twenty years? Even if she had a clue, apparently she didn't care. Maybe she just figured that her looks had so often worked against her—making people resent her or think she was dim—that it just made things honors-even if she exploited those looks to good advantage.

"Then I told him to go out to the outer office and ask Hilda for a glass of water. Well, I figured that would keep him away for at least five minutes, since Hilda was bound to pounce all over him for treating her as though her job description required she wait hand and foot on every single person who'd ever lived.

"While he was gone," continued Dodo, "I struck a deal with Minerva."

"A deal?"

"Yes. I promised her that, for a term of one year, I would personally see to it that she only had to work on promoting authors who were clearly promotable."

"And that worked?"

"Of course it did. Minerva loves her job, always has, provided it's worth doing. You should have seen her eyes light up. I could see visions of Garcia Marquez plums dancing in her head."

"But we'll never have Garcia Marquez, or anyone like him, come to that."

Dodo shrugged. "Doesn't matter. You should have seen how happy just the fantasy made her. Besides, she has been a smidgen more content since you found Mona Shakespeare for us. And while Mona is no Garcia Marquez—"

"So then what happened?"

"So then Stephen came back and Minerva told him that, despite some of your past inventions, she believed you to be a force for good in the world. And then she left. See? I told you," she said, putting her feet up and crossing them on her desk, which, coming from her and despite the skirt, was not unladylike at all. "Minerva finally came down on the side of decency and common sense."

"So what will you do when Minerva expects you to deliver Garcia Marquezes?"

Dodo's legs came down again and for the first time she looked puzzled.

"Well, I don't know," she said, frowning. But then she brightened, leaning back again, hands clasped behind her head as she swiveled. "I know. I'll give her more Colin Smythe."

I was on hold for Simon Smock and it appeared they were going to keep me holding forever.

Since our luncheon, I'd received my copy of the manuscript everyone in the city was so hot for. Title: Unknown. Author: Anonymous. Well, I thought, at least they knew how many words were in the damn thing: 120,000, which seemed like an awful lot of sex to me. But then, what did I know? It had been way too long since I'd had any.

Of course, I'd read all 120,000 words, just as quickly as I could after having got my hands on it. Then, I'd made my pitch to acquire the book in the weekly editorial meeting. I hadn't had to make much of a pitch, given the industry buzz, even though no one who'd merely read about it could get their minds wrapped around quite what it was.

In fact, Stan from Accounting had been the only dissenting voice.

"So, we'll spend—what?—more than we've ever spent to acquire any book before on this overrated four-way teddy-ripper that will probably never even earn out its advance, just so we can get pissing rights over every other publisher in London?"

I had been about to defend the book, which really was just like what Stan was describing, when Dexter Schlager of all people jumped in. I say "of all people," because he nearly never said anything and, whenever he did, we nearly never listened.

"What business are you in?" Dexter demanded. "Of course that's what we will do. What the hell do you think publishing is all about?"

"I dunno," Stan shrugged. "Making money?"

"Pfft," pffted Dexter. "Publishing isn't about that at all. It's about gaining power."

"Excuse me," piped up Constance, who had on her serious brown contact lenses that day, since it was Tuesday and Tuesday always meant editorial meeting and she did so want to be taken seriously, the hoped-for effect of seriousness compromised completely by the square ring in her pierced brow that said Write Free or Die. "But isn't publishing supposed to be about the romantic pursuit of wonderfully seminal material that will both entertain and educate?"

"Christ!" Dexter looked at Dodo accusingly. "Whose idea was it to promote little Don Quixote here?"

Before the meeting had the chance to degenerate into the usual round of name-calling our happy little family was prone to, I'd suggested we come up with a plan. If we wanted Simon Smock's anonymous author's untitled book, and we desperately did, we were going to need to offer him more than just money. After all, what if we were outbid by a competing firm? We needed to sweeten the pot so we'd be irresistible.

Naturally, being the brilliant people that we were, we came up with a plan to offer Simon Smock.

"Anything," Dexter Schlager had said.

"Anything?" Stan's eyebrows went up so high they'd topped his glasses.

"Anything," Dexter reiterated. "If we want to make sure no one else gets it, we have to promise them whatever they want." He nodded at me with his chin. "By the way, Taylor, is it any good?"

I shrugged. "Honestly? It's just okay."

Dexter nodded. "That's what I figured."

And now, here I was on the phone, waiting for Simon to...

"Hello, Jane. Sorry to keep you waiting."

I pictured him on the other end with that Dali hair and Zorro mustache. For so long now, I'd been feeling so outblonded by the world, longing to have another dark-haired person on the scene. But honestly, this? Was this man, not to mention Stephen Triplecorn, the best the world could do for me?

"Hello, Simon. I'm prepared to make an offer."

"What have you got for me?"

I gave him the financials, heard him grunt at the other end over every deal point.

"Huh," he said. "I've heard better."

"For this book?"

"Yes. Just five minutes ago, in fact."

C-rap!

"So," he said, "if that's all you've got…"

"Anything!" I shouted.

"Excuse me?"

"Anything! I've been authorized to offer you anything your client wants!" Can you tell this was my first time doing this?

"More money?" he asked cagily.

"Er, no, not that." Dexter had been firm that our bottom line on this one, being higher than our bottom had ever been before, was as far as we would go financially. "But anything else. Really, a-ny-thing."

Simon made hemming and hawing noises, which I was sure he was doing merely for the fun of having me squirm. "My client did say she wanted certain artistic guarantees."

C-rap! Another writer who thought she was some kind of fucking artiste just because she could put together over 100,000 words and have it all come out making a fair amount of sense in the end.

"Whatever she wants," I said sweetly.

"She wants you to let her design her own cover."

"Does she have any art training?"

"Does it matter?" he countered. "It's what she wants."

She'd probably draw something with stick figures.

"Okay," I agreed brightly. After watching Dodo for years, I'd at least mastered the art of saying things brightly.

"She doesn't want anyone giving her grief over the title of the book," Simon said. "She says it's called what it is and she doesn't want the publisher changing it."

"What's she worried about?" I laughed. "I'm pretty sure hers will be the only book titled *Untitled* out there. Or did she decide to change it to *Ishtar?*"

But apparently Simon didn't think that was funny.

"Does it matter?" he asked again, his tone having taken on a rote quality. "It's what she—"

"Right," I said. "Okay, fine. Well—" brightly again "—is that all?"

"Not quite. There's also the matter of her name."

"Her name?"

"Yes. She's been publishing under a pseudonym for years now, having been pressured to do so by her previous publisher. Now though, she says, now that she's writing things that are more true to her heart, she wants the world to recognize her by her real name."

"Which is?"

"To you? For now, it's still Anonymous."

"You want me to put Anonymous down as the author on the contract?"

"I'll work it out with your legal department. Just make sure you have them put my client's terms in writing."

I could feel myself experiencing a giddy sense of excitement that I was sure Dodo was familiar with, but that I'd never enjoyed before (well, except with Mona Shakespeare).

"Does this mean that we have a deal?" I asked, not daring to believe.

"Sure," he said. "Why not?"

As I hung up the phone, I couldn't believe my good luck. I'd paid a small fortune, beating out everyone else in London, for a mediocre untitled book by an anonymous author who was going to do her own artwork.

C-rap!

Just to prove how desperate I was to get to the bottom of the truth regarding my mother and her new lover, which had been gnawing on my back burner ever since I'd broken into her house, I actually phoned my mother.

The last time I'd phoned my mother it had been to invite

her to my place in order to announce my pregnancy over a year ago. And, of course, she hadn't come, having her nails done being much more important. Even the times she'd come to my place since Emma's arrival, I'd first phoned Sophie and then told Sophie to call Mum up and invite her.

I knew all of this, because my mother was only too happy to remind me of it as soon as she realized that it was my voice saying "Hello."

Well, except the part about her nails.

"Yes, I remember all that, Mother, thanks so much for reminding me."

How to delicately bring up the fact that I now knew she had a lover and I was curious about it…?

It occurred to me that I should have taken the time to work these details out in advance. After all, I couldn't just say, "While I was going through the desk in your bedroom, I discovered…"

"Sophie says you're sleeping with somebody!" I blurted, needing to say something and having failed to think of anything better.

I was sure I was hearing surprise on the other end of the line. There was certainly a sharp intake of breath. Then, on the exhale:

"Sophie's right, of course."

"She *is?*"

I couldn't believe my mother wasn't playing games with me about this, that she was simply answering straightforwardly.

"Yes, although it's more than sleeping. I've been seeing someone for some time now."

"I see."

But of course I didn't. None of it made sense. Why, my mother and I were having an adult conversation!

"What's his name, this person you've been seeing?"

"Vic. The person's name is Vic."

I couldn't believe it! She was telling me everything!

"So," I said, "when do I get to meet Vic?"

"Oh, eventually, Jane. I just want to see where things are headed first. After all, you of all people should understand the importance of not rushing things. Didn't you start, have and finish an entire relationship with Tolkien before anyone in the family even knew he existed?"

I hated it when she was right.

I'd asked Tolkien out on a date.

Not wanting to go again to Meat! *Meat!! MEAT!!!,* even if it was good enough for Kevin Spacey, I'd selected a Japanese restaurant that had red lacquer walls and low lighting, the low lighting of the couples-in-love variety as opposed to the hide-the-food-while-saving-on-the-electric variety I was more accustomed to. I'd had the foresight to book us the private room with the table on floor level that had a well beneath it for our legs, figuring it was worth the extra money. At the very least, when the meal was over, he'd have to offer me his hand to help me up, being the gentleman that he was. And I'd really need help since I'd elected to wear a teal satin Mandarin minidress that was very snug in the hips and upper thigh, making it not all that easy to execute the kind of move necessary to remove one's legs from a restaurant well. I did realize that by wearing my Mandarin dress to a Japanese restaurant I was mixing my Asia, but the snugness was sexy on me and there was that well he'd need to help me out of. So I knew there'd be that much physical contact, at any rate.

Ever since that day Tolkien had taken Emma and me to the park, had kissed me on the head, I'd been waiting for him to ask me out again. That call not coming, I'd steeled my own bravery and invited him here.

The way I figured it, once again, I'd been passive for far too long. It wasn't like me to be so passive, me being the more bull-by-the-horns type. But I supposed I'd let the day-to-day busyness of new motherhood, coupled with a sincere desire to give him what space he needed, tripled by a fear of rejection...well, I'd let the combination of it all guide me. But now I was tired of waiting. I wanted him back. How? I had no idea. The only thing I knew for certain was that it was time for Action Jane.

Thankfully, when Action Jane had timidly asked him out, he hadn't told me to stuff it; he'd said yes.

Of course, now that I had him here, I hadn't a clue as to what to say. It was that awkward.

Before the ginger salad dishes were even on the table, we'd dispensed with Emma's latest accomplishments—her attempts to pull herself to a standing position from sitting—and what was going on at work, both mine and what he could talk about involving his.

What to say...what to say...?

"Your work!" I half shouted, my sudden excitement so high at having come up with something concerning his work that we could discuss, I knocked over my wineglass, the contents landing right in his lap.

He gave a half jump backwards and bumped his knee on the table in the well as I reached to help him wipe what I'd done, but I felt him stiffen as I dabbed at the place on his pants where the wine had spilled.

"Sorry," I said, drawing back, no doubt blushing a red color as deep as the wine.

"That's okay," he said, in an attempt to shrug it off. "Everyone thinks C.I.D. are all on the take or drunks anyway. Might as well give the taxpayers what they expect for their money."

He must have seen that I was still dreadfully embarrassed, since he chose to keep the subject matter aboveboard.

"And my work is so exciting, why?"

"Right! Your work!" I half shouted again.

He lunged to keep his own wineglass safe from my sweeping reach.

Ignoring his self-protective lunge, I rooted in my handbag for what I wanted to show him.

"Here!" I said. I pushed the photo across the table.

"Who's this?" he asked, looking at the snap of the sad girl.

"It's Sarah Johnson, Mary Jr.'s niece. Remember I told you about the playgroup I've been bringing Emma to?"

"Right, Mary Jr.—the woman you met when you were standing behind her in line at the market."

"That's right."

"Her niece looks sad," he said, moving to return the photo as our entrées came: shrimp teriyaki for me, steak tempura for him.

"No, keep the photo," I said.

"Why? And why show me her photo in the first place?"

So I explained to him what little I knew: that Sarah would be just sixteen years old now, that she was Luke Johnson's daughter, that she'd been missing from her family for over a year, that no one knew why, that there had been no note.

Then I explained to him that I'd asked Mary Jr. for a copy of Sarah's school photo.

Tolkien looked at me, clearly puzzled.

"I want you to start looking for Sarah Johnson," I said.

"You want me to…?"

"Yes," I said. "I want you to find her."

He put his napkin down. "You make it sound so easy," he said. "If it were that easy, don't you think she'd have been found already?"

"I'm sure the local cops devoted some time to looking for her…*in the beginning.* But she's been gone for over a year now. Do you really think that, given where she comes from and how long she's been gone, that they're devoting a lot of manpower and hours to bringing her back home?"

"No," he conceded, "I expect not."

"If someone doesn't get involved soon, someone who knows how to do certain things, how to properly look for a person who might not want to be found, but might also *need* to be found…" I let my voice trail off.

Still, he said nothing.

"I'd do it myself, but—"

"No, you can't do it yourself. You have Emma to take care of. Besides, you wouldn't know where to start."

"But you would," I said.

He sighed. "Did Mary Jr. give you anything at all to start with? Did she know what Sarah was wearing on the day she disappeared? Did Sarah have any special mates? A boyfriend?"

I smiled, as I leaned forward, prepared to tell him what I'd learned.

Good thing Dodo had said to just leave Emma with her overnight just in case.

When Tolkien and I got back to my place, we were so eager

to get each other's clothes off that I doubt we would have noticed had Emma needed anything.

I hadn't been with another man, not since that last time I'd been with Tolkien, oh so long ago. And if I had to lay money on it? I'd say that he hadn't been with another woman either.

Had he been with another woman?

I realized that I didn't want to know the answer to that question, didn't ever want to know. If he hadn't been with anyone else, I'd feel guilty, responsible for his loneliness. If he had been, despite the lack of rationality in my reasoning and my total lack of rights regarding him, it would kill me.

All those nights Tolkien had stayed here right after Emma came home with me, sleeping in the same bed each night, we'd never once made love. Believe me, it hadn't been from lack of desire, not on my part, but because I knew that Tolkien's feelings for me were conflicted. It wouldn't have been right, wouldn't have been fair, for me to seduce him. As for him, he spent those days, when he wasn't holding Emma, with his hands studiously clasped behind his back. I sensed that he was afraid to touch me, that if he did we would both burn.

Apparently, though, something about tonight's dinner had gotten him past his reticence, for now we were crashing around my flat, bumping into furniture in our joint single-minded mission to remove cloth from skin.

People have remarked, once or twice, that I'm a funny girl. How surprising is it, then, that even when I have sex, it tends to be funny?

"It's okay," I whispered in his ear, alternating whispering in it with nibbling on it, "if you still want to change your mind."

I realized that I was treating him like some timid virgin sacrifice, but I couldn't stop myself. As much as I wanted this, I didn't want it if he didn't really want it.

He took hold of my face on both sides with his hands, looked me deep in the eyes. "Are you fucking nuts, Jane?" he asked. "I want to fuck your brains out!"

Oh my! all the more timid Janes in me cried out—Jane Austen, Jane Eyre, Jane Fonda (during her Ted Turner phase). *My man never talked to me like that before!*

But it was Jane Taylor who ultimately triumphed.

"Good." Between kissing him hard and fumbling with the buckle on his belt, I backed him into my bedroom. "Because I want you to."

It was no one's idea of a smooth lovemaking session. Like two people with the same destination, but with different screwed-up maps, we kept missing each other's rhythm.

He started to snake his tongue down my body, and that felt so good, but then I realized I wanted to be doing that to him and in my efforts to turn him over, I managed to bang my head on his chin.

For a while, we were all about tongues, and that was very good, but then I could see that he wanted something different and we became all elbowy awkwardness again. I know there was at least one big "ouch!" in there when, meaning to stroke his brow, I somehow managed to poke him in the eye.

But then there was that imperfect perfection of us coming together and Tolkien was inside me again—he was inside me!— and all of a sudden, nothing that had gone before mattered any longer.

Emma could now pull up to a standing position from sitting, get into a sitting position from her stomach, pick up a tiny object with any part of thumb and finger. (I do know that some people would have trouble believing that a baby of that age could do those things, but those people should look under the May Even Be Able To sections of *What to Expect the First Year.* Emma was definitely a May Even Be Able To kind of baby.)

But best of all?

Not only did she say "mama," but she also said "dada." So what if, as the book suggested, she was still doing it indiscriminately? So what if "mama" was sometimes the fuzzy bunny and "dada" was sometimes Christopher? Whenever she said the "dada" thing to Tolkien, I could see that it made his heart sing as much as mine.

July, the seventh month

My mother was coming for a visit.

She'd called early that Saturday morning, saying she wanted to stop by. To realize how strange this was, you have to know that in all the years I'd been living here, she'd never once said she wanted to stop by. If she asked to see me at all, it was always at some neutral zone, like David's restaurant, where we could take up our opposite corners and come out fighting, where there would be other people standing by should the need to "break it up" arise. But she'd certainly never granted me home advantage before. Could it be that she wanted to talk some more with me about her relationship with Vic?

But that wasn't it at all.

She came in like a whirlwind of motherhood, thrusting a wrapped package at me "for that baby," sniffing at my decorating choices and demanding to use the bathroom right away.

When she emerged, every champagne tinted hair in place, a sapphire-blue summer frock pulled down neatly over her hips, it was apparent that whatever else she'd been doing in there—*flush!*—she'd also managed to take the time to note evidence of

Tolkien: the second toothbrush, the shaving things, his bathing trunks drying over the shower rod.

"Who…?" she asked, not needing to say anything else.

"Tolkien," I answered, not wanting to say more.

It was all too new, Tolkien moving in with me. I felt that were I to say too much about it to anyone, were I to betray my eagerness for this to the world, it would somehow jinx my dream.

"Is he…?" she asked.

"Not officially, at least we haven't said anything formal about it yet, but he keeps a lot of his things here."

And then she asked a strange thing; for my mother, that is.

"And you're happy about this?"

It seemed important to get the answer right. "I'm happy that he's here," I said. "I'm very happy about that."

"I'll never understand your life, Jane," she said, and I could see where she would feel that way. Despite the way the rest of the world was currently spinning, I was the first Taylor woman to live with a man she wasn't married to, living first with Trevor; and now, sort of, with Tolkien. Okay, so maybe Mum was living with Vic on the weekends, sometimes at his place sometimes at hers, but I was the first Taylor woman to live with a man more or less full-time that she wasn't married to.

I heard Emma stirring from her nap.

I went to get her, brought her out, got her something to drink, and rubbed her back until she burped.

"Can I get you something?" I called out to my mother from the kitchen, going through the cupboard to see what I had. "Raisins, perhaps?"

"Er, no, Jane, thank you."

Emma shrugged. I shrugged.

"The baby's gotten a lot bigger," my mother observed, as Emma and I returned to the living room.

"Babies do that."

"Here," she said, picking up the present she'd brought from where I'd laid it down. "Open it," she instructed Emma.

"She's a bit young to be opening her own presents," I pointed out. I moved to hand Emma plus bottle to my mother. "Why don't you take her and I'll open it?"

My mother drew back. "Are you sure?"

"Of course I'm sure."

But when my mother finally took her, she was all awkwardness. The way she was holding her, Emma's feet were higher than her head.

"Here," I said, adjusting Emma more properly on my mother's lap. Then I looked at her. "Are you sure you've done this before?"

"Yes," my mother replied icily. "With Sophie. And with you."

"No matter," I shrugged, noting that Emma had settled down. "Babies are incredibly forgiving creatures."

"It's only when they grow up to be people," she pointed out, "that they suddenly remember every wrong you've ever done them and won't let you forget."

I knew that was meant for me, but I chose to ignore it. Why go down the road of recriminations now?

I tore open the wrapping on the box. "Look, Em! Look what Mum's mummy brought you!" Of course, I hadn't seen what was actually inside the box yet.

Inside the box were three items: a frilly dress big enough for a four-year-old; a doll that came with a tag clearly marked Warning! Small parts! Not for children under age 3; and a five-pound note, with a hand-scribbled note on it, "For ice cream."

It took all of my will to hide my exasperation. I suppose she had tried her best. "She'll enjoy these things when she gets older. Thanks."

"Do you really think she'll still be here then?" my mother asked.

"What does that mean?"

"It's just that, I don't think it pays to get your hopes up. I know from talking to Sophie that they're still searching for her real mother."

"Emma and I like to think I'm her real mother."

"Yes, but…"

My mother was so stiff with Emma that I could see Emma starting to fuss. Quickly, I got the fuzzy bunny and offered it to my mother.

"Here," I offered, smiling, "give this to her. She'll be your best friend for life."

My mother listened to me, for once, and like the magic that it always was the fuzzy bunny made Emma happy. In fact, Emma was so happy with my mother that she looked right at her, smiled and clapped.

"You never did say," I asked my mother, "why is it you wanted to come see me today?"

But my mother wasn't looking at me. She was looking at Emma.

"Do I need an excuse?" she said. "I came because I wanted to see my granddaughter."

Dodo was nervous about being interviewed by Stephen Triplecorn. She was so nervous, in fact, that she was wearing red—the color of power—to overcompensate.

"What are you nervous about?" I asked her. "I can understand why you'd have been nervous about Constance and Minerva, and we'll still need to get through Stan and Louise down the road, but why ever would you be nervous about talking to him yourself? Surely, you must not have any worries that you'll have to stop yourself from saying the wrong thing."

"But that's just it," she fretted. "With the others, I have my radar up. I know some of them have it in for you—or, in Constance's case, she's just plain whacky and unpredictable and likely to put her foot wrong without there even being any malice whatsoever. When they're involved, I don't even think about it. I just play defense. They say something stupid, or something purposely destructive, and I deflect it. Sort of like Wimbledon without the net."

"But how is this any different?"

"Because he'll be asking *me* direct questions. You know me…if someone asks me a direct question, I can't lie."

"What will you do then?"

But Dodo had already stumbled on her solution. I could tell this by the sudden brightness of her eyes.

"I'll ask him out on a date," she said.

"A *date?*" Boy, that came out of the blue.

"Yes. I'll invite him over to my place for dinner. Surely, even Social Services workers have to eat sometime."

* * *

Tolkien, Emma and I were going to Tolkien's parents' house for a party.

Tolkien had finally told his parents that we were seeing each other again, that we were kind of living together, and that I now had a baby, which was technically true: he never said I'd *had* a baby, which would have been a lie, but simply that I now *had* a baby, as though I were a doll who'd suddenly been accessorized: "Get the Crazy Jane Doll! Now with real live baby!" He'd also told them the baby wasn't his. His parents, being the people they were, had said not a single judgmental thing to him, one way or the other. Of course, this was the first time I'd be seeing them since before Tolkien and I had broken up and I was naturally nervous about how they'd receive me, the woman who had broken their son's heart once already—plus, this was the first time they'd be meeting Em.

Back in their hippie days, Tolkien's parents had been known as Elrond and Galadriel. Since then, they'd made a fortune in the bond market and retired from it, and they now went by their original names of Ron and Claire John. While Tolkien had originally been Donald John, just because his parents had switched, they'd seen no reason to expect their grown son to change his name back, so he was still Tolkien Donald.

Got that? And see? I told you before not to ask.

I'd been to their estate once before, when Tolkien and I had been dating the first time around. At the time, I hadn't seen much other than the entryway, the study where they'd served us drinks, the bathroom when I'd needed to pee. Now, for the first time, I got to see the rolling grounds of their estate up close.

There was a lot of rolling, I must say.

Tolkien had informed me that this was their annual Fourth of July party.

Not knowing how to put my question delicately, and failing, I'd asked, "Isn't that, um, quirky?"

"That's them all over," he smiled. "Quirks."

"But they're British. Isn't it strange to be celebrating America's Independence?"

He shrugged. "Not to them it isn't. They've got this thing about being good sports whenever you lose. They set off fire-crackers at night and everything."

"Do a lot of people come to these parties?"

"Oh, masses. Their friends are used to them, not that they agree with the principle, mind you, but it's a fun time and the drinks are free."

By the time we pulled up, the party was already in full swing. Everything—the grounds and the people—was rolling. And everyone was so...*white.*

Oh, I don't mean they had no tans. I mean that, among the three hundred people there, Emma was the only one of a sub-stantially different color.

It gave me an inkling of what might lie ahead in her future. I remembered being the only white person at Mary Sr.'s funeral and how odd that had felt. True, since I'd had Emma, there were the few times I'd had family and friends over, and Emma had been the only black person those times, too. But somehow, I hadn't noticed it then. Maybe because it was our place, the place I shared with her, and so it was home. Maybe it was be-cause it was fewer than a dozen people each time, and all of them were, if not necessarily close, people I was familiar with.

But this, this felt so *outnumbered.* And, growing up with me, with rare exception, it would always be like this for Emma.

Despite the midsummer heat I felt a chill and moved closer to Tolkien. But I didn't have long to dwell on Emma's future or the peculiarity of feeling cold in July, because...

"Jane! Tolkien! Baby!"

It was Claire, her hennaed hair in a chignon, floating at us through the separation in the crowd, looking like she wasn't even attached to the ground. Ron was at her side, white hair flow-ing, moving the same way.

I was never quite sure whether the way they moved in such a moony, floaty way was some kind of holdover from their days of smoking too much dope or whether it was the acquired phys-ical quirks of noblesse oblige in the nouveau riche, as if they'd gone to the moneyed people's version of dog-grooming school or something...

"Baby! Tolkien! Jane!" said Ron.

"We're so glad you could come," Claire said.

It looked like I needn't have worried about how they'd receive me. They were clearly tickled to see us all together.

"Oh, what a beautiful hobbit you have there," said Ron, referring to Emma.

"Does she have furry feet?" Claire smiled.

Do you see what I mean about these people? "No, she—"

"We're kidding, of course," laughed Ron.

Claire chimed in, "It's just that we remember when our Tolkien was just a little hobbit and we start to get all…"

"There, there," said Ron. "Don't cry, my dear. Our little hobbit has his own hobbit now and everything's as it should be. Come on," he added, "might as well meet the masses."

It was an odd assortment of human beings, to say the least. Apparently, Ron and Claire, no matter where they'd gone in life, had never seen fit to discard anyone afterwards. Thus, there was their old hippie crowd, who were all themselves still hippies, though Claire and Ron no longer technically were, like the long-haired middle-aged women in all the tie-dye and the man they all referred to as Acid ("babies are like little human beings—way cool!"); there was the investment-days crowd, the men in suits, the women in summer dresses, spectator pumps and hats, as though waiting for the Queen's garden party to start ("Do you think Emma'll be a Cambridge or Oxford girl?"); there were the neighbors from their second home in Barcelona (*"Niña habla espanol?"*); and the extended John family, who repeatedly commented, one and all, "She doesn't look much like Jane, but I do see a lot of Tolkien in her."

This last perplexed me so much that with each repetition, I felt the exasperation inside me growing at an unreasonable rate, until finally, Ron said to one of the uncles, "I know. She has Tolkien's ears," to which I responded:

"What is *wrong* with you people? You do realize she's black, don't you?" Apparently, I shouted it loud enough to stop all the noise and the chatter and the band.

It just made me so crazy for some reason. In my world, with my family and friends—well, except for David and Christopher—Emma's color was the first thing anyone ever remarked upon. But here, with these people, where there was only one of her and so many of them, they talked right around it, as if it didn't exist. It was too confusing. Couldn't the world make up its mind?

Claire looked at me, perplexed, as did everyone else, I might add.

"Of course we realize that," she said, head slightly tilted to one side. "But what does it matter?"

"She's your baby," added Ron. "And you are with Tolkien…" He shrugged.

Everybody shrugged.

I felt like a complete arse.

"And she really does look more like Tolkien than you," Claire pointed out. "Oh, not the coloring. After all, you have dark hair and his is much lighter."

"It's in the way she looks at people," said Ron. "She looks at people in the same way that Tolkien looks at people."

And somehow I knew exactly what he meant. What's more, I knew that he was right.

Several hours later, while the fireworks exploded overhead, Tolkien kissed me as we sat on a blanket on his parents' rolling lawn. They had pink fireworks and blue fireworks and green fireworks and they even had a fireworks of America's Old Glory, which would have been odd on anyone else's lawn and yet seemed perfectly right on theirs. I supposed they must be breaking all sorts of laws, and what laws they weren't breaking, Acid was. But there was a cop on the premises and he didn't seem to mind a bit.

He was too busy kissing me.

I had yet to talk to the author of *Untitled*.

For the past few weeks, I'd been deep into the editing of the work, making extensive revision notes against the day I might actually get to communicate my ideas with the author.

It's not like *Untitled* was bad per se. I mean, I'd seen worse, which may sound like faint praise but went a long way towards making me feel not completely awful that we'd spent so much money on the book. And since we'd spent so much on it, we'd need to spend a ton of money to promote it, no matter how well or poorly written it was.

Now I'd reached the point where I simply couldn't do any more work on it without a live body.

Feeling a bit frustrated, I phoned Simon Smock, hoping he'd be willing to finally set up a meet for me with the author, whose name I still didn't know. Even though I'd seen the signed contracts, the author's signature looked like "Cake" to me and I was fairly certain *that* couldn't be it.

Lucky for me, or so I thought, Simon was in. Although once I'd posed my request, his answer was a resounding "No."

"No?"

"Is it the *N* you're having trouble with or the *O*, Jane? No, I'm sorry but the author is not ready to meet with you yet. She has good cause to be shy of editors and she's been working on her own revisions preparatory to any meetings."

Great. Now the author was editing herself. Just what the hell had I been doing here these past few weeks?

"Oh," was the best I could come up with.

"Can I ask you something?"

"Hmm?"

"Before, when you were first stumbling through your request, why did you keep referring to the author as 'Cake'?"

Apparently, I'd been wrong. Grateful for the phone, I was glad he couldn't see me blushing.

"Because the signature looked like that's what it said?" Well, it *had* looked like that.

I heard him chuckle.

"Yes," he said, "I can see where you might read it that way. Tell you what."

"What?"

"She's finally come up with a title for it."

"She has?" We were finally making progress! "Great!"

"Yes." Now I thought I heard a devilish smile. "She's made an acronym from the names of the four main characters."

I reviewed the four names from *Untitled,* which was soon to be titled, in my head: Layla, Ipanema, Sara and Twinkle. She'd named them all, I'd learned from Simon during a previous discussion, from women in song. Layla and Sara I could understand. But Ipanema struck me as sad: apparently, Anonymous didn't get that the girl was *from* there; she thought she *was* Ipanema. As for Twinkle as in Twinkle, Twinkle, Little Star, that was easy to understand as well, for even I couldn't think of a female name beginning with T that had been celebrated in song. But then, why hadn't she just named her a name beginning with another letter, like Angie or Delilah?

But then it occurred to me: Maybe the acronym had come before the names and she'd simply selected the names to fit the acronym!

"The List!" I practically leaped up in my seat, like a quiz-show contestant all excited I'd guessed correctly.

But then I checked my own enthusiasm. "I hate to say this, Simon, but haven't there already been a lot of books published with that title? I mean, it's not exactly original…"

I could hear him chuckle again. "Oh, but that's not the title," he said.

"It's not?" Apparently, it was the consolation prize for me. "Then what is?"

"Slit."

"Excuse me?"

"Slit."

"But isn't that, um, vulgar beyond belief?"

"Not at all. It's feminist."

"A Rashomon-like novel that's kind of a cross-pollination of *Divine Secrets of the Ya-Ya Sisterhood* and *The Story of O* that's called *Slit* is somehow feminist?"

"Well," he said, "since Cake says it is…"

Great. Now I had a feminist book called *Slit* to sell. I'd have been better off with *Untitled*.

Dodo's date with Stephen Triplecorn had been, er, interesting.

"What did he say? What did he say? What did he say?"

We were at the little Chinese place around the corner from Churchill & Stewart. The food was of questionable origin, but the lighting in the place was dark at least, so it was honors-even.

"Can we at least order first, Jane?" Dodo scanned the menu.

"No, we can't bloody well order first. Besides, the food here sucks."

"Well, I'm still hungry, so I'll have the Moo Goo Gai Pan."

"Wonderful," I said, "great. Now, will you tell me about this date?"

"First, you tell me, what are you more concerned with, my dating life or how it affects you?"

"What a question! Of course I care about how it affects me!"

"Of course."

"Because how it affects me is directly tied to how it affects Emma."

"True." Dodo looked a tiny bit embarrassed for having made a fuss.

"And, of course, I also care about your dating life. I always have." This, of course, was an exaggeration. I hadn't always cared about Dodo's dating life other than in the abstract, certainly not back in the days I'd only seen her as my boss. But the more I'd got to know Dodo, the more I liked her, and the more I liked her, the more I cared about her dating life. So the general sentiment was true. It had just taken me a while to arrive at the specific.

"I know that, Jane." She smiled. "At any rate, it really wasn't a date, not in the technical sense."

"Well, he came to your home."

"But not to see me. He came to talk to me about you."

And here we were, back at me again.

"Frankly," Dodo said, "I think Stephen Triplecorn is obsessed with you."

"Obsessed with me? That's ridiculous!"

"Yes. The only way I could think to keep him from asking me questions, which I would feel compelled to answer honestly, was by turning the tables on him, by asking him questions instead."

"What did you ask him?"

"Well, I asked him why this case was taking so long. It seems to me, I said, that what's taken him months could have been accomplished in a few days."

"And what did he say?"

"Oh, he gave me that line again about 'these things take time' and being 'underfunded.'"

"But you don't believe that?"

"Do you?"

"I don't know," I said. "I have done some research on foster care and adoption, you know, against the day. Everything I've read does point to things taking a ridiculously long time. Everyone says they have the best interests of the children at heart, but you'd think that if that were so, these things would move more quickly, there would be more of an effort made to put babies in situations where they could have a secure and permanent home, rather than drawing it out."

"Well, and that's exactly what I mean," said Dodo. "It's not like Emma's birth mother has come forward—or anyone else for that matter—to claim her. I would think, in light of that, that Stephen Triplecorn would want to move more quickly. But instead, he seems content to wait until he's uncovered every scrap there is to uncover about you."

I squirmed in my seat. The idea of that made me uncomfortable.

"Don't worry," Dodo said. "I didn't tell him anything he could use against you."

"What did you tell him?"

"I told him that I'd known you for several years, that you were clever and resourceful and determined. I said that Emma couldn't hope for anyone stronger in her corner."

"Do you really mean all that?"

"Yes, I do."

"And what did he say to that?"

"He said the same thing he kept saying to everyone. 'There's something about that Jane Taylor woman. I can't place my finger on it, but there's something not quite right there.'"

"Oh no! What did you tell him?"

"I said it was just your determination, that it's rare to meet anyone as single-mindedly determined as you are, and that that's what he was reacting to. I told him that at work we call you Dog With A Bone."

"But you don't call me that at work!"

"No, but we should."

I could see that something else was troubling her. "What is it, Dodo? What's wrong? What aren't you telling me?"

She gave me one of those bright-eyed, Dodo-trying-to-smile-but-looking-sad looks. "I *like* him, Jane."

I was shocked. "You *like* Stephen Triplecorn?"

Who knew? Even though she'd never admitted it, probably never would, she had to have noticed his large, er, package. Maybe that was it? I certainly couldn't think of anything else to recommend him.

"Yes, Jane, I like Stephen Triplecorn. He's nice and gentle and determined and very dedicated to his work."

"He has no sense of humor."

"Details." She shrugged.

I supposed that I could have pointed out that Dodo was similarly lacking in the humor department—well, except for that Dog With A Bone remark; that was pretty funny—but I kept mum.

"At any rate," she sighed, "it doesn't matter what I think of Stephen Triplecorn, since I'm fairly certain he's in love with you."

"Please. Isn't that laying it on a bit thick?"

"He's certainly obsessed with you, and in my book, obsession and love are just one murderous killing spree apart."

"Just what book are you reading?"

"Oh," she said, "I'm not serious. I mean, I don't think he's romantic enough to *kill* anyone over you." Then she nodded wisely. "But he is a man obsessed."

Oh, please God, I thought, she had to be wrong about that one. Whether he was obsessed about *me* (doubtful) or obsessed about my case (more likely) it didn't bode well.

Emma was beginning to discover games.

She liked playing peek-a-boo (David was her favorite for this), could play patty-cake (believe it or not, it was my mother who taught her this one), and was particularly proud of her new-found talent of waving bye-bye.

I knew she was very proud of that last achievement, but I couldn't help it: every time she did it, it made me a bit sad. It made me worry that one day she'd be waving bye-bye to me.

I hoped that, when the time came, it would be because she was going off to school and not because life had somehow conspired to take her from me.

August, the eighth month

Christopher had something to show us.

"Call Mary Jr.," he said. "Tell her to meet us at the playground. Tell her to call the other women, too."

Even though it had only been a couple of months since I'd come up with the idea of his redoing the playground, it was finished. It hadn't taken long to get the town council to approve it, since it wasn't like we were asking for anything huge, like better neighborhood housing or anything like that. What money they didn't have, I'd contributed, no one the wiser.

Still, I hadn't expected...

"It's *beautiful!*" Mary Jr. said, as we all stood there trying not to sweat too much, being caught in the midst of the hottest August that Britain had ever known.

And it *was* beautiful.

Oh, you know, it wasn't anything grand like something Disney might dream up, but for a neighborhood playground in a poor part of town...

I looked at it through Mary Jr.'s eyes.

Going to her home the way I had been these past several months, I'd had a lot of occasion to reflect on how amazingly fine the line was between having not much really and having just enough: for me, that line came in the form of having my own bathroom, no sharing with anyone down the hall.

So, looking at the playground not just through my great-expectations eyes, but through hers, I saw:

A trimmed-back grass area; equipment that was new, sturdy, colorful and arranged for maximum use, with not one, but four slides, each a different color, one in each corner so there'd be no fighting or jam-ups, regular swings for bigger kids, bucket swings for smaller ones, a sandbox with a closeable chest next to it for storing buckets and things, and a large multicolored jungle-gym/treehouse thing in the center for the more adventurous, of which I was sure Emma would be one day; plus umbrella/table/bench combos for the mummies with small babies.

As I watched Mary Jr. and the other women move off to experiment with all the new stuff, I grabbed on to Christopher's arm.

"It *is* the fucking Louvre!" I said.

He actually blushed.

"It's amazing," David spoke quietly. "I'm very proud of you."

"Yes, well…" Christopher's voice trailed off.

"So what's next for you," I asked, "now that this is done?"

"Next?" Christopher took a deep breath. "I suppose that next I'll be going back into business."

David took Christopher's hand in his.

"I couldn't be happier." David smiled.

Stan from Accounting was next on Stephen Triplecorn's list. I'd been dreading this day, knowing it must inevitably come.

In the intervening months since Stan had hacked into Stephen's computer, our relationship had not only gone back to its previous each-other's-nemesis state; if possible, it had worsened.

Whenever we had an editorial meeting—every week, in other words—he blocked my ideas. Basically, every time I wanted to say "yes" to something, he said "no."

And he got everyone else to say it, too.

He was also back to making breast jokes, calling me Taylor instead of Jane and, whenever I threatened to get the better of him, reminding everyone, "Remember when Taylor had that fake-pregnancy scam running for nine months?"

None of which boded well for his meeting with Stephen Triplecorn.

As Stan sauntered out of Dodo's office after the meeting, he gave me a bit of a sneer, before heading off to his own office.

This was beginning to look worse and worse.

Nearly right behind Stan was Stephen Triplecorn, talking over his shoulder to Dodo. "Right, then. Friday at eight." When he saw me, he gave a surprised backward jump, before nodding curtly and hurrying on.

I immediately went into Dodo's office, closed the door behind me.

"What was that all about?" I asked her. " 'Friday at eight'?"

"Oh. That." She waved me off. "He just wants to talk some more about you. I swear the man's obsessed. I've never seen anyone so in love before."

Was Dodo nuts? I'd never seen anyone act less in love with someone than Stephen acted with me. It was all he could do not to spit on me when our paths crossed. Still, I remembered when I was little, and Gran Taylor used to say that the boy who made fun of me most in the schoolyard only did it because he liked me so much. I supposed that Stephen's behavior might be an adult version of that. And yet the thought made me shudder, not least of all because Dodo, sweet Dodo, clearly was besotted with the jerk.

Maybe that's what it was, I thought. Maybe Dodo's own vision where Stephen Triplecorn was concerned was so cloudy that she was projecting her own strong feelings for him onto him as being his strong feelings for me. Got that?

I shrugged it all off. As important as Dodo's happiness was to me, I needed to worry about Stan right now, because Stan in a strange way equaled me, and I equaled Emma.

Dodo didn't seem to mind changing the subject. On the contrary, she was clearly relieved to no longer be discussing what she perceived as Stephen's romantic inclinations towards me.

"Stan was *amazing!*" Dodo crowed.

"You're kidding, right?"

"No, I'm not. He stuck strictly to the truth, but he was selective about it. He told Stephen, and I quote—" and, by the way, her ability to exactly quote Stan didn't surprise me; like many good editors, she had an amazing memory for text and was one of those ones who could do "Ozymandias" while popping peanuts at cocktail parties, which may also explain why she didn't get asked out much " '—Jane and I have never really gotten along. No. Scratch that. Jane and I particularly detest one another. When she says "yes," I say "no" and vice versa—and not because we necessarily hold the opposing view either, but because we *like* being opposed to one another. We're like a battery—if you have two positive ends or two negative ends, you may have a matched set, but you've got no light. All of that said, I can't imagine a better woman, apart from my sisters, to be a mother. Around here, we like to call Jane Dog With A Bone—' "

"You told him to say that!"

Dodo blushed. "Well, yes. I did prep him on that one. May I go on?"

"You mean there's more?"

She nodded. "And then Stan said, 'Can you think of anyone better to have taking care of a baby than a woman who's known as Dog With A Bone? I don't even *like* Jane Taylor, but I'll tell you this…if I had a baby needed taking care of, and for some reason I couldn't do it myself, I can think of no one else I'd rather trust that baby to than Dog With A Bone.' And then he left."

"But if he said all that in my defense, then why did he sneer at me on his way out?"

Dodo frowned, clearly as puzzled as I. "I dunno," she shrugged. "You'll have to ask him that yourself."

Knock! Knock!

Stan's voice: "Yeah?"

I entered, closing the door behind me.

"Stan," I said, "I want to know, I *have* to know, why did you sneer at me on your way out of Dodo's office?"

"Oh. That." He snorted. "Because that's what you and I do with each other, isn't it?"

"I know that's what we've always done, but I don't understand. If we have such a sneering-at-each-other relationship, then why did you stand up for me with Stephen Triplecorn?"

"You call what I did standing up for you? That whole Dog With A Bone thing?"

"Coming from you? Yes."

"Fine. I'll tell you why I did it. I did it because psycho-bitches are a pound a dozen. But good mothers? Got to encourage them wherever you find them, however unlikely they may seem."

Who would have ever guessed? Stan had a soft spot for what he perceived as good mothers and, wonder of wonders, he thought I was one of them. I must have been beaming at him too much, because he reddened.

"Don't think that just because I helped you out today, I'm going to stop saying 'no' whenever you say 'yes,' because I'm not."

"Okay." I beamed.

"And I'm going to keep saying 'yes' whenever you say 'no,' too."

"Okay." I beamed still.

"And stop smiling at me like that!"

I figured that, in the interests of our new camaraderie, I'd best change the subject to one Stan would be comfortable with.

"Did you notice anything particularly different about Stephen Triplecorn?"

"Christ, yes! The guy's got the biggest John Thomas in England!"

For Stan, that was like coming home.

Perhaps it was finally feeling a grandmotherly instinct towards Emma that was making my mother act differently.

Was such a thing possible? Could family members ever really change? Whatever my mother's reasons, she'd called me on the phone and it wasn't even for anything negative.

As she invited me, in a rather nice—if cautious—tone of voice, to meet her and Vic at an upscale bar called Tarquin's, I thought over the past several months, during which time it seemed as though at least once a month we either talked to each other or saw each other at some event like the shower or her visit to see Emma. For us, that was a lot of contact. Weren't we supposed to keep on being absent from each other's lives in the vain hope of becoming fonder? Was it really possible that one day we might remotely resemble a nice family?

And now here she was, inviting me to meet her lover.

"Of course, I'll come," I said, feeling far more ambivalent about it than I was endeavoring to sound.

"There's something you should know about Vic."

"Okay," I said, hoping my "okay" projected a note of openness.

"Oh, never mind," she said, sounding nervous, my "okay" clearly not having been okay enough. "We'll just meet you at the bar."

Tarquin's catered to the well-heeled set, but it also really did look like the kind of place your mother would go to. The wait-staff, as I sat in mahogany-and-red-leather comfort, were far more polite than I was accustomed to. In addition to some polo prints on the walls, there were some photos of the large woman who owned the place shaking hands with celebrities, like that Patricia woman from *Keeping Up Appearances* and another woman who was a dead ringer for Emma Thompson. In fact, something about the room made me feel tempted to order a Dubonnet, save that I didn't know what a Dubonnet was. So I settled for a decent Chardonnay and watching the door.

My mother entered first, and as I saw her step through the doorway, throwing a smiling glance over her shoulder at her companion behind, it was as though I were getting a slow-motion glimpse of a younger version of my mother that I had never known before.

Then she was through the doorway and coming through behind her was…the most beautiful middle-aged woman I'd ever seen.

I didn't know what I was feeling as I came to the realization of the thing I should have guessed: Vic was Victoria.

My mother was in love with another woman.

I kept the news of the revelation involving my mother to myself. The news was too new, and somehow I couldn't sort it out immediately, so I kept it to myself, kept it even from Tolkien.

When Tolkien had sort-of moved in with me, the first thing we'd done was gone out to buy a new bed. The queen-size sleigh bed I'd had the past few years still had a lifetime's worth of service left in it, but I didn't want to spend my new life with Tolkien sleeping in the same bed I'd shared with Trevor, did I? It would be daring the gods or something, like wearing the same wedding dress twice, so we'd gone and picked out something just for us: a pencil-post bed that we'd liked the style of and Emma had liked its height from the floor (it was extraordinarily high) because she could roll under it.

I lay next to Tolkien in the pencil-post bed, propped up on one elbow, idly caressing his chest.

I was trying to pay attention to his words, since he was talking to me about something important, but I was so grateful on a daily basis that I'd been granted a second chance with him, that each night in bed felt as though I was rediscovering the world. I sometimes told myself it must be a bit like what Emma experienced the very first time she opened her eyes: the attractively shiny newness of everything and, yes, the scariness of the unknown. And, oh, did he an amazing body! It was hard to stop myself from admiring the way a muscle was shaped here, the way his hair lay there...

"Would you rather do this later?" Tolkien asked, referring to the papers he'd been about to tell me about.

"Sorry," I said, exercising a superhuman will and tearing myself away from that chest. "You were going to tell me about your search for Sarah?"

I'd been sleeping when he'd come in late from work, sliding in next to me and whispering that he had news. I guess the fact that he was naked when he told me was what had made my natural inclination to ignore the talk and go for the comfort. What can I say? Once self-involved, always—

"I'm finally getting somewhere." He spoke with such enthusiasm that his enthusiasm made me get enthusiastic and actually made me forget about having sex with him for the moment.

"What is it? What?" I asked, sitting up.

"Well, remember I was going to interview some of Sarah's friends?"

"Right. The same ones the local cops had already talked to."

"That's right. Anyway, it looks like they didn't tell everything they knew before. Apparently, Sarah had a boyfriend that no one else had bothered to mention. Her family didn't know about him, of course, she'd kept it a secret. It looks like he went missing the same time Sarah did."

"So you think they went together?" I didn't give him a chance to answer. "But why wouldn't someone have put this together before? Two kids go missing at the same time—"

"He was several years older, out of school, living on his own, so it wasn't like anyone at school would have put it together and her friends weren't talking. You know how that is with teenagers—they think loyalty means keeping their mouths shut, with no thought that to do so might result in a far greater danger. As for the boyfriend, I suspect that when he disappeared people just assumed he'd moved on."

"Do you have any idea where they might have gone?"

"No. But at least I've got something more to go on now."

"Mary Jr. will be so excited!" I said, but then I stopped myself. "But I don't think I'd best say anything to her yet. Why get her hopes up before we know something more concrete?"

"That sounds smart," he said.

I settled down into the welcoming crook of his arm, head against his chest, and recommenced idly playing with his body.

"Can I ask you something?" I asked.

"Mmm?" he responded. Apparently, my idling was starting his motor.

"Do you think I'm a bad person?"

That stopped his engine cold. He looked down at me, tilted my head up so that I had to meet his eyes.

"Why do you ask that?"

"Because I've asked you to use your spare time to find Mary Jr.'s niece and while I could have asked you to do the same for Emma's mother, I haven't."

"I see," he said softly. Then he laid his cheek against my hair.

"No, Jane, I don't think you're a bad person for not actively going the extra step in searching for Emma's mother. I think you're human. You can't be expected to go after that which might cause you lots of pain. Besides, Social Services says they're looking for her, right? It's not like you're obstructing their search in any way. Honestly, it's not your responsibility to do any more."

"I suppose."

"I mean, how good would it be for Emma, if someone else showed up now, wanting her back?"

I thought about it hard, not just from my viewpoint, but from Emma's. I thought about how happy she was with me.

"It wouldn't be good at all." I shivered.

"And then there's this," he said.

"What?"

"In all these months, no one has come forward to claim Emma. I'd say the field looks pretty good for you and her."

"I'm worried about Emma." I poured forth my fears to David and Christopher in their apartment. It was such a happier place up there once again, now that Christopher knew what he wanted to do and knew that David was fine with it.

I hadn't told Tolkien about the revelation concerning my mother, and I wasn't ready yet to talk to David and Christopher about it either, even though I did feel they could help me sort it out. I was still too busy coping with my own conflicted emotions, though, to let the prism of other people affect those feelings just yet.

"Oh dear God," said David. "Is this like when that book had you worried she wasn't rolling over quickly enough and then she just rolled right over?"

"No," I said a trifle testily, "this isn't at all like that. I think she needs religion."

"What are you talking about, Jane?" David looked at her playing on the carpet. Then he sniffed the air. "I think she may need a new nappy, but religion?"

I moved to change her, but Christopher got there first. "I'll get this round," he said.

"Thanks," I said to Christopher as he went off to get the supplies for Emma they kept up there.

As he proceeded to change her on a small blanket he'd laid on the carpet—the bigger she got, the easier it was to just change her on the floor, since she'd begun to twist too much for a changing table—we continued with the matter at hand, the subject of my latest motherhood anxiety attack.

"Why do you say Emma needs religion?" David asked.

"Be-*cause*," I Jane-whined, "that's what people *do* with babies!"

"They do?" he asked.

"Yes! Where do you come from?"

"Israel."

"Right. I knew that."

"Then why did you ask?"

"Be-*cause* you don't appear to be getting it!"

"Well, then, why don't you explain it to us, so we *will* get it," suggested Christopher, pulling Emma's pants back up. "There you go, Em."

"Okay," I said, "fine. Haven't you ever noticed, that when people have a baby, they start going to church again?"

"Well, not everybody," said Christopher.

"Of course not," said David. "I would imagine that some people go to synagogues."

"Or mosques," added Christopher.

"Okay, fine. Be semantically precise if you must. The point is, that when people have babies, they return to some sort of house of worship."

"Right," said Christopher. "Babies make people hypocritical."

"What? Why are you not getting it?"

"It's just that, I can see where you're heading with this. And it does seem hypocritical to me, in light of what you yourself have previously said on that subject, stuff along the lines of people not needing any specific organized religion provided they could be inspired on their own not to murder one another."

"That does sound like me," I conceded.

"Yes, it does," agreed David.

"So you think it's hypocritical when anyone does it?" I asked.

"If we're talking about people who haven't set foot themselves in a church or a synagogue or a mosque since they've gotten big enough to say 'no' when their parents tried to make them," said Christopher, "and now that they have kids of their own, they're starting that same whole empty process again, then yes."

"I respectfully disagree," I said.

"That's a new one from you." David snorted, and I ignored his snort.

"I'm not convinced it's empty at all," I said. "In fact, I think it's a great way to give Emma a sense of community."

"How many communities does Emma need?" David asked. "You've given her the community of us, of your friends and co-workers and family, of Mary Jr. and her friends. Come to that, you've given her the community of you—why, you're like an entire community unto yourself. How many more communities does she need?"

"I just think she could use a religious community as well."

"For what?" asked Christopher. "For small-mindedness and us/them face-offs?"

"Do you honestly believe," said David, "that a person needs to be a member of a specific religious group to have a moral center?"

"Do you mean that we need to save her soul?" asked Christopher.

"We could always get that Jewel girl." David shrugged.

"Or REM," suggested Christopher.

"I don't know!" I said, growing frustrated. "I don't know what I mean! Maybe I just think that, when Christmas eventually rolls around again, it should mean more to her than *just* the decorations and *just* the presents. Maybe I just think she should be going to potluck suppers."

David's and Christopher's eyes met right over my head.

"She makes a persuasive argument," David said with a shrug.

"I like casseroles," said Christopher.

"Then you agree with me?" I asked.

"About the casseroles?" Charistopher said. "Sure. You can't ever have enough of those."

Well, it was a start at least.

"Great!" I said. "Where do you think we should start?"

"We?" said Christopher. "Oh, no. Count me out of this one. I'm C of E. We don't have to go to church. We've got the Queen, you know."

"But what about the casseroles?"

"Oh, I'll still come for those, but only for those. I doubt wherever you wind up, they'll be having potluck every Sunday."

Wherever I wind up? Yes, I still didn't know to what church I'd be taking Emma. I still needed to figure that one out. And, according to Christopher, C of E was out, since there wouldn't be any need for us to show up at all. Well, unless another Royal got married.

As so often happened, when stumped by life, I looked to David for inspiration.

"What about you?" I asked. "What church do you belong to?"

My best friend was clearly annoyed with me.

"I'm Jewish!"

"Oh. Right."

Christopher, perhaps hoping to deflect the annoyance David was so visibly feeling, turned the spotlight on me.

"What are you, Jane?" he asked.

Now there was a stumper.

"I dunno," I said. "Episcopalian?"

My Emma could now understand the word "no"—not that she always, or even sometimes, obeyed it. She was also a mobile little girl. She could already stand alone momentarily and could walk while holding on to furniture.

It occurred to me that whenever a woman has a child, whether that child has come from her body or not, each succeeding moment from the child's birth takes it an independent step at a time away from where it began.

It was my job, much as I loved having her with me, to see to it that Emma kept taking those independent steps away; and if at all possible, for her to take those steps joyfully.

September, the ninth month

Tolkien and I were going out on a date.

Yes, I do realize that we'd done that part already—we'd technically gone out on a first date twice in fact—but this was a bit different.

Tolkien pointed out that since Christmas Eve of the previous year, I had yet to spend a full night away from Emma.

"You're wrong," I countered. "There was that one time Dodo kept her overnight and we had all that mind-blowing sex, which eventually led to your sort-of moving in here."

Tolkien looked sheepish at being caught out. "But you can't really blame a guy for trying to get more mind-blowing sex, can you? So couldn't we have another one—a night away from Emma, that is?"

"You make it sound as though 'a night away from Emma' is some kind of great thing," I said, "but I don't see it that way at all."

"Well, of course, the not-Emma part of it isn't the selling point. It's the us-being-completely-alone that I was looking for."

"But what can we do without Emma there that we're not doing already with her in the next room?"

I guess he was too embarrassed to say it aloud, because he whispered it in my ear.

I can tell you this much: it involved me playing Scotland Yard detective and arresting him for crimes against the Crown, upon which I would interrogate him using any method I saw fit; then we were going to switch, and he could arrest me.

"I can see what you're saying. That game would work better without interruption."

And so we'd decided on a location for our first just-us-since-he-sort-of-moved-in date. His apartment, which he hadn't given up yet.

I suppose I might have been offended at his keeping his options open like that, but with the past history I'd given him, I couldn't blame him. And, as for the fact that we weren't going somewhere more exotic, I couldn't care less that it was going to be in his nondescript apartment (which was now even more nondescript since he'd moved his CD player and CD collection to my place). I was going to get to play a detective from Scotland Yard!

So, having a perfect location, the only thing we were still in need of was a sitter.

Unfortunately, however, neither David nor Christopher could do it, because David was working and Christopher had a project he was working on; Dodo couldn't do it, because she was going out on yet another "interview" with Stephen Triplecorn and, God bless her, I didn't want to do anything to tip that cart; Sophie couldn't do it because Baby Jack was sick, not that she would have anyway; and my mother wouldn't do it because she was just plain scared to.

"But why does it have to be this Saturday night?" I asked Tolkien.

"Because it's one of those now-or-never things. I'm guessing that if I don't get you away for a whole night now, my next chance will be when Emma leaves for university."

I could feel my lower lip begin to quiver. "Emma's going to have to leave to go to university?"

Yes. Well. Even I could see his point.

That left us with…

"I think it's just *brilliant* what you've done with this place since I was last here!"

Ladies and Gentlemen, we'd been forced to rely upon the baby-sitting generosities of Our Constance.

"But it hasn't changed any since you were here last," I said, letting the vampire in, "save that Emma's cot is now in the living room—" which is where it would be until we moved somewhere with a second bedroom "—and we've got Tolkien's CD things set up."

"But those two things are just so—" and here she did her flapping-seal clap "—*brilliant!* You've got the baby's things taken care of and the man-you're-sleeping-with's things taken care of. *Brilliant! Brilliant! Brilliant!*"

I pitied poor Emma that she was going to have to put up with this whackjob for the entire night, but I was glad that Tolkien and I would soon be able to get the hell away from her—Constance, that is. And who knew? Babies were always taking to the strangest things—why, look at Emma and my mother. It was entirely possible that like the birds that always seemed to trail after Constance whenever we happened to be outside together, Emma would be enchanted with her, too. And if Constance kept changing her contact lens color for her, or perhaps flashed a few pretty healing crystals, Em would probably be mesmerized.

"Off you go," Constance said, Emma on her hip. "You two have a brilliant time. We two will be just fine here."

No sooner did Tolkien and I enter his apartment, than the phone rang.

"It's for you," he said. "Constance."

"Yes, Constance?"

"Emma was thirsty and I was wondering…how long do you boil the milk bottle for?"

"You don't boil the milk bottle! Take it off the stove before you blow the place up!"

Constance laughed. "I wasn't going to boil it on the stove! I was going to put it in the micro. I was thinking, what? A minute? Two?"

"No, Constance! You just pour it from the container in the fridge and then give it to her."

"You mean cold?"

"Yes, that's exactly what I mean."

"But I always like mine—"

"Trust me, Em likes it that way. Was there anything else?"

"Oh, no. We're having a ball."

Kiss, kiss, kiss.

Even though I was supposed to be the interrogating Scotland Yard detective first, Tolkien had my bra off and was quite intent…

Ring!

"Constance again," Tolkien said, running his fingers through his hair.

"Yes, Constance?"

I have to admit, I felt distinctly strange talking to Constance, even over the phone, with my bra off.

"I was thinking…maybe steak for dinner?"

"For you or for Emma?"

"Oh, certainly not for me. I'm a vegetarian—you know that."

"Well, Emma can't have steak either."

"Whyever not?"

"Because, Constance, she's…a…ba…by."

"Ah." Then: "And babies can't eat steak? But I would have thought the protein—"

"No, Constance. There are some baby food jars in the cupboard. She likes the lasagna best."

I heard the cupboard door open, heard Constance crack open a jar, heard her sniff.

"It smells awful! Like dirty socks."

"Well, you don't have to eat it. Emma does, and she likes it."

"Well, all right. Bye now!"

Tongue between my breasts.

At least I was getting closer to where I wanted to be.

Ring!

This time, I just answered it myself.

"Yes, Constance?"

"I was getting ready to give Em her bath. Do you think she'd like it if I washed her hair in beer?"

"No!"

"My mother used to—"

"No."

"I hate to say it," Tolkien said when I rang off, "but at this rate, I'm going to forget what we're supposed to be doing here. Do you know what's on TV?"

"Stop that," I said, throwing the remote across the room. "I'll remind you." I proceeded to get serious about my interrogation.

I was warming up to the good part, the part where I'd make Tolkien scream for mercy…

Ring!

"What. Is. It. Now. Constance."

"You don't have to get so huffy," she said, sounding truly wounded. "I'm just trying to do a good job."

"Yes, I do realize that," I sighed. "What is it?"

"Well, there's this really great horror flick on tonight," she said. I could hear her excitement get the better of her. "It's about a monster and, oh, I don't know, a city that needs to be eaten or something. Anyway, in order to prepare Em for the cruelties of the real world—"

"No!"

"But you don't think—"

"No, *you* don't think."

"Excuse me?"

"Emma likes that blasted purple dinosaur. Or those four Aussie boys who won't stop singing. Her videos are in the cabinet under the TV. If you must watch something while she's still awake, watch one of those with her."

I heard the sound of the cabinet opening and Constance rooting around.

"Do you mean this?" she asked, as if I could see the box.

"I can't see the box you're holding, Constance."

"It must be the Aussie one you mentioned. I don't know if this one is such a good idea. These guys all look so…excitable."

I ran my fingers through my hair, making the exasperated man's favorite gesture. Damn, but now I could see why guys did that.

"Constance."

"I mean, the guy in the purple shirt—"

"Constance."

"But if you really think she'll like this kind of thing—"

"*Constance!*"

"Yes?"

"Do me a favor. On second thought, make that two favors. First, put Emma on."

"But I don't think she's really ready for conversation yet—"

"Just. Put. Her. On."

"Ga!"

"Hey, Em, how's it going?"

"Ga!"

"Are you enjoying yourself with Auntie Constance?"

"Ga!!!"

"That's just great. Mummy loves you, Em. Can you put Auntie Constance back on the phone again?"

"Hello?" said Constance.

"Apparently, Em's having a great time with you."

"I'm so relieved to hear that," she said, and she did sound relieved. Then: "You could tell that from…how?"

"By the way she said 'ga.' She wouldn't have said it like that if she were miserable."

"Oh no? What'd she be doing?"

"She'd be crying, Constance. That's what babies do when they're unhappy."

"Well, she must be happy then, because she hasn't cried since I've been here."

"That's great."

"You said there was a second favor?"

"I did, and here it is… Don't use the microwave or the stove or anything else that might blow up, don't bathe Emma in juice or beer, don't watch horror shows or porn with her, and don't, I repeat, *don't* call here again *unless it's an emergency!*"

"There are an awful lot of don'ts in there, which inclines me to point out that you're asking for—one, two, three, four, five don'ts—five favors rather than one."

"Just. Do. It. Constance. *Just do the don'ts.*"

"Now is that really grammatically sound?"

I know it was rude but, rather than answering that last, I merely hung up. I knew that if I went on marginally obeying the laws of polite conversation, I'd probably never get to have sex again.

And, oddly enough, that last exchange appeared to do the trick, for there were no more peeps out of the Constance quarter for the duration.

This meant, in effect, that, once I woke Tolkien up, I got to play interrogating Scotland Yard detective with him—my finest hour being when I got him to go looking for the missing Crown Jewels with his tongue. Then he got to play the interrogating Scotland Yard detective, which he was extremely good at, I suppose because he was one, but he'd liked the Crown Jewels hunt so much the first time that he wanted to do it again, which was fine by me. Then we had great looking-each-other-in-the-eyes sex, ate whatever we could find to eat that wasn't moldy and passed out.

I woke as the dawn was breaking.

Oh, it was nothing so romantic as wanting to make love again with my lover as the sun rose over sleepy London; it was that I was used to Em waking me then. She may not have been my natural-born child, but she clearly had the key to my biological clock.

I punched Tolkien awake.

"We need to go see Em."

"Can't we sleep some more?"

"No. She'll be up now."

"Can we at least have sex again?"

"No," I said, throwing his pants at him. "I miss her."

When we got back to my place, I put the key in the lock, turned the knob, pushed open the door, only to hear…snoring.

I looked at Tolkien and whispered, "My word, but Constance is loud for a little woman."

But when we got farther into the room, we realized that the hibernating-bear sounds weren't coming from Constance, who was asleep in the chair. They were coming from the open mouth of Stan from Accounting, asleep sitting up on the couch, Emma sleeping on his chest.

The door clicking shut must have wakened him, because Stan

blinked alert. Seeing me, he rose, and handed me the still sleeping Emma.

"What are you doing here?" I hiss-whispered.

"The little raving loony," he said, indicating Constance with a nod of his head as he put on his rumpled suit jacket, "went into a little raving loony panic, and her Uncle Stan was the only person she knew who was home."

"What was she panicked about?"

"I dunno. The Aussie guys in that video you had her watch? Whoever knows with Constance."

"Well," I said, "thanks for helping out."

"Oh, no problem." He gave sleeping Emma a light chuck under the chin. "She really is a cute little bugger. But next time, don't even bother with Constance. Just call your Uncle Stan. All those sisters, you know. I may not look it when I've got my calculator out, but I know babies."

A few days later, Tolkien, David, Christopher and I were all sitting on the floor of my flat, sharing some shrimp pizza—David doesn't bother with kosher—while Emma napped in her cot in the corner, fuzzy bunny held tight. The get-together was ostensibly to celebrate Tolkien and I buying a new carpet for the living room together—progress towards us finally, at last, completely living together!—which was a nice off-white Berber with garnet and emerald colored threads woven into the nap. In reality, the get-together was because I wanted to talk to them about Mother and Vic.

Ever since that night in Tarquin's, I'd been trying to sort out my feelings.

Vic had certainly been nice enough. She'd been downright deferential to me, as though I were somehow my mother's parent, a force to be reckoned with. Given how low a regard I knew my mother to hold me in, this was almost laughable.

And Vic was very pretty. She was tall and had that lanky I-could-have-once-been-a-model body, but without the anorexic face. Her face, on the contrary, was warm, with chestnut hair framing brown eyes and a sunny complexion, the lines of which she didn't bother trying to conceal with makeup. In fact, the confidence with which she wore her looks transformed features that might just have been pretty into an overall impression that was somehow stunning.

Maybe it was the perfect smile, the warm laugh.

And she was a sharp dresser, on that occasion having worn a white linen shirt and pants, which I knew would have instantly become a wrinkled mess on me were I to try to wear such a thing, with a matching tan jacket over her shoulders. She even had on somewhat high-heeled strappy sandals, which I would have killed for and which proved she wasn't bothered by her height.

"She sounds like a real beast," said David with dramatic sarcasm. "I can understand why you would despise her."

"I never said I despised her," I protested. "I simply said that I didn't know *how* I felt about her."

Christopher took another slice from the box. "Maybe you just don't like gay people."

"That's not helpful." I glared at him. Then I really thought about it for a second.

"Oh God," I groaned. "Do you think that could be it? Do you think it's possible that, here, all along, while I've been thinking that I'm some open-minded person, I'm really just another self-righteous git who doesn't know what she's talking about?"

"Well, sometimes you don't know what you're talking about," Tolkien said gently.

"Like when?" I was outraged.

"Like all that stuff with Emma about the Babinski reflex and then trying to get her to roll over on some kind of timetable—"

"The book *said*—"

"I really don't think anti-gay or anti-lesbian sentiment is your problem," David cut in.

"It's not?"

"No, it's not. I think you are simply, perhaps even understandably, ambivalent about seeing your mother with someone other than your father."

"But he's been dead a long time." I was surprised at how

blunt I sounded, as if the length of how long he'd been gone should somehow make my feelings about him less.

"So what?" said Tolkien. "You've certainly told me before that you always felt he was your only champion in the family."

"In a way," put in Christopher, "your late father has somehow been the full-body equivalent of a phantom limb. You can't see him anymore, but he is felt by you quite often and that feeling somehow affects everything else."

I was intrigued and appalled at the same time. "What a bunch of amateur psychoanalysts you three are!"

"Perhaps, but we make a weird kind of sense." Tolkien shrugged.

"About as much sense as the Weird Sisters in *Macbeth*," I muttered.

"Exactly!" David said. "And they knew what they were talking about too! What do you want for your mother?" he asked me.

"What do I *want* for her?" I'd certainly never given that any thought before. "What a bizarre question."

"Well, think about it," he pressed as, in an effort to delay confronting whatever it was he wanted me to confront, I excused myself to the kitchen to search for dessert options.

I returned in a moment, offering the open canister around.

"Raisin, anybody?" I popped one into my mouth.

"No, I don't want a *raisin!*" David said. "And since when do you eat raisins?"

"I dunno," I said, popping another one. "It must be the Emma Factor."

"We were talking about your mother, Jane. Do you want her to be happy or do you want her to be miserable?"

I thought about my long history with my mother, all of which somehow involved each of us trying to make the other miserable, not through any hugely overt acts but rather through small annoyances. While this behavior might not have passed for normal in everyone else's families, for us it defined the dysfunctional way in which we functioned. But did I want outsiders or even life its own self making my mother miserable?

No, I realized with a shock, I didn't.

"Oh my gosh," I said tentatively, feeling slightly awed. "I think I want my mother to be happy."

Then I remembered something David had told me the previous November, on the occasion of his wedding to Christopher. He'd said that true love is what human beings live for and that it was rare, very rare.

I looked around me—at Emma sleeping, at David and Christopher loving each other, at Tolkien just being himself—and it occurred to me that not only was David right, but moreover: love is love wherever one finds it and because of its rareness should never be turned away from.

"There is one thing I'd like to know," Tolkien said.

"Hmm…" I was still caught up in my musings on love.

"You said before that it was Sophie who first told you about your mother having an affair. Does she know who Vic really is?"

I hadn't thought of that. Then I shrugged. "I doubt it. Whoever tells Sophie anything if they can help it?"

"The author has received your revision notes," said Simon over the phone, as I pictured him sitting there in what were undoubtedly plush offices, this man who had put the flame in buoyant. I'd sent the revisions to the author through him, since I had as yet to receive a name or address for Anonymous.

Uh-oh, I thought. Anyone who was as much a hands-on control freak as Anonymous—the woman even insisted on designing her own cover, for Christ's sake!—would undoubtedly fight me tooth and nail on every editorial suggestion. Hell, she'd probably insist we print it in some impossible typeface.

"And?" I asked, trying to keep my tone brightly Dodo-ish.

"And she thinks you're brilliant."

"She *does?*"

"Yes. She thinks you're right that the dream sequence slows things down and that Ipanema isn't as sympathetic as she should be. Of course, there are a few minor details she disagrees with…"

We spent the next half hour going over the minor details, me surreptitiously munching on my salad, hoping all the while he couldn't hear me. He'd caught me just starting to eat when he'd phoned and I was too hungry to stop. Relative happiness with the universe having returned my appetite to me, I'd recently discovered that if I didn't eat when the hunger pains started, I got downright mean.

The minor details went well, with him winning some points but also agreeing to ask Anonymous again about others. And they really were just minor details, the kind of niggling things editors need to point out so that the writer will at least stop and think a moment before saying, "Oh, it's fine the way it is." The big things—making Ipanema, who I truly detested, a bit nicer; editing out the entire boring dream sequence—were things I won hands down.

"So," said Simon, "I'll just get back to my client with these further notes…"

"That's great," I said, unable to keep a tetchy note out of my voice. "I can't wait to hear what Anonymous has to say."

"It's really bothering you, not knowing who the author is, isn't it?"

"Yes, well…"

"Fine, I'll tell you."

"Rurry???" I was so shocked that I couldn't stop myself from speaking around the huge wedge of tomato that was already in my mouth.

"Uh, rurry," he said. "Do you remember that trilogy of novels about the Welsh au pair with the shoe-buying problem?"

"Omigod!" I said. "You mean the author of *Slit* is Gayla Gladsone?"

Gayla Gladstone was a supremely successful novelist whose books were very popular with women in the 18-34 demographic. She was also stunningly blond, given to wearing only white and gold and fur—which got her into a lot of trouble with certain groups—and she was very good at getting herself on television.

"I'm really not that crazy about the fur," I said.

He sighed. "I have tried talking to her about it. Many times."

So now I finally had a name for Anonymous. But wait a minute! Simon had said that she didn't want to publish any more books under the name of Gayla Gladstone.

"Why would she want to stop using the name of Gayla Gladstone?" I asked. "It's practically a household word. It has great recognition."

"My client says that her previous publisher strong-armed her into using it. They said her real name would present a problem in marketing her work, that no one would ever take her seriously. But now she feels that she's famous enough that her fans will forgive her anything. You know how these celebrities are—John Mellencamp, Hillary Rodham Clinton, the Artist Formerly Known as Prince…once they achieve a certain level of fame, that which they rejected as a career expedient becomes desirable again."

"Well," I objected, "that's not really true of Prince. I mean, he wasn't originally called that by his parents, was he? Anyway, doesn't he just go by a symbol now?"

"Who the hell knows anymore."

I was becoming fairly certain that I did not want to know the answer to the question I now had to ask.

"Simon, what's Gayla Gladstone's real name, the one she insists on using now?"

"She claims the last name is Polish, Jane."

"Yes?"

"It's Candy Likme," he said, spelling it for me.

Great. I was now the proud editor of *Slit* by Candy Likme. This just kept getting better and better.

My mother's church, unsurprisingly, was a sea of white, with Emma the only black pearl.

Was it Anglican? Methodist? Lutheran? It was hard for me to say. All I knew was, I had brought Emma into yet another situation in which she was in a minority of one.

When I'd phoned my mother, asking if she'd be willing to take us to her church, she'd been thrilled at the prospect.

"I've always wished you were more religious, Jane," she'd said. "I've never quite understood just what it is, the problem you have with God."

"I don't know if it's so much me having a problem with God, Mother," I'd said. "It's more like I suspect God of having a problem with me."

Still, she was pleased that I was coming and that Emma would be coming, too.

"She can't start too early on the road to salvation," my mother pointed out as we walked into the church.

I wanted to point out that, to my mind, Emma didn't need salvation. What, after all, did she have to repent so far in life—her inexplicable adoration for those four video boys from Australia? It seemed to me more like the rest of the world was in need of salvation for not providing her with a better world to live in. But I kept mum with Mum—no need to rock the ark and make waves in what were comparatively calm waters.

As I said, I really wasn't quite sure what denomination church I'd stumbled into, but I knew it wasn't Jewish or Muslim, since Jesus apparently figured strongly into the equation.

While still on the phone, I'd asked Mother if Vic would be coming with us.

"Oh, no," she said, although she did sound glad I'd asked. "Vic isn't much interested in the conventional side of religion."

"But things are still going well with you two?"

"Oh, yes," she said, again sounding pleased.

"Have you told Sophie yet?"

"Yes."

"How did it go?"

"Oh, you know Sophie."

I did. But I'd always assumed that the Sophie I knew was far different from the Sophie my mother knew.

"What did she say?" I asked.

"She said she was shocked, but then Baby Jack gurgled something to her and she had to go. Of course, by then she was all smiley-sounding and said, 'This is the greatest thing to ever happen to the Taylors yet!' before ringing off." She sighed. "I don't know about her moods, Jane. Could she still be breastfeeding?"

When I looked back on that day at church, I realized that the strongest impression I'd come away from it with had been one of *hats*. Meeting my mother on the steps in front of the church, I'd noticed she had on her head a sedate navy and cream number.

"Here," she said, pulling a pristine white bonnet from out of a purse that matched the hat.

"Thanks but I'm not really the type who—"

"Not for *you,* Jane! For Emma."

I proceeded to put the bonnet on Emma, which made her look silly, I thought, but she didn't seem to mind and it made my mother happy.

"She looks a bit *Scarlet Letter*-ish in it," I said.

My mother looked pointedly at my spiky-haired, unhatted head.

"I would have said that was more *you,*" she said.

Touché.

But once we were inside, there were hushed tones and Jesus on the cross and about four hundred hats.

There were straw hats and felt hats. There were white hats and hats of every other color imaginable, some hats having more than one color. There were hats with feathers and hats with flowers. There was even a hat with a stuffed bird on the brim, which I thought kind of scary in a pre-serial killer kind of way but that Emma found a treat.

Aside from the hats, there was a lot of hushed talking from the man at the altar—no, not Jesus; the other one—and hushed, off-key singing and hushed whispers as everyone stared throughout the service at unhatted me and my black-pearl daughter.

I couldn't wait to get out of there. Not that Emma wasn't well behaved; she hardly fussed at all except for when the minister—reverend?—said something about "unsaved souls going to Hell," which she rather seemed to take exception to. It was just that it was all so airless in there. And I was a bit worried that this particular preacher might be the scaffold-carrying type, and that he'd begun readying it for me, what with my *Scarlet Letter* vibe.

I thought we'd be able to just walk away afterwards, perhaps go grab some brunch, maybe some chocolate chip pancakes for me and a glass of milk for my little friend. After all, isn't that what church-going families do together on Sunday after church? But my mother was in no hurry. Apparently, we first had to talk to the minister. Reverend?

"Mis-*sus* Tay-*lor,*" the man in black intoned to her.

"Reverend Pauling." She gripped his hand with a smile I'd thought she'd reserved for getting an extra slice or two of cheese off the man in the cheese shop.

Well, she'd called him Reverend, so at least that was cleared up for me.

"And this must be Little Janie," he said, looking at me.

Little Janie? He looked at me like he'd known me once, which I guess is just barely possible, although I really didn't remember the church at all and, oh, I don't know, I'd think I would have remembered that particular Jesus on the cross.

"Do I know you?" I asked, taking his hand.

"No, but I know you. Your mother talks about you all the time."

Now there was a revelation that wasn't in the New Testament: my mother was talking about me to reverends; and, when she was doing it, she was calling me Little Janie.

"We here at Little Divine Divinity United Reform—" so that's where we were! "—think it's just so marvelous the way you've opened up your home to that little black child."

"Well, it's not like—"

"No, I'm sure it's not easy."

"That wasn't what I—"

"But we want you to know we're here to help. And of course you'll be wanting to bring her every Sunday."

"No, actually, I—"

"And, when she gets a little older, we'll want her in the choir..."

It was time to stop him. If I let him go on any longer, he'd have me signing Emma up for the convent just to get him to shut up.

"I'm sorry to disappoint you, Reverend Pauling, but I'm afraid Emma and I won't be able to become members of your church."

I saw my mother's face fall, and felt a rare twinge of guilt.

"Oh, you know," I said, "maybe we'll still come here for the big things—Christmas, Easter, potluck—but I just don't think we could do it every week."

"And may I ask why not?" The reverend asked, looking at me earnestly.

"It's, um, er, it's the, *it's the hats!*"

"The *what??*" The words came from both Reverend Pauling and my mother.

"The hats! They're very scary for Emma."

"They *are???*" and here they both looked at Emma, who was

of course not cooperating at all on this one, but was giggling again at the woman's hat that had the taxidermy.

"Yes, they really are," I said in as solemn a tone as I could muster. "I'm not even sure where it comes from exactly. All I know is that she has bad...*associations* with them."

"I've never heard of such a thing."

"Maybe it comes from when Constance sat with her?" I babbled on. "I do believe they watched some Hitchcock. Maybe it was *The Birds*." And here I gave a head jerk towards the taxidermy lady again but Emma was still not helping, because she was too busy giggling.

"You can see how hysterical she's getting," I said. "I'm afraid we really must go."

But I'd only taken a single step before I felt a hand on my shoulder.

It was my mother.

"You do realize, Jane, that you're an intensely odd young woman?"

Well, it wouldn't be a year in my life if at least one person didn't say that to me.

"Yes." I smiled back at her. "I did know that."

Constance, Minerva, Dodo, Stan.

Stephen Triplecorn had interviewed everyone at Churchill & Stewart who had been on his list except for one person, but now the time had come for him to talk to Louise.

One thing had been bothering me, ever since this whole Home Study thing had started. Any two idiots could get together, exchange a few bodily fluids, and, if a baby came out of it nine months later, no one would question their right to keep the baby; much less subject them to a study to test their fitness. And yet here was Stephen Triplecorn, tossing through every corner of my life, to see if it was okay for Emma to keep living with me.

Did I think it was wrong for them to examine prospective parents so closely?

Bloody no! I thought they should subject *every* prospective parent, natural or just waiting in line, to some sort of examination for fitness. If a closer eye were kept on things, who knew but that there might not be less abuse in the world.

That said, as much as I might endorse some kind of examination for all parents, I could yet see the fly in my ointment: where a person had enemies—and how many of us don't?—it would be easy for one to come forward to say that one was unfit.

So, as much as I'd dreaded Stephen Triplecorn talking to Constance or Minerva or Stan—or even Dodo, who might feel ethically compelled to tell an inconvenient truth—it was nothing compared to the dread I felt over him talking to Louise.

In the months since I'd been back at C&S, in the months since Louise had been assigned as my assistant there had been no easing of tensions between us. If anything, the situation had worsened. The way I figured it, the only way she would give a kind interview about me would be if I managed to throw a sack over her head and lobotomized her in the hall closet prior to Stephen Triplecorn's arrival. And, since physical violence was one of the few things that was beyond me, that wasn't on.

How I would have loved to have been a fly on the wall to see what she would say when she was interviewed by Stephen. I supposed I'd just have to rely on Dodo once again to tell me all about it later.

As it turned out, Louise and I were of a single mind for once. Apparently, she wanted me to be a fly on the wall, too. She even suggested it!

"Jane should be there too," she said sweetly to Stephen and Dodo. "Why, I'd almost say it was her *right* to hear what's said about her."

And so, there we all four were, in the conference room at C&S, since three people in Dodo's office had been stretching its capacity limits and four was just that one too many.

Louise was seated where I suspected she'd always wanted to be in life: at the head of the table. To her left, was Stephen Triplecorn. Dodo was at her right and I was next to Dodo.

Before Stephen Triplecorn could even ask a single question, Louise began talking in a voice that brooked no interruption.

"Let me tell you about Jane Taylor.

"Jane Taylor and I began working here at Churchill & Stewart within a week of one another over eight years ago. To be frank, our relationship has never been good. Jane has always been soooo much her own person, that who could ever stand her, really? She always has to have these...*opinions* about everything, always thinks she's right.

"But I suppose that's neither here nor there.

"No, the thing I think you'll be most interested in is Jane's pregnancy."

Here Dodo tried to stop her, but Louise wasn't having any of it.

"It all started a year ago April when Jane thought she was pregnant but then wasn't. First, she lied to the man she lived with at the time, Trevor Rhys-Davies, who somehow has managed to get lost in the shuffle since. I guess Jane thought that eventually she'd just get pregnant and that would be that. Of course, she didn't get pregnant, but she continued telling everyone, including all of us here at Churchill & Stewart, that she was.

"First, she tried to pretend that she shared the same obstetrician as Princess Niquie. But then, when she began to worry that we might catch her out in that lie, she invented a tarot-card reading midwife, Madame Zora, who was to deliver her baby. As the months wore on, Jane accepted all sorts of perks at work—days off, a footstool under her desk, *attention*. Eventually, I suppose she must have realized that someone might question a pregnant woman not getting any bigger, so she took to wearing padding under her clothes so that no one would be any the wiser."

"And how long did she keep this up?"

"*For nine months*. As a matter of fact, it is my belief that if the baby she'd found on those church steps had been white, she'd still be scamming everybody."

"Louise!" Dodo shouted.

Louise held a hand up.

"Before anyone says another thing," she said, "I have something to show you."

While she was gone, I stole a surreptitious glance at Stephen Triplecorn. If that wasn't smoke pouring out of his ears, it was close enough.

When Louise returned, she was pushing a trolley with a TV/VCR on it. She punched play. At first, there were just squiggly lines as she fiddled with the remote. Then there was a picture shot from overhead of me, undeniably looking pregnant, with a date and time stamped in the lower corner as Louise hit freeze frame: November 5, 2:00 p.m.

Apparently, Louise had gotten the guys from Security to go through old tapes of people entering the building, and they'd located me returning from lunch. The time stamp proved that, for once, I'd returned on time, but I doubted that was going to carry any weight for me in this room.

I was ruined. More importantly, Emma was ruined.

Dodo was the first to recover.

"Thank you so much, Louise," she said icily. "I think we've seen and heard enough. You may go now."

"I'd say I've seen enough," said Stephen Triplecorn, starting to rise, after Louise had left.

"Oh, no," said Dodo, "I don't think you have. Sit."

He sat. And then Dodo did something I'd never seen her do before, something I would never have imagined her doing in a million years. She *lied.*

Oh, how she lied.

"I've never told anyone this before," she said to Stephen Triplecorn, "so please keep this in the strictest confidence. Louise is my cousin."

"Louise is your cousin," he stated, not asked, as though unsure which particular room in the madhouse he was going to find himself in now, which turned out to be topically appropriate as it happened.

"Yes, Louise is my cousin. But she comes from the known-to-be-mentally-unstable branch of the Lane tree."

"Except she's not a Lane at all," pointed out Stephen Triplecorn. "Her last name is—"

"Yes, that's right," said Dodo. "And the Lane branch doesn't like to talk about that other branch very much. But they are an insane bunch and Louise is the worst. Anyway, a few years back, within the week of our hiring Jane, as Louise mentioned, I got a call from Louise's mother, saying she'd been sacked from yet an-

other job for being a pathological liar, some story about her saying everyone at the firm—man, woman, receptionist—had made
passes at her. Can you believe it? It's quite enough to accuse one
person in a firm of sexual harassment—nearly expected, in some
jobs—but the whole firm? It would have been more believable
if Louise were even remotely likable. But the idea of an entire
firm with the hots for Louise? At any rate, Louise's mother didn't
think that anyone would ever hire her again. I mean, would *you*
hire someone like that?"

Dodo didn't wait for an answer.

"No, I thought not. At any rate, I took pity on Louise, got her
a job here at C&S."

"Weren't you at all concerned she'd try to pull the same stunt
here?" asked Stephen Triplecorn.

"Here?" Dodo looked indignant. "Nobody would ever try to
pull that here, because who would ever believe it? Do I look like
a harasser to you? Does Jane? True, there's Stan from Accounting," she conceded, "but he's such an equal-opportunity harasser that nobody ever takes him seriously. Does Constance—"

"Wait just a second," said Stephen Triplecorn. "Didn't you tell
me before that Constance was insane and that you'd given *her*
a job out of pity?"

"Yes," said Dodo, determinedly looking obtuse. "What of it?"

"It just makes me curious, that's all," he said. "I mean, what
are you all running here, a publishing firm or a home for way-
ward whackos?"

"Well," said Dodo, "we try to do our part."

"And, if you felt so sorry for Louise, why'd you give her to
someone else at the firm?" asked Stephen Triplecorn. "Why not
keep her as your own assistant?"

Dodo feigned shock.

"But that would be nepotism!" she said.

"Isn't it nepotism anyway," he pointed out, "to hire your pathologically lying cousin, even if it's to work for another editor?"

"Well, if you want to be *picky.* May I please go on?"

"Please do."

"Right away, Louise became jealous of Jane working for me,
felt I played favorites. To cut to the chase, ever since then, she's

made up the most horrendous lies about Jane, trying to ruin Jane's life."

Stephen Triplecorn didn't say anything to that. He merely looked pointedly at the video equipment.

"Oh, that!" Dodo laughed.

"Yes," he said, "that."

"It was a costume party!"

"A costume party?"

"We were celebrating Guy Fawkes Day. Everyone was supposed to get dressed up, for the party, and that's what Jane went as—a pregnant lady! I do think you need to give Jane credit for that one. Why, most people are so unoriginal that there's usually more than one nun in the mix."

"And that's how you celebrate Guy Fawkes Day here—with a costume party?"

Dodo leveled a look of seriousness at him. "But of course. Don't you?"

"No," he said. "What's more, I never heard of anyone who does."

"We are publishing people," Dodo said, going all haughty again. "I suppose we must do things more artistically than you bureaucratic types."

Oddly enough, the situation had become so absurd that Stephen Triplecorn, not knowing what to do, did nothing for the moment. In fact, the poor man looked positively deflated.

"And now that your pathologically lying cousin has tried to ruin the life of another worker here, a costume-happy worker, what do you intend to do about it?"

"I'm going to keep her," said Dodo. "After all, she is family."

Emma could drink from a cup independently, she could stand alone momentarily, she could respond to a one-step command from me with gestures ("give that to me," with hand out, the bloody book sometimes making me feel as though I were a dog trainer) and she'd added to her game-playing repertoire (after months of bringing balls to playgroup, she liked to "play ball" now, rolling the ball back to whoever would roll it to her). In fact, "ball" was her first word other than "mama" or "dada."

And, the nugget I'd been waiting to tell you: she'd begun saying "dada" and "mama" with discrimination. The latter was always me, of course (thank God!), the former was now always Tolkien.

October, the tenth month

Even though I'd told my mother I'd be going back to her church—for Christmas and Easter, at least—I knew that wasn't the place for me or Em. Maybe Emma could have stuck it with those hats, but I certainly couldn't.

At any rate, the hats at Mother's church had thrown me so much, I was determined to try Mary Jr.'s church instead. And, for good measure, I asked David to join us, figuring that two fish out of water were better than one.

So there we were, back at the Shakespeare Baptist Revival Church, and there were...

"More hats," I hissed at David as we walked down the aisle.

It turned out, though, that David, at least, had come prepared. As we sat down in the pew next to Mary Jr. and the rest of the Johnson family, he whipped out a yarmulke, put it on.

"I've never seen you wear one of those before."

He shrugged. "You've never seen me go to the bathroom before either. Doesn't mean I don't do it."

"You do realize," I said, "that this religion isn't that religion?"

He looked at the crucifix on the altar.

"I did realize that," he said. "But so? I always put on a yarmulke whenever I go into a house of worship."

"Even when it's not your house of worship?"

He shrugged again. "I'll close my eyes and pretend."

Emma didn't seem to have any problem with fidgeting in church at all, but I was certainly fidgety.

"I should have worn a hat," I muttered.

"Why do the hats bother you so much?" he asked.

I looked around me at the sea of color and I realized suddenly that the hats here didn't bother me, not in the way they had at my mother's church.

"I don't know," I said. "Maybe I just feel like the odd man out."

And of course I was the odd man out. Correction, *we* were the odd duo out, at any rate, hatless me and my yarmulke-wearing escort. Emma, on the other hand, was right at home.

Everyone who passed her smiled, despite her odd companions. And she didn't at all elicit the kind of reactions you expect from a crowd of adults gathered to do something solemn; you know, the looks that say, "Oh God no—not a baby! It will be so loud! It will do smelly things at inopportune moments!" On the contrary, the congregation seemed very welcoming of her and she was very happy there, particularly since Mary Jr. had baby Martha with her.

I leaned over to David to whisper, "I think I'd just feel better if—"

But then the preacher took his place on the altar and I figured it was time to shut up as the solemnities were about to begin. *Time to hear all about going to Hell.*

But it wasn't like that at all!

There was a choir and singing and hand-clapping. Before I knew it, I was up on my feet with the rest of them, Emma bouncing in my arms, as David and I shouted along to "Praise the Lord!" There were lots of "Hallelujahs" too.

I was enchanted, and I grabbed on to Mary Jr.'s arm to tell her so.

"This is so…this is so…*happy-clappy!!!*"

As soon as the words were out of my mouth, and I saw the look on Mary Jr.'s face, I felt like the biggest jerk who ever lived—or like Constance with one of her "brilliant!" sputterings, at any rate.

Mary Jr.'s voice was quiet as she spoke. "We don't call it that."

"No, of course not," I said. "I'm so sorry. It's just that—"

"We're not a spectacle, you know?" she said. "We're just people." As she turned her attention back to the reverend I poked David in the ribs.

"Do something!" I begged.

"What do you want me to do?"

"I don't know! But *something*. I've offended her."

He leaned across me and gently tapped Mary Jr. on the arm.

"If I promise to make Jane wear a hat," he said, "can we come back here again?"

Mary Jr. just smiled.

It was amazing how much forgiveness one could find in a smile and it occurred to me that, ever since I'd met her, Mary Jr. had been all about forgiveness. She'd been the first to extend a warm hand of welcome to me at her mother's funeral. She'd allowed me to invite my way into her playgroup, and whenever I'd say something stupid or unintentionally insensitive (and, God knows, I did that many times!) she'd find a way to smooth it over, make everything okay again. Maybe, I thought, her instincts were better than mine? Maybe she was better able to, for whatever reason, empathize. Maybe she knew that were the situation somehow reversed, were she to find herself among my odd assortment of family and friends—and, knowing me and having met David, she had good reason to assume we were all bonkers—she knew that the best she could hope for would be a friendly smile from someone who held a map to the lay of the land.

Forgiveness was an amazing grace, I thought, as I happy-clapped along with everybody else.

I blame it all on Stephen Spielberg.

To be more specific, I blame it on *E.T.*

Prior to that film's release, sure, we'd celebrated Halloween, but nothing like it since. Halloween was originally Scottish, the jack-o'-lanterns carved out of turnips, then it went to the United States with the immigrants, who eventually re-exported it back across the water. There are those who claim the whole "pay up or we'll trash your house" theme (i.e., the trick being the flip side of the treat coin) is a folk memory of the pagan holiday of the night before Samhain, November 1, which was the first day of winter in the Celtic calendar.

As I say, though, the celebration here had been rather tepid before *E.T.*

Prior to finding Emma, my own Halloweens had been restricted to eating sweets as a child and, as an adult, going to costume parties where the sole purpose was to get drunk. Or laid. Or both.

But a baby changes everything, they say, and they for once were right. Now, I had Emma, and I wanted us to join in the festivities in a big way. Naturally, she had to have the most perfect costume there ever was, since she was the most perfect child there ever was.

Wrack my brain as I might, I couldn't figure out what that costume should be.

Once I'd exhausted all of my ideas, I started polling people.

Constance: "She could be a tiny little tarot-card reading midwife. I'll bet no one else will think to be that."

Me: "She's. Just. A. Baby."

Stan: "What about having her go as one of those Aussie guys from that video she likes so much? All you need is a yellow, blue, purple or red shirt and black pants, and you're all set."

Me: "Over my dead body."

Mother: "She should be a pumpkin."

Me: "Too traditional."

Sophie: "She could be Tweedledee to Baby Jack's Tweedledum."

Me: "No one will know what she is and we'll only have to keep telling them."

David: "I honestly don't know what all the fuss is about."

The effect of his words was like plate glass crashing to the floor. *"It's her first Halloween!"*

"Yes. And?"

"And I want it to be bloody special!"

"I can understand that. But you do realize, that whatever you put her in, she'll still be the cutest thing out there, don't you? Because she is."

"But it's her first Halloween!"

"So? There will be others."

"But it's her first Halloween!"

Christ! How many times was I going to have to say that?

And so we went, round and round.

Finally, David suggested I call Dodo, who'd been out of the office when I'd quizzed everyone else.

Dodo (dreamily): "A fairy princess."

Me: "That's an awful idea."

Dodo: "Why?"

Me: "Because she's too small. Make a baby a fairy princess and, before long, some witch'll come along and place a spell on her. No, I'm afraid that won't do at all."

I also rejected further suggestions of a ghost (too obvious), a beadle (too British) and Minnie Mouse (too Disney).

Minerva from Publicity took one final stab at it: "Why not dress her up as a miniature editor?"

I just glared at her.

Apparently, I glared too long, because she came up with an alternate idea.

"I know!" she said with glee. "Why not dress her up as an editor impersonating a pregnant woman?"

Oh, these people were just sooooo much help.

Even Kick the Cat let me down.

Kick: "Meow!"

Me: "No, she can't be a cat."

Kick: "Meow!"

Me: "Because you're the cat."

Kick: "Meow!"

Me: "Oh, come on now. There's no reason to go off all offended."

I'd been spending the whole first three weeks of October doing this. Now, with just a little over a week left until Halloween, I had the most beautiful baby in all of London and no costume to put her in. It was like being at the ball with just one shoe. How the hell were you supposed to be the belle, when you kept hobbling along on one stiletto and a sock? It may not sound like exactly the same thing, but I can assure you, it was.

I sat on the floor in the outer office of Churchill & Stewart, dejected, back against the wall.

"That's not very professional, you know." This from Hilda, who hadn't even bothered to look up from her typing, as she clipped along at her trillion-word-a-minute pace.

"Perhaps not," I conceded, "but I'm tired."

"Well, do it somewhere else. Can't you see I'm trying to run a business here?"

"You're trying to—?" I stopped myself. Good God. Another one who thought she owned the place. And I'd thought there was only room for one of those—me—around here.

Still not bothering to look up, she asked, "What *is* your problem, Jane?"

Lacking the required oomph to make the obvious comeback of "you," I told her.

Finally she said, halting the typing, "You're sitting here on the floor of the office, dejected, with your back against the wall, because you can't come up with the perfect costume for your foundling daughter to wear for Halloween?"

When she put it like that, it did have that small-in-the-greater-scheme-of-things ring to it, not quite up there with peace in the Middle East or whether to vote for Blair again next go-round.

I realized there was nothing I could say that would make it seem bigger, plus I was tired, so I merely shrugged.

"God!" she said in disgust, finally looking up. "What is *wrong* with you people?"

"Excuse me? Which people?"

"I'm talking about *you people.* I'm talking about *mothers.*"

"I don't know," I said. "What's wrong with us?"

"I'll tell you what's wrong. You all get flummoxed by the simplest decisions. Baby with a high fever? Train speeding down the tracks? You all know what to do. But the little things? Like soccer v. ballet or what to wear for some stupid holiday? You're bloody useless!"

"I'm sorry, Hilda." I wasn't really sure why I should be sorry, but feeling as though an apology from someone was required, given her level of distress. "I'm sorry the mothers of England have let you down so."

"I suppose that's all right then," she said, un-huffing herself. "Just don't let Emma down."

"What do you suggest I do?"

"It's simple, really." She folded her arms across her chest, the very picture of A Challenge. "What's Emma's favorite thing in the world?"

"Me," I said. There was no contest and I wasn't being immodest.

"Besides you!" She was clearly exasperated. "And anyway, you already rejected Minerva's suggestion that she go out as Mummy."

"I did?"

"Of course. What do you think Minerva meant when she suggested you dress your baby as a pregnancy-faking editor?"

"I dunno," I said. "I thought maybe it was one of those sick ideas, like when rugby players dress up as tampons or something."

"Gross!"

I shrugged. "Hey, I never did that."

"Think," she prompted. "Besides you, what's Emma's favorite thing in the whole world? Not person. *Thing.*"

Well, that one was easy too. "Fuzzy bunny!" I shouted, jumping up.

"Perfect!" shouted Hilda, also excited, having solved my dilemma. "Now, then, who's fuzzy bunny?"

I explained it to her.

"Well, there you've got it," she said. "Dress your baby up as something she really loves—this fuzzy thing—and you'll be happy because in later years, when you look at the snaps, you'll remember why she was dressed like that. And she'll be so much happier herself, dressing up as one of her personal gods, than she ever would have been dressed up in some stupid costume that makes no sense to her."

"Thanks, Hilda," I said, and I meant it.

"No problem." She shrugged it off. "Anyway, I blame *E.T.*"

"You too?" I was shocked at having found common ground.

"Yeah, once you let the Americans in, things get altogether too cute or too violent by half."

"Indeed," I said, just to be agreeable. "Be that as it may, I'm off to find a fabric shop."

"A fabric shop? Whatever for?"

"You don't think I'm going to buy Emma's costume for her very first Halloween ever, do you?"

"You're good with a needle, are you?"

"Are you kidding? I've never sewn a thing in my life." Well, there was that one time I'd sewn extra cloth onto my cloth baby so my fake-pregnancy tummy would grow bigger, but there was no point in bringing *that* whole thing up again. "How hard can it be?"

Making a costume that would look like fuzzy bunny proved harder than one would imagine, and I was in my office, trying to get the sleeve right as opposed to editing anything, when Hilda buzzed me to say that Simon Smock was there for a surprise visit and that he'd brought with him the Author Formerly Known As Gayla Gladstone.

"Oh, God!" I muttered, shoving costume, needle and thread into the first drawer I could get open. You'd think they could have given me some warning.

"She's wearing a whole forest full of foxes," Hilda whispered.

"I'll try to make her stop," I whispered back.

I greeted them at the door. "Please sit down." I indicated the chairs. Then I looked at my new author in all her gold lamé glory and more pointedly at her controversial coat. "Perhaps you'd care to…"

"This?" she asked belligerently. Okay, I admit to being reluctant to use her name. Let's try that again. "This?" Candy Likme asked belligerently.

"Er, yes," I said, unsure why I was feeling sheepish.

She removed it, then tossed it over the back of her chair as Simon leaned his cane against my desk.

"You don't like it, do you?" she accused.

"It's, um, very pretty in its own way," I said. "If only it weren't made up of—"

"What?" she demanded. "You don't think it's real, do you?"

"I've always assumed that with the way you're always defending your right to wear it in the press...that, yes, it is."

"Well, it's not."

"No? Then why ever do you go through all the trouble of arguing about it, of letting everybody get angry with you about it?"

"Because I get tired of the hypocrisy. If it's wrong, make it illegal. It's like Americans with all of their anti-smoking nonsense. Say it's okay or declare it illegal, but don't demonize people for doing something that's not breaking any laws."

"So you think people should shut up about furs?"

"God no!" She looked at me as though she were having second thoughts about whether or not I was smart enough to edit her. "I think they should make it illegal, and fast, because it's damned hot in this thing!" She gave her fake fur an angry flick.

"And you think smoking should be illegal too, then?"

"God no," she said again, rooting around in her gold bag and coming up with a smoke. "Can I light this in here?"

"Afraid not," I said. "We're owned by an American."

As Candy Likme dejectedly put her cigarette back in her purse, Simon withdrew something from his satchel.

"We came by today," he said, "because Candy has finished her drawings for the cover art and she was eager to share them with you."

He laid them out before me on my desk.

There were four of them and, unlike my previous suspicions, there wasn't a stick figure in sight. Rather, each was a variation on a Georgia O'Keefe theme. Maybe if the book hadn't been called *Slit,* maybe if its author wasn't Candy Likme, it would have all been somehow okay. As it were...

"Don't you think these are all, er, rather labial?" I asked.

"What?" said Candy, her eyes feigning an innocence that clearly wasn't there. "Are you scared of a little controversy?"

It's amazing the things you never plan on, the big-ticket items that are so big, you never take them into account as they hide there in plain sight, waiting to blow your world apart. You think you have all the plot threads of your life under control. And then...

The moment I'd been waiting for forever was finally here. My book came out.

People who want to be writers live their whole lives waiting for a single moment. For each one, it's different. Some are waiting for that first call from an editor, the calls that we in publishing love to make the most, those life-changing moments when you get to hand someone their dream by saying: "I want to buy your book." Some are waiting for that first paycheck, sometimes the amount doesn't even matter, just so that they have financial validation of themselves as A Writer. And then there are those of us who, for all the excitement of having our books bought by publishers or receiving money, are waiting for what we think will be the grandest moment of all: seeing our books, with our own names on the spine, on the shelves of our local bookstore.

For some of us, that is the dream. We know, if we are smart at all, that the dream is ephemeral and human memory all too often short. We know that as soon as the moment passes, even while it is yet passing, we'll move past that dream to a new level of wanting: we'll want the book to be bought, to be read, to be reviewed, to be reviewed well, to sell, to sell well, to sell phenomenally, to sell internationally, to outpace Harry Potter XXII, to outpace England, the United Kingdom, Europe, planet Earth, the universe.

And then we want the next contracted book to do even better and earn more money.

That's the foolish stuff we writers are made of. And, for at least some of us, there's no point at all in dreaming the dream, if we're not going to dream it larger than our imaginations, larger than life.

And, if we are smart enough to be smarter than the smart part of us that knows we'll only want more, better, bigger tomorrow, we do take that first moment in a bookstore with our own book in our hands and we freeze that virgin moment of pure joy in our memories, an investment against future disappointment.

After a lifetime of wanting to be a writer, after months writing the book, months revising the book and months of just plain waiting…

"My book is out! This is my book!"

Then the moment was past, part of my history.

But what do you know? There were new moments!

It turned out that, my book, *The Cloth Baby,* had struck some sort of cultural nerve.

Back when I'd first contracted with Alice Simms to write the book, she'd been excited about it mostly because she thought the idea so original.

"Either fact or fiction," she'd told me at one point, "it's a safe bet that your book will be the only fake-pregnancy book on the market." And she was right about that, as far as it went, but what she hadn't planned on, what neither of us had ever guessed, was that two things would happen.

One, women would actually identify with acerbic-as-acid me. Oh, not the acerbic part. But apparently people were more familiar than they liked to let on with the theme of someone wanting a thing more for the shape of it than for the actual thing itself.

Two, it seemed that every other person who got in touch with me, had a similar, crazy story.

Them: "My cousin did that."

Me: "Did what?"

Them: "Faked a pregnancy."

Me: "For how long?"

Them: "Why, for the entire nine months, of course."

Who knew there were so many of us out there?

I'll tell you one thing. I didn't want people to start mistaking my book for some sort of prescription for behavior.

It got so bad, so quickly, I called Alice Simms.

"Do you think we could put some sort of warning sticker on the jacket?" I asked.

"What sort of warning?" she asked.

"I dunno," I said. "Maybe something along the lines of 'Hey, kids, don't try this at home'?"

"You worry too much, Jane," she replied with a laugh. "People might do this sort of thing on their own, but nobody is going to do it because you did it."

"Why do you say that?" I asked.

Then she explained, something along the lines of me being "not role-model material" and rang off before I could get offended.

But who cared really?

My book was out, mybookwasout, *mybookwasout!!!*

And people were buying it. Not only were they buying it, but they were talking about it.

And not only were they talking about it, but the talk shows wanted me to come on and talk about it some more.

I was an overnight success.

And then the bottom dropped out.

Once upon a time, Alice Simms had told me that I'd be forgiven all my previous lies if my book were successful enough. She'd pointed out that people have a romantic notion about writers and writing and they'd be willing to let a lot go, provided I was published and published well.

And how right she'd turned out to be, in so many ways.

My mother—Ladies and Gentlemen, *my mother*—was even proud of me. So what if my book revealed me to be something of a nutcase? I was a nutcase who was a writer and who had received payment for her work. What mother wouldn't be proud?

Even Martin Amis had loved *The Cloth Baby,* calling it a "bizarrely pro-creative tour de farce" in the *Guardian.*

As for the people at work, they couldn't be happier, except for Louise, of course.

We were crammed into Dodo's office—Minerva, Stan, Constance, Hilda and me—making it quite a tight cram. Even Louise was there, because we were drinking champagne, and even Louise won't pass up free champers, whatever the reason for drinking it.

"To Jane," said Dodo, glass held aloft. "May *The Cloth Baby* sit on the bestseller lists until her next book comes out!"

And it was on the bestseller lists! Every now and then, a book comes along that goes miles beyond expectation. For whatever lucky-star reason, *The Cloth Baby* was this year's surprise winner, an instant bestseller. We'd just gotten the news, hence the drinking of the champagne.

Everyone except Louise held their glass in the air.

"To Jane!"

I had my glass to my lips, was ready to take the first sip from my celebratory drink, when there came a hard knock on Dodo's opened door, the kind of knock that demanded attention. No "excuse me, so sorry to interrupt you" about it. It was a knock from hell.

It was Stephen Triplecorn, of course, with an angry look on his face, of course, carrying a copy of *The Cloth Baby* clenched tight in his hand, of course.

I was surprised; shocked senseless, I would have said, if I could only speak. But just one single heartbeat later, I saw how inevitable this all had been. In my efforts to plug up all the leaky holes, I'd forgotten about the book. Oh, not about the publication; I'd remembered my book was coming out and the date. But somehow, the writing thread of my life and the Emma thread ran parallel. I'd never stopped to think that one day they would intersect.

And if I had stopped to think? Would I have done things differently?

Are you kidding me? I would have called up Alice Simms. I would have told her I wanted out of the contract. When she told me, as she undoubtedly would, that they'd already paid me the money, I'd offer to return it, all of it, if I had to work three jobs for the rest of my life to pay back the part I'd already spent. When she said that wasn't good enough, I'd tell her I was getting a lawyer. She'd laugh and tell me she had at her disposal the law offices of one of the finest firms in London, which she did. But I'd tell her I didn't care about that, and I didn't. I'd tell her she could financially and professionally ruin me, destroy me, it didn't matter what she did to *me,* because the train was now rolling down the tracks, I knew exactly where that train was heading, knew exactly what it was going to hit, and I'd do anything, lose my dream of being a published writer, anything, lie down on the tracks, anything, to avoid—

"You *lied* to me!" Stephen Triplecorn j'accused, except that he wasn't pointing at me. He was pointing at Dodo.

"I—" was all he let her get out.

"You told me Louise was lying! You said Louise was your crazy cousin!"

"You said *what?*" Louise whipped her head around to stare at Dodo.

"You said the story about Jane's fake pregnancy was a lie!"

Nobody said anything.

"What did you think?" Stephen Triplecorn fired away, waving my book in the air. "Did you think I was the only person in England who can't read?"

"Well, heh," said Stan from Accounting, "you do work for Social Services."

There was a nasty gleam in Stephen Triplecorn's eyes. "That's exactly right," he said, nodding in angry rhythm to his words. "I *do* work for Social Services. And, as such, it is my duty to tell you, *Jane Taylor,* that we will be removing…"

Here came the train.

"…the baby…"

No longer Emma, she was the baby now.

"…from your care."

NO! my mind screamed and in the very same instant, "No!" yelled Dodo.

"What do you mean, *no?*" demanded Stephen Triplecorn.

"I mean *no,*" said Dodo. "*No,* you *can't* take Emma away from Jane."

"Of course I can," he said. "She's a pathological liar. She fabricated an entire pregnancy."

Her expression was one of wonder. "How can you take Emma from Jane, when you're in love with her?"

"In love with *who?*" asked Stephen Triplecorn.

"In love with *Jane,*" said Dodo.

"In love with *Jane? *Are you bleeding mad, woman? No one in their right mind could be in love with Jane. She's nuts!"

"But you like her," Dodo protested. "That's why you've dragged this case out so long, so you'd have an excuse to keep on coming to see her."

"This case has gone on so long," he said, "because we're bloody underfunded. And I didn't keep coming by because I was in love with Jane, you stupid cow." There was the Triplecorn charm. "I kept coming by because I was in love with *you.*"

Now we were all speechless, and I have to say, despite what

I knew had to be coming next, I felt sorry for him. He may have been showing his anger at Dodo, but it was the pain of her betrayal of him that I was seeing.

"But none of that matters now," he said, just prior to taking that j'accusing arm and sweeping any powers I had ever had of empathy, sweeping my life away, "because you lied to me," he said pointing at Dodo. "And you lied to me—" he pointed at me "—and by the time you get home—" he pointed at me a second time "—that baby will be gone."

I raced home so quickly I could have sworn I had beaten the wind.

But I hadn't, of course.

As I fumbled with the lock on the door, let myself in, I realized it was too quiet. It was too goddamned quiet.

There was no sound of happy gurgling, or even I-want-my-milk-now crying. There was just Tolkien, who had been watching Emma, standing there in the middle of the room, silent tears running down his face.

Over on the sofa, was the costume I'd made for Emma. We had been planning on taking her out in it that night.

It wasn't the greatest costume in the world—one arm was a little longer than the other, never having been able to get it right after that day Simon and Candy had visited me at the office—but I'd gotten the ears in the right spot, the cottontail as well.

I picked up the costume, held it to my face. I could still smell Emma on it—she'd laughed when I tried it on her, laughed when I'd shown her what she looked like in the mirror. It smelled like baby, like Emma-baby, like milk and soap.

I held it to my cheek and I cried.

And I cried.

And I cried.

Over the course of her tenth month, Emma had mastered two new accomplishments. One, she could indicate her wants in ways other than crying. Oh, I don't mean she was saying, "Mummy, may I have another biscuit, please?" But she had primitive-sounding utterances for particular desired objects, however no-reasoning-behind-them they might seem to an outsider. "Ca" was for "cookie," because I kept them in the cupboard, "ball" was now for the fuzzy bunny, because she liked to pretend she was playing ball with it all the time.

Her other accomplishment?

She was walking.

Ever hear that one about "be careful what you ask for"?

Mothers the world over buy books like *What to Expect* so we know what milestones to anticipate and work towards. So what happens?

You wind up encouraging a tiny creature, whom you could formerly expect to stay in a reasonably small geographical place, to start walking.

As a result, Emma was into everything now. There was just no stopping her. No stopping her eagerness to explore the world. Walking also meant that one day, and not just to chase after the ball, Emma would be walking away from me.

I'd dreaded that day, thought it was far in our future still.

But it had already happened.

Emma was gone.

November, the eleventh month

Halloween was officially behind us and we were now two hours into All Saints' Day.

I picked up the phone, dialed David's number.

"Yes?" he answered.

"It's Jane."

"Where are you?"

"Downstairs."

"Can you tell me why you're calling me at 2:00 a.m. from downstairs?"

"Because I miss you."

I couldn't bring myself to tell him yet that we'd lost her, we'd lost Em. I could tell him the next morning. There would be time enough then, it would be better when there was some light once again in the sky.

"That's strange," he said. "I am, after all, right up here."

"And I'm feeling kind of strange."

"Hardly surprising, given your life."

"Tell me something, David. Why does my life have to be so strange?"

He made a sound I'd been hearing him make often, ever since

he'd begun spending more time with Christopher's circle of friends: "Heh." It sounded incongruous on him. "Heh. Good question. A lot of it is a result of the choices you make. As I believe I have remarked once or twice before, you have a larger-than-life quality about you. I'm afraid an ordinary life just isn't in your cards."

"I sometimes wish that were different. Or, at least, if I have to live an extraordinary life, that it was a different extraordinary life."

"Yes, I believe you. Still, life can be different. If you were to live a different extraordinary life, what would it be?"

"I dunno." I sighed. "Tax inspector. Ambassador to Bora Bora. *Queen.*"

He laughed softly. "No point in ever aiming low, right, Jane? Good to see you haven't lost your sense of humor."

"Who said I was joking?"

"There's things one can change, you know."

"But change is so hard for me," I said.

"You're kidding, right? Please tell me you're kidding, Jane."

"Excuse me?"

"You are the embodiment of change. I've never known anyone before who was so much of a whirlwind of evolution."

"A whirlwind of *what?*"

"I'm just trying to say that whatever you want to change, whatever you want to do or be, you can. That's not true of everyone, you know. But it is most definitely true of you."

It's tough when you've been a funny person all your life— both funny ha-ha and funny strange—when tragedy strikes. Where does the funny part of you go?

Losing Emma was a grief unlike any I had ever known. It was a bottomless pit.

I'd tried calling Stephen Triplecorn—called him daily, several times a day, as a matter of fact—to ask him where he'd taken her. But he wouldn't tell me.

I suppose I could have gotten an attorney, tried to challenge Emma's removal, but given my track record, even I wouldn't represent me.

I even tried trailing Stephen Triplecorn one day, to see if I could figure out where he'd placed her—if only I could see that she was all right!—but he caught me at it and told me I had to stop.

"Emma's care is no longer any concern of yours," he said. He said it over and over again. "Emma's care…"

Emma's care. Without Emma, I suddenly had time on my hands. Where for the past ten months my life had revolved around fulfilling the needs of another, there was now just an aching emptiness. There was no more worrying if she was getting enough to eat, there was no more splashing in the bath, there was no more lying on our backs on my big bed with me holding a book high over us, watching her face scrunch up in delight as she looked at pictures of Horton hearing the Who. If I had never known it, I wouldn't have missed it. But I had and I did. In a way, I realized, my life had revolved around a fiction—the notion that I would somehow be able to keep this baby I had found—and now that fiction had been smashed, taken away, the ending I'd longed for had been rewritten even before I had the chance to read it.

In my grief, my incredible raging grief, I threw myself into Tolkien, took everything he had to give, and he gave everything.

Then, I threw myself into the search for Sarah Johnson. Somehow, I knew, that if there was any salvation left for me in this world, it lay there; it lay in bringing Mary Jr.'s niece back home to her.

November 11, Armistice Day, was coming up on us.

Some say that World War I, the war Armistice Day commemorates, was the shaping trauma of the British people in living memory. Before 1914, the British hadn't fought a war in Europe since the Crimean War in the 1850s—in fact, the phrase "The Thin Red Line" originated in that war—and before that Waterloo. And even those wars were fought entirely by long-service career military volunteers.

World War I, on the other hand, sparked a huge patriotic outburst and thousands of civilians joined up, many in the so-called "Pal's Battalions." These were battalions that promised if you joined together, you'd serve together. Every walk of life formed Pal's Battalions. The London Stock Exchange clerks had one.

I liked to think that Mary Jr. and I and her friends—and even Sophie and her set—had formed a Pal's Battalion: women who banded together in the common pursuit of a different kind of battle, the battle against so many odds to see that you raised your children healthy and well.

Now Mary Jr. and I were still in the Pal's Battalion, only now it was one of loss. Her family had, long ago, lost Sarah. And I had now lost Em.

Since losing Em, I'd heard from everyone—my mother, Soph, the people at work, even Tolkien's parents called—all of who were sorry for my "loss."

But after that, the conversations quickly devolved into silence. After all, what could people say? "I'm sorry that, previously, you lived your life in such a screwy fashion that you were bound to one day lose the one thing you could not bear to lose?"

People just don't say things like that; if, for no other reason, because they're simply not that long-winded. I hadn't been back to work since the day I'd dropped my unsipped-from champagne glass, the glass shattering against the floor as I'd run out, racing to beat the unbeatable wind. If something desperately needed doing for Churchill & Stewart, if Simon Smock needed an answer to one of the many nervous-author questions Candy was forever asking or if one of my other authors needed anything, I could do those things from the relative safety of my home, that safeness being an illusion, since every square centimeter was a reminding cut of the loss of Emma.

I also hadn't accepted the calls from newspapers, magazines, TV either, all calling to interview me about *The Cloth Baby.* What did any of that matter now?

In fact, the only time I'd left the house had been to go with Tolkien to talk to Sarah's friends, to look at places she'd been seen early on after going missing, to chase a child—a teen—that might still be brought back.

But now Armistice Day was upon us, the following Sunday being Remembrance Day. In previous years, I'd never bothered much—I guess, not at all—with Remembrance Day. After all, what had it to do with me? It mourned people I'd never known in a world I'd never known. Each year, special services were held, but I'd never taken part. Each year, there was a big ceremony in London with the royal family participating, with two minutes of silence at 11:00 a.m., which was widely, but not completely, observed.

Whatever I'd been doing in previous years, I hadn't been observing any silence.

But this year was different.

In the week previous, I'd seen the paper poppies for sale everywhere, as always, only this year I bought one of my own, so that when the day came, I had my own red poppy to wear with nearly everyone else.

I went to Mary Jr.'s church, the Shakespeare Baptist Revival Church, and stood there between her and David, all of us with our red poppies, listening to the service to commemorate the loss of those no longer with us.

I held tight to the hand of my Battalion Pal, feeling the loss of her niece all over again. Sarah had been gone so long, no one in the family believed she would ever be coming home again, at least not alive.

And as I stood there, holding my Battalion Pal's hand, I realized that, of we two, I was surely the luckier. For while she believed that she would never see her niece again, and while I believed I would never see my daughter again, our losses were different. Whatever else I might think of Stephen Triplecorn, however much I might hate him for taking Emma from me, I knew that, wherever he had taken her, it would be a good home and that he would see to it that she was safe and well cared for.

When Mary Jr. started to cry, I put my arm around her, realizing that as great as my loss was personally, it would be far worse to believe that Emma no longer existed in this world.

I've never found what I think you're supposed to find in churches, never found anyone else's definition of religion, certainly. But I'd found other things there that day, as David and I "Hallelujah"-ed once again and "Praise the Lord"-ed and clapped with everyone else. I'd found hope in the form of Mary Jr., found hope in the belief in Emma, still loose out there somewhere in the world.

* * *

The night I'd broken into my mother's house to see if I could discover any evidence of her lover, I'd seen the changes she'd made to the living room, kitchen and bedroom. But, not wanting to get caught, I hadn't taken the time to check out any of the other rooms: like Sophie's, to see if it was still a pink testimony to all of Sophie's schooldays glory; or mine, to see if my poster of the mouse wizard with a joint wrapped in Union Jack rolling paper still hung on the wall. Nor had I seen the changes in the dining room.

But I was seeing them now, since Mother and Vic had invited me and Sophie over for dinner. Replacing the dull oak family dinner table was a Romanesque-looking long dark wooden table with eight high-backed chairs covered in crushed crimson velvet. On the wall hung a beautiful tapestry depicting a pastoral scene from another era. To lighten the heaviness of the rest of the decor, there were loads of live plants, which somehow made things balanced.

I'd arrived first (for a change). My mother and Vic were busy in the kitchen, so I let Sophie in.

"Why isn't Baby Jack with you?" I asked in a slightly caustic tone. "Still afraid I'll be a bad influence?"

She looked earnestly surprised, stopping in the midst of taking off her coat. "I just thought it might be painful for you to see a baby who is so close to, well, Emma's age."

This is what my life had come down to: being pitied by my sister. Of all the things I'd aspired to have my family and others feel for me over the years, pity had never been one of them. Empathy? Always. Sympathy? Sometimes. But pity? Never.

"That's okay, Soph," I murmured, making a vague pat at her arm that just missed. "Mum and Vic are in the kitchen."

As we sat down at the table to eat, it quickly became apparent that my mother's cooking habits had altered as well. The diet she used to prepare for us consisted mostly of overcooked vegetables and boiled beef, but now the paella she served was positively refreshing.

It also became quickly apparent that someone, either Sophie or my mother, had taken the time to fill Vic in about some of the details of my past. She knew about the fake pregnancy. She knew about finding Emma and losing her.

Vic spoke to me with a certain carefulness, but with strength as well. "Have you ever stopped to think," she said, "that you've played a role in the things that have happened to you?"

"Isn't that a bit harsh?" Sophie surprised me, defending my honor.

"I don't mean it harshly," Vic said. "But you have to admit, Jane makes things harder on herself than they need to be."

"Do you mind my asking what you mean by that?" I asked.

My mother spoke for Vic, "You know, Jane, you've always had a problem with doing things in a straightforward manner."

"True," Sophie agreed.

"Can you give me an example?" I felt somewhat attacked on all sides.

"Take for instance your breaking in here and going through your mother's drawers to find out about *me*," Vic said, spearing a shrimp.

"How did you—"

"You put the date book back in the wrong drawer," my mother said, with a surprising degree of gentleness. "Since nothing was missing and the door was locked that night when I got home, I knew it had to be someone with a key, which leaves just you and Sophie..." Her voice trailed off, the implication being that it could never be Sophie.

And of course it could never be Sophie. It could only ever be me, doing something like that. Still...

I put my fork down carefully. "Let me get this straight... Are you saying it's my own fault I lost Em?"

Sophie covered my hand with hers. "No, Jane. It's just that—"

"Because," I continued, "it's not like if I'd told the truth from the start, about my past, they'd ever have let me kept her, not for a single night."

Nobody could argue with the accuracy of that statement. Nor did they try. However, I felt Vic studying me. What was she seeing? Did she see my loss? Did she see the depth of my pain?

She shook her head slowly. "No, of course you're right," she said. "They'd never have let you keep her at all. It's just that…"

"Just what?" I demanded.

"I don't know, maybe things would have turned out the same no matter what you'd done. Or maybe, if you'd been more straightforward at times, oh, I don't know, you might feel differently about the outcome."

Between the main course and sweet, I helped Vic clear the former and prepare for the latter—something intensely chocolaty, since my mother does know me (a bit)—while Mum and Soph leafed through photo albums in the living room. Sophie'd mentioned she was trying to put a special album together for Baby Jack, so he'd know who all of his relatives were, even the dead ones, and Mum was helping her.

Since I'd grown up in this house, it was odd to see Vic loading the dishwasher while I assisted her by hand-drying the special things, as though she took precedence there and now I was a guest.

"It must be hard on you," Vic said carefully, rinsing off a plate, "going through everything you're going through right now. You might be better off if you talked about it more."

"Who would I talk to?" I asked. "Besides," I added, "I have Tolkien." Although he and I didn't talk about Em anymore, not really; the pain was too great, she lived in every corner of the flat we shared, in every cupboard and cabinet where there were still her boxes of biscuits, her special videos, but we couldn't talk about her. "I have David, and Christopher too, come to that." But we didn't talk about her either. How could I turn to them for comfort when I could see how much they were hurting too?

"You could try talking to your mother," Vic suggested.

"You're kidding." I snorted. I've never been much of a snorter, but, honestly, her suggestion did invite snorting.

"No," she said. "I'm quite serious. Why wouldn't you talk to her about things that are troubling you?"

"He-*llo*," I said, surprising even my thirty-year-old self with my ability to impersonate a snotty teenager. "Have you even been paying any attention at all to the family dynamics here?"

"What do you mean?"

I led her over to the doorway of the kitchen, from which we could see on a diagonal through the dining room to Mum and Sophie sitting on the sofa in the living room beyond.

Vic wiped her hands off on her apron. "What am I supposed to be seeing?"

"Them," I said.

She looked at me like I was nuts. "Now, that's cryptic."

"Look how they sit there, with their heads together. It's always been like that, ever since Dad died. There's them together and then there's me."

Vic studied my face for a long moment, considering. "You really don't get it," she finally said.

"Get what?"

"You look." She gently turned my chin so I was looking again at Mum and Soph together.

"The reason your mother focuses on Sophie so much is because Sophie *asks* for it, Sophie *needs* to be taken care of. But you? You never let people get close enough to help you, you never let your mother in."

"What are you saying?"

"I'm saying that you've built up such armor around yourself that you don't even see it when people love you, when they want to help you. Some day, Jane, you really should think about letting your mother in."

I am a writer.

I am a writer who wrote a funny book. I know this to be true, because the reviews, the reviews I no longer look at, all said it was so.

Actors are always saying that comedy is harder to do than drama. You hear it said less in the world of books, but it's true nonetheless.

In comic writing, if you have a book that's supposed to be funny, but the laughs just aren't there or they're of the tight-smile tepid-laugh variety, then your literary house of cards comes tumbling down around your ears.

But drama? It's much easier to write drama; it's more forgiving. All you need do is create a moving moment, a heart-breakingly sad moment, and you have your story.

The evidence of that was right in the room, with me all the time. All I needed do was pick up Emma's misshapen bunny costume one more time, hold it to my face one more time, inhale the slowly-slipping-away scent of her one more time, that scent that grew a little fainter with each passing day:

The evidence of it was all right there.

It was Tolkien's voice on the phone.

"I've found her," he said. "I've found Sarah Johnson."

I hurried to Mary Jr.'s home, knowing now that it was impossible to ever beat the wind, but hurrying just the same.

When I got there, breathless, it was Tolkien who answered the door, Mary Jr.'s baby Martha in his arms.

It was hard to see him like that, with a baby in his arms once again, the baby not being Emma.

"They're in the bath," Tolkien explained of Mary Jr. and Sarah. "When I found her, Sarah was...*dirty,* to say the least."

"Where did you find her?"

"Would you believe sleeping on a bench in London? She's been under our noses the whole time."

"But why? Why did she run away? Where has she been? What has she been doing?"

"She wouldn't tell me," he said. "She was just there, on a bench, sleeping with a newspaper for a blanket. I recognized her face from the snap, despite the dirt. I simply waited for her to wake up."

"And when she did?"

"I didn't want to scare her, but I did tell her I knew who she was, that her family had been looking for her, that they were worried sick."

"And?"

"And then I asked her if she'd like to go home. And then she just got up and came with me. She didn't struggle in the slightest. It was as though she'd merely been waiting all these months for someone to come along and ask."

For the first time in a long time, I felt an incredible joy spreading inside of me. Whatever else was wrong with the world—and there was a lot—this one thing was at last right.

Sarah Johnson had come home.

And then there she was, fresh from the shower, a robe of Mary Jr.'s swimming around her.

In Sarah Johnson's school picture, despite the sadness of her face, there had been a mystique, something almost regal about her. In the flesh, that impression still came across, in the high cheekbones, in the way she carried her head high.

But when she opened her mouth to speak, she was all teenager, her speech liberally peppered with today's jargon of youth.

"Yo, man," she said to me, toweling her hair. "Who you be?"

"I be Jane Taylor," I said. "I be a friend of your aunt."

"No need to mock me," said Sarah. "Just be yourself."

Would you believe it when I say that that's one thing I'm rarely advised to do?

"She's the one who got Tolkien to look for you," smiled Mary Jr.

"Wicked." Sarah smiled.

But when we tried to get her to tell us where she had been all this time, why she'd left in the first place, she was unwilling to talk about it.

"What did my mates tell you?" she asked, eyes narrowed.

"They just told us about an older boyfriend that no one in your family had heard about before," Tolkien said. "That's all. I figured you must have taken off with him, since he disappeared right around the time you did."

"Right. Him," Sarah said. "It looks like you come around the right time, innit? Another winter on the streets might've killed me. Yo, Auntie Mary—" she turned from Tolkien "—got anything to eat 'round here?"

And that was all she'd say on the subject, for the time being. She just wanted to eat—which she did a lot—and then she just wanted to sleep in a bed.

Mary Jr., who'd called Sarah's parents to let them know she was alive, was the kind of aunt who was smart enough to just let Sarah call the shots for at least one night, content to leave her questions unanswered just a little longer, content because one she'd counted gone for good was finally back home.

"Isn't it amazing," Tolkien said to Mary Jr., "that this all came out of Jane being behind you in line one day at the supermarket?"

Mary Jr. was clearly puzzled. "The supermarket?"

"Yes, where you two met for the first time."

"But we didn't meet at the supermarket. We met for the first time at Mum's funeral."

"But I thought…"

They both looked at me for explanation.

"Jane?" Tolkien asked.

So I explained. With a feeling of dread in the pit of my stomach, I explained how I'd gone to Mary Sr.'s funeral, hoping somehow to come up with some ideas of how I could better give Emma the cultural background she had the genetic right to.

I could actually see Tolkien harden against me.

"Let me get this straight," he said. "You exploited a moment of grief for something you needed?"

I didn't know what to say to that. What could I say in my defense? I said nothing.

Then Mary Jr. spoke, slowly at first, as though recovering from the shock. "I could see where you might see it that way, but I don't see it that way at all."

"No?" Tolkien asked, jaw set firm.

"No. Maybe, in the beginning, Jane came for the wrong reason. Although I wouldn't even say it was the wrong reason completely. She did, after all, want to help Emma."

"But she lied to you!" said Tolkien. "She lied to you and to your whole family, your friends."

"But who did she hurt?" Mary Jr. asked.

"You're kidding, right?" Tolkien replied. "She hurt all of you. She hurt you by lying."

"But she was trying to do something good for Emma." Mary Jr. raised a brow. "Besides, you lie to people sometimes in the course of your duty, for the greater good, don't you?"

"But that's different!"

"Is it?" Mary Jr. asked. "Besides, look what she did afterwards. She changed our lives."

"How so?"

"Well, just look at this place."

Tolkien did. He looked at the toys, the books, the clothes on baby Martha—things I had brought.

"Those are just material things," he said.

"She got the new playground built, didn't she?"

"That's still just money," he said. "She took from you."

"What did she take from us?"

"Information. What she came for in the first place."

It was true. I had originally come there for information, information that would help Emma and I make our way in the multicultural world.

But what had I found? I'd found that people I assumed to be different than people like me, different than people I couldn't help but think of as "us," were no different than us at all. They were just like us—loved like us, fought like us, worried about their children like us. So maybe the music was different, the food was different, some of the words were different. But the love and humanity and desire for something more were just the same. We all wanted the exact same thing: a better life for our kids.

"Hah!" Mary Jr. laughed, but there was no malice in it. "She took information from us? Are you kidding? The first day she came, she could have learned everything she wanted to know— what we talk like, how we are with our kids, what we eat, what we listen to. She could have got all that the first day. Then she could have left and never returned. So, why did she keep coming back?"

Tolkien was at a loss. "But she *took* from you," he repeated.

"And she *gave back*," said Mary Jr. evenly. "Sure, she lied in the first place, but she didn't mean any harm by it. She meant to do good. And when she could have stopped coming, because she'd already got everything from us that she needed, she didn't stop. She kept coming, every week. Besides me, she was the only one who never missed. She came, and she didn't just bring things. She listened to us. She listened to Charmaine's concerns and Chantelle's and Jade's, she listened to Marisa's obsessions, and she listened to my worries, too. And she tried to help."

I felt so humbled by her. "I didn't do anything, Mary," I said. "It was you who all listened to me, helping me with my worries about being a new mother and all, helping me with everything— helping me get through these last weeks without Emma."

"We all helped each other," Mary Jr. said.

Finally, Mary Jr. looked Tolkien dead in the eyes, hands on hips. "And she got *you* to bring Sarah home to us. Oh, yeah. I'd say that for whatever Jane took, she gave back plenty."

But Tolkien didn't see it that way. I could see that, looking at him. It was just that one lie too many and he could no longer forgive.

I watched him go—how many times in my life would I have to watch that man, the only man in the world I wanted, walk away from me?—and I knew that it was useless to follow him.

I knew where he was going, what he was going to do.

I knew that by the time I got home, his things would be gone.

Rather than going home, I stayed on Mary Jr.'s couch. She didn't seem to mind, seemed to understand that whatever my previous definition of "my home," that geography no longer existed.

So I was there the next morning when Sarah rose, was there to hear her as she began the tale, which would spin out over several tellings.

"Denny said it would be great, didn't he," Sarah said.

"Who's Denny?" Mary Jr. asked gently.

"He is," Sarah said, "he *was* my main man."

"She means he was her boyfriend," Mary Jr. translated for me.

"Ah," I said. Of course, even color-challenged me knew that, but this was not time to be making that point with Mary.

"He had a couple of hundred pounds saved, see, from working the odd job…"

"What kind of work did he do?" asked Mary Jr.

But Sarah didn't answer that. "He said we were both old enough to be living on our own. Well, he was anyway. He was eighteen when we left. He knew Dad and the rest of the family would never take to him."

"Why did he think that?" Mary Jr. was nervously wringing her hands.

"Dunno," shrugged Sarah. "Because he was a singer. Because of the drugs."

I could see Mary Jr. fighting with herself, wanting to ask the tough questions, wanting simply to be grateful that Sarah was back.

"Do you know," Sarah asked, "that a couple hundred pounds don't last very long?"

Mary Jr. smiled. "Yeah," she said, looking around. "I do know that."

"We thought he'd get a good job, you know, playing in a club or something. But I guess he wasn't as good as we thought, because no one would hire him. And then the money ran out, and then we lived on the streets..."

I could see the war in Mary Jr., wanting to ask, because she should know; not wanting to ask more questions, because she really didn't.

It didn't matter, though, because Sarah had said all she was going to for the time being.

"If it's all the same to you," said Sarah, "I don't want to talk about it no more."

I could see she was holding something back, something big, something that caused her both pain and shame, but it wasn't my place to say.

"What I'd really like," Sarah said, "is to see the rest of the family. I'll bet the little ones have gotten bigger."

Seeing how easily and unconditionally Mary Jr. welcomed Sarah back, it was easy for me to understand why Sarah would turn first to her aunt in times of trouble rather than to her parents. Mary Jr., being so much closer to Sarah in age, must have seemed more like Sarah's own wise big sister, rather than her father's youngest sibling.

Emma, wherever she was, could now say three words other than "mama" or "dada"—I was sure of it. In addition to "ball," she could say "cat" and—yes!—she could say "book." I was sure of that, too.

In just one more month, my baby would be a year old.

December, the twelfth month

I imagined what my life would be like if Emma were still with me.

According to *What to Expect the First Year,* it was time to plan Emma's first birthday party, a prospect that thrilled and saddened me at the same time. Life, the whole "things are going forward as the past is receding" stuff, was getting to me.

As I looked at the beginning of the last chapter heading of *What to Expect the First Year,* I saw that Emma—the Emma that kept growing in my mind, if not right in front of me any longer—could do everything they said she should be able to do, would probably be able to do, might possibly be able to do and might even be able to do. My dream Emma could even do the very last thing on the list, which was to respond to a one-step command without gestures. In other words, if I asked her for the fuzzy bunny, and if she was inclined to let me have it—which she often was (she was a good sharer)—she would give it to me without me needing to put my hand out, a feat most children wouldn't reach until after their first birthday, some not until after sixteen months.

Yeah, Emma was all that.

And if she hadn't been?

I couldn't imagine ever loving her any less.

Even in her absence, she still took up the whole world.

In a moment of weakness, grief-stricken at the thought that I wouldn't be there when Emma's birthday came on Christmas Eve at the end of the month, I went knocking on Tolkien's door. I knew, even as the rain pelted me as I waited for him to answer, that it was a selfish thing to do. But I'd lost Emma and losing him as well was just too hard.

Like the Good Samaritan he was, he let me in.

"I just don't understand," I said, my tears mingling with the rain that was already on my face, so you couldn't tell one from the other. "Why can't we try…?"

I reached out my arms towards him and felt him grab on to my wrists, hard. I couldn't help but wonder if it was me he needed to restrain or himself?

"Because you're always making things harder than they need to be," he said with a strangled kind of exasperation.

"It was bad enough when I first learned about your pregnancy charade," he went on. "But then, when you somehow tied it in to your not wanting to hurt Dodo, I believed you. I *wanted* to believe you. And yes, given the cast of characters in your life that you were duping, and how poorly they'd treated you in the past, I reasoned that their behavior somehow made it okay. But to dupe someone like Mary Jr.…"

"But she said she didn't mind!"

"It doesn't matter if she didn't mind! Is it okay to…I don't know, rob a bank, if the teller doesn't mind? You told unnecessary lies. And for what? Are you self-destructive?"

"I don't know." I tried to smile. "Maybe."

"Actions have consequences, Jane. You can't always get away with things that easily. Sometimes you lose."

I knew that!

"Why can't you be more like normal people, Jane?" His voice had a pleading quality as though he still wished things could somehow end differently. "Why did you have to crash someone's funeral? Why couldn't you have just…put up a flyer on the church bulletin board where the funeral took place, simply asking for what you wanted?"

"I don't know," I said, and I didn't. "Maybe I just never expect to be given what I ask for."

After that, there really didn't seem to be any more to say. I'd caused pain before. I was causing it still.

It was time for me to go.

I got on with my life.

Emma was with me all the time now. I imagined her in her new life, happy, loved. How else could I imagine her? I didn't want to think about her sad, crying, missing me, wondering where I had gone to.

So I imagined her happy, getting on with the business of living.

There comes a time when no matter how big the grief, a person has to return to work. If I didn't show my face at Churchill & Stewart soon, even though I'd been taking care of many of my responsibilities from home, I'd return to find Louise sitting in my chair. And I did need my work right now, if for no other reason than to silence the sounds from the monkeys constantly scurrying around in my brain.

I'd phoned ahead to Dodo to let her know I was coming. My hope was that in doing so, my return could be treated as just another day at the office for everybody.

Of course, it wasn't like that at all.

Every time I passed anyone in the hall, I saw a look of pity that I recognized because it was the same look I'd seen on Sophie's face at my mother's house.

But they'd get over it, I told myself. Eventually, everyone would learn to act normally around me once again. Either that, or they'd redefine normal; after all, this walking-on-eggshells treatment I was getting from everyone couldn't go on forever. It was good to be back, I told myself.

Still, did it have to turn out that on my first day back I was confronted with Schmuck and Likme?

"Simon Schmuck and his Candy are here to see you," came Hilda's voice over my phone.

"It's Smock," I pointed out. "And he doesn't have an appointment." But that didn't stop Simon and Candy from coming in anyway.

"Candy had me ask Dodo to let us know when you returned to work," Simon said, settling himself into the chair across from me as golden Candy took the chair next to him.

Candy was the only author I'd ever known who couldn't even meet with an editor without her agent present. What did she think I was going to do—bully her? Actually make her write better?

"What's wrong?" I asked a trifle testily. There was a time I would have smiled brightly at anything where an agent or author were concerned. But those days were gone. Too much had happened for me to present my feelings as anything but what they were. "Is there a problem with the cover? Have you decided to do your own author photo now, too?"

"I heard about your loss," said Candy, "and I wanted to tell you about how sorry I am."

Did *everybody* in London know my life story? Apparently, they kind of did. Simon explained. "There was an article in the *Globe* about it. Now that your book has made you a literary celebrity of sorts, and you did cancel all your interviews, some reporter, presumably annoyed at you for leaving him with print space to fill, decided to run a story on your finding and losing your foundling."

"Emma," I said. "Her name isn't 'foundling.' It's Emma."

Simon coughed, clearly embarrassed. "Of course. Emma."

Candy ignored Simon. "I wanted to come," she said, "because I've been there. I know what you're going through."

"Excuse me?" I heard her words, but they made no sense to me.

"I lost a child too." A tear came to her eye.

"How?"

"I wasn't looking." She shrugged, tried to smile, failed. "My ex and I had a bitter breakup and he lost custody. I thought he'd finally accepted that, but then one day I went to pick up Robert at school and apparently my ex had beat me there. Of course I called the police, but I haven't seen him since."

I vaguely remembered reading something in the papers about such a tragedy befalling Gayla Gladstone—maybe that was one of the reasons for wanting to change her name? A desire to start fresh?—but I couldn't remember how long ago that had been. I thought to ask her, but I couldn't bring myself to lift the spear, poke it around in the wound.

"I'm sorry."

"I know," she said, and this time she really did smile. Then she tossed her head. "But I didn't come here for sympathy. I just came to say I understand. It doesn't matter how the loss happens. It doesn't matter what the world thinks you should or shouldn't have done. In the end, the pain is just the same."

I looked at her with new respect. For an all-white-clothes, too-much-gold, fake-fur-masquerading-as-real-fur-to-make-some-bizarre-sort-of-point kind of woman, she was smart.

"Of course, there's always some good that comes out of tragedy," Candy added, spoiling my newfound respect for her nearly instantaneously. That sort of platitude-impersonating-wisdom always makes me wince with annoyance; that and the one about it being "part of God's plan," as if God were some kind of capricious bastard saying "I feel like saving you today, but today I also feel like pissing on *you*."

Yes, loss can make one bitter.

"And what might that be?" I asked Candy, tiredly, since her statement demanded the question. Then I pre-empted her response, "That tragedy makes you a better person?"

"No, of course not." She looked at me as though I were an idiot. "There's nothing across-the-board ennobling about tragedy. Tragedy sucks. But it does somehow liberate you to finally be yourself. You realize that life is simply too short to keep being someone you're not."

I was in my kitchen, doing the most uncharacteristic of things. I was making dinner.

I'd been feeling lonely but disinclined to impose on the usual suspects. David wouldn't be home anyway since it was Saturday night and you can't miss Saturday night in the restaurant business. And just Christopher without David was, oh, I don't know, like the vegetable without the main course. As for my family, although the saying goes that they are the people who, when the world turns you away, have to take you in, I still had some doubts. So I'd phoned up Dodo, who was available with no notice on a Saturday night—no surprise there.

"What would you like to do?" she'd asked over the phone. "Go to a film?"

"No," I'd said, realizing exactly what I wanted as I said it. "I want you to come here. I want to make you dinner."

And I did want to do that. Dodo had done so much for me, it was a little thing to be able to do in return.

"But, um, can you really cook, Jane?"

"I'll see if I can learn how before you get here." I tried not to sound testy, since my intentions *were* to do a nice thing.

By the time Dodo arrived, I had the water boiling for the pasta. Even if salad and pasta doesn't qualify me as the next Jamie Oliver, I'd made the dressing (balsamic vinaigrette) and the sauce (whole tomatoes, chicken, broccoli and mozzarella cheese) myself and I'd opened a nice bottle of Chianti just in case the food sucked.

I was startled, when I answered the door, to see Dodo in jeans. I'd never seen Dodo in anything other than business clothes before and it seemed somehow *wrong,* like seeing the Archbishop of Canterbury in a grass skirt or something. Of course, I had jeans on too, but that was somehow different. My jeans I wore with an old purple V-necked T-shirt I'd used when painting the flat, figuring more splatters from the sauce wouldn't show. Dodo's jeans were worn belted with a red jersey top tucked in and a silk scarf of red, white, blue and gold draped around her shoulders in a casual manner I'd never be able to perfect.

I poured Dodo a glass of the Chianti, brought it to her as she sat down on the sofa, taking my own position on the floor across the coffee table from her.

"Do you need any help?" she suggested brightly, chin going in the direction of the kitchen.

"No," I said, "the water's rolling so much, I need only stir it a time or two."

"Ah." She looked at her wineglass. "Well." She took a sip. "This is—"

"—awkward, isn't it?" I finished for her, making a face.

"Actually," she said rather primly, "I was going to say 'This is nice.'"

"And awkward." I squinched my nose a bit. "Admit it. It's awkward."

She tried to look serious. "It's…" She began to fail, a smirk creeping up on her mouth. "It's fucking *amazingly* awkward!" She burst out laughing. "Why do you think that is?"

"I don't know," I said, having laughed along until there were tears in my eyes. "Because the dynamic's different? Because we're used to having the office as our common ground and whenever we're together outside of it, we're always either surrounded by other people or are engaged in some joint purpose?"

"You're right, Jane. This is just too casual for us."

"We don't know how to do casual," I added.

And then for some reason, we were laughing again and were still laughing, off and on, as she helped me put the salad things out and kept me company as I stirred the pasta, served it on big heaping plates, and poured more wine.

"Oh, this looks good," Dodo said, picking up her fork. "And things are so much more relaxed, now that we're not—"

"Awkward anymore?" I finished again for her, which set us off laughing once again.

"Oh, we have to stop." I had one hand on my side. "My mother always used to warn that if I laughed too hard, someone would die."

"What a truly awful thing to say to a little girl," she said.

I shrugged. "Her mum probably said it to her."

"How do you think we ended up like this?" Dodo asked, serious. "Alone. You and I having dinner together. Do you think somehow our mothers—"

"Bollocks," I said, pouring us another round. "It's not our mothers' faults we're doing this on a Saturday night. A lot of it is simply the life decisions we ourselves made."

Dodo looked wistful all of a sudden. "I *liked* him, Jane," she said softly.

I knew she was talking about Stephen Triplecorn and even though I didn't like him myself, I knew that she did and that her hurt was very real.

"I know," I said, feeling helpless to help, covering her lovely hand with one of my so-so hands. "I know."

"You must mind terribly," she said, "me still feeling this way, after what he put you through."

"No." I shook my head. "You can't help it. You feel what you feel."

She picked her pasta fork up, set it down again without eating anything.

"Besides," I said, "you need to remember, we put him through a lot, too."

She laughed a bit. "Oh, but didn't we? Remember the thing with me telling him Constance was nuts?"

"And the whole thing with Stan from Accounting," I added, "and Dog With A Bone? Woof!"

She laughed harder. "And remember when Louise…" But then she stopped herself abruptly. That was too close to when things turned serious, too close to the end.

"It's okay, Dodo," I said, rubbing the back of her hand once more before taking mine away, tiredly picking up my fork again. "We did the best we could."

"What can we do now?" she asked balefully, which may have been the wine, but somehow I knew she was talking about our futures. Hers without Stephen, mine without Tolkien.

"I don't know," I said, and I didn't. But I did know one thing: I was glad to finally recognize Dodo, not just as my boss, but as my very good friend.

"Eventually," I added, "we'll think of something."

Sarah was ready to tell the rest of her story. And she wanted to tell it to Mary Jr., in my presence.

Having met Luke Johnson, Sarah's father, just once, and having seen how Mary Jr. and Sarah were together on my last visit, I could well imagine why she'd prefer to tell it to gentle Mary Jr. As for the latter, all I could be was honored that, as Mary Jr.'s friend, she trusted me too.

"Not long after Denny and I ran off, and the money ran out, I found myself pregnant."

"Oh no!" Mary Jr. couldn't help herself from exclaiming. "You must have been so scared…"

"Scared? I was bleedin' terrified. But Denny said that we'd

manage somehow. I wanted to go home, but he said that we were adults now, weren't we, with a baby coming. He kept saying it would be okay."

"What did you do?" I asked.

"He had a friend who knew someone at a clinic who was able to get some of those prenatal vitamins for me."

"But how did you live?" asked Mary Jr.

"Oh, we were still on the streets," said Sarah mildly, as if it was the most normal thing in the world.

It all seemed so foreign to me, the kind of thing that never happened to anyone you really knew. But then I thought about those people you see on the streets sometimes, about the stories you read about young girls getting in trouble and fearing to tell anyone about it, and I realized there's a whole other world that most of us are lucky enough to never have to see.

"When it got to be close to the end, I started to get really scared, that's for sure. It was December then, last December, and it was very cold out. Denny still kept saying that it was all going to be okay, but I kept saying, 'How? How is this all going to be okay?'"

I was hearing the words, but it was beyond me to imagine the reality of it.

"Denny borrowed a room in a friend's flat. He'd got a job, he said—I didn't ask doing what. And he got some books. He said that we could do it ourselves, that no one would ever need know. He said that people had been delivering their own babies at home for centuries, that it was only in modern times that people thought they needed hospitals for what women throughout time had been doing all on their own. He got his friend at the clinic to get him things, scissors…"

My mind nearly shut down at this. I didn't want to hear any more, didn't want to hear how lonely, how scary it must have been for her, giving birth in someone else's place, with no one to help her but a guy with a book and a pair of scissors.

I had to ask. "Why didn't you go to a hospital?"

Sarah shrugged. "Denny said we couldn't. That if we did, my dad or someone would come and take the baby away."

I shook my head, started to object, but then stopped at the futility of it. It was done. What point was there now in telling her that she could have done things differently, that she might have avoided some of the pain and loneliness?

"It wasn't so bad, really," said Sarah, trying to smile, failing, "but then the baby was there, she was *right there,* and I thought this was going to be the part that Denny'd kept promising about, this was the part where everything was going to be okay. Except it wasn't okay, because he began freaking out, saying that it'd been hard enough for him to keep both him and me alive, and how could he do it now with a little baby to take care of too? He couldn't do it, I couldn't do it, he said, the only way for us to keep ourselves alive was to give her up…"

Oh no.

"But we were scared of being caught." It was obviously difficult for her to say the words. "We were scared of being caught *abandoning* her, so we didn't want to bring her to the cops or to the hospital, although we knew we should. And then Denny said 'What about a church?'"

Oh no.

"And even though I was still so sore, I couldn't let him be the one to leave her there. I had to be there to make sure there would be someone on the street who would see me do it. And so that's what I did. I waited outside a church, late last Christmas Eve, when the streets were deserted, waited until I heard someone coming and then I placed her on the steps—she was so beautiful!—and moved on up the street and then turned, just in time to see a pregnant woman coming and I knew that she had to have heard my little girl cry when I'd set her down and I told myself that Denny was right, that he'd been wrong about the way in which things would become okay, but that it would somehow be okay all the same."

Oh no.

"Not long afterwards," Sarah said, visibly tired now, "Denny took off. I think the guilt did him in. And I've lived on my own ever since, until Jane's friend found me. I never stopped wondering about my baby, of course, what became of her, not for a second. But I had to stay alive, didn't I? If nothing else, Denny was right about that… I was in no position to take care of a baby. Still, I've wondered…"

I knew that in telling her, I would probably lose any remaining chance—as if there were any remaining chances—of getting Emma back. After all, if there had been one thing I'd known all along, it was that if the birth mother ever came back, there would be no contest over who would get to raise Emma. But I had to do it. Sarah had to know.

"Sarah." I put my hand gently on hers. "I think I can tell you what happened to your baby."

My fingers were shaking as I dialed Tolkien's number.

"Yes?" he answered.

"It's me," I said.

We hadn't talked since that night I'd visited him at his place. After I'd gotten home after his revelation at Mary Jr.'s, after I'd seen his things were all gone, I'd experienced a different kind of loss than the one I had upon losing Emma. It was a separate ache altogether. I'd thought of the last time we'd made love—an uncharacteristically solemn lovemaking, and yet of course there had been some laughter; there was always laughter—and I didn't want to let myself think, didn't want to wrap my mind around the impossible idea that it was the last time I would make love with him in this lifetime.

But that night I'd visited him in the rain, I'd been forced to recognize that that was exactly the way things were going to be.

"What do you want?" he asked.

I told him what had happened, how, through listening to Sarah's tale, I'd come to realize that the baby I'd found had been her baby. Emma was her child.

"What did you do?" he asked.

"I told her," I said. "And then I called Stephen Triplecorn. And then I left before he could arrive with Emma."

"That must have been hard for you," he said.

I suppose he could have been referring to any single one of those things. But they'd all been hard, each in their own awful way. There was no point belaboring it, however. There weren't enough words in the English language to describe just how hard it all had been.

"Yes" was all I had left to cover it.

"Well," he said, "thank you for calling."

"I just thought you'd want to know. After all, you loved her, you *love* her too."

I lay on my bed, alone, imagining Emma's return to the Johnsons.

I allowed myself to picture what Emma's homecoming had been like, her coming to the home of someone other than me.

Before, when they'd taken her from me, I hadn't allowed myself to picture Emma with her new foster family, not really, because a part of me still entertained the small hope that the situation might somehow be temporary, that fortune could somehow be reversed.

But now I had to face the facts: Emma was with her real family. There was no turning back from this.

They would all be so excited to see her, of course, Sarah, Mary Jr., Luke—all the Johnsons. She belonged to them. Something Sarah had believed was missing forever, something the rest hadn't even known was theirs, had returned.

And how would Emma feel? How *had* Emma felt, that first time Stephen Triplecorn had taken her, after she'd lived with me for ten months, after ten months of knowing me as the center of her world, as she'd been mine?

I knew that, if she never saw me again, she wouldn't remember me, not years later; I'd just be a story people told her. Or didn't tell her. But what about now, right now, after six, seven, eight weeks? Did she remember me still?

I *knew* that Emma would be happy with the Johnsons. I *knew* that if I wanted to, they'd let me come visit her; Mary Jr. had said as much. I *knew* that it would kill me to watch Emma grow up at a remove, a visitor to her life.

I did not know if I could bear that.

I pictured myself, at some point, doing the Jane thing: standing on the street across from Mary Jr.'s place or going to the playground Christopher had made for the kids, watching, waiting, hoping to get a glimpse of Emma.

But then I realized that whatever I saw would break my heart: if Emma looked as though she'd grown unhappy without me, my heart would break in one helpless direction; if she looked happy, relieved as I would be by that, my heart would break in a different, selfish direction.

And the ultimate truth had not escaped me. Whatever I'd done, no matter what—if I had never been the fake-pregnancy woman, if I'd been the most normal person in the world when I found Emma on those church steps, if I'd been the blessed Virgin Mary—Sarah would have still come home. Sarah would still have decided, as she had clearly done, that she wanted Emma back.

No matter what I'd done, I would have still lost Em.

December 24, last chapter

Stephen Triplecorn had called to say he wanted to see me in his office, that the Johnsons had wanted a meeting.

I was in a dither.

I called Tolkien.

"Please come with me," I said. "They probably want to arrest me for never having done the right thing in the first place."

And Tolkien, perhaps feeling guilty about his own part in that—he had, after all, fixed all of Stephen Triplecorn's parking problems, so that he'd be more amenable to cutting me a little slack—agreed.

Then, for good measure, I called up David and Christopher, and Dodo, hoping for some extra support.

Against what? I didn't know. I guess I figured that if I got enough people who knew me in one room, one of them was bound to be willing to speak up for my character.

Dodo was the only one who objected.

"I don't want to see him again," she said, "not after what he did to you."

What was left unsaid was that she also didn't want to see him again because of how she still felt, because of what seeing him would do to her.

But I was feeling selfish. "Please, Dodo," I said. "Do it for me. If they're going to have me arrested, I'm going to need all the friends there that I can get."

"All right, Jane," she said, "if it's what you want."

When I arrived at the office, they were all already there. The one thing I hadn't counted on, however, was...

"Mama!" It was Emma, her face lit up with glee, straining to get away from Sarah and come to me.

She hadn't forgotten me at all.

"She's been asking for you ever since he brought her back to us," said Sarah, nodding at Stephen Triplecorn, a sad look on her face. "We tried to tell her that I was her mum now, but she wasn't having any."

"You're the only mother she's ever known," said Mary Jr., gently, sadly. "You took care of her from nearly the moment she was born, did everything for her. She loves you more than anybody."

"Mama!"

"It's not right, us keeping her," said Mary Jr. "It's not right to take her off the track that she's been set on."

"What do you want, Sarah?" Stephen Triplecorn asked.

Sarah looked at Emma long and hard, with such a look of wistful longing, but then she tore her eyes away.

"I want to go back to school," she said. "I don't want to live hard anymore. I want to go back to school, get a good job, have something better. And, one day, if I'm very lucky, I want to have another baby, one I can properly care for."

I couldn't believe what I was hearing.

From birth, due to circumstances neither of us had chosen, our life paths, Sarah's and mine, had been on different tracks, each somehow lacking an important ingredient.

In my case, I had education, an adult life, successful career and the support of those around me, whether I deserved it at all times or not. And yet I was certainly willing to give up those things or modify the time devoted to them, if that's what was somehow called for in caring for Emma. I was yet smart enough to realize that it was having had those things that made it possible for me to sacrifice them.

Sarah's situation was almost the reverse. She had an incomplete education, an interrupted teenaged life and no certainty that she'd ever even have a career, although she clearly wanted one. I will say this, she had a family who obviously loved her. It was apparent from the way Mary Jr. and her parents stood by her. Whatever she decided, they would give her their full support.

For me what was lacking was another being that I could put whole-heartedly ahead of my selfish self; in Emma, I had that. For Sarah, what was lacking was the simple time that a few more years might have given her to feel confident enough in herself to reach for that which was already there. And so…

Sarah took in a great lungful of air. "I want Jane to keep Emma," she said.

"Are you sure?" Stephen Triplecorn asked.

"We're sure," said Mary Jr. gently, speaking for Sarah, who had tears in her eyes.

"But maybe Sarah's parents would like to—" Stephen Triplecorn tried again, looking this time questioningly at Luke and his wife.

"No," said Mary Jr. firmly. "It would be one thing if Emma were still a newborn. Do you honestly think we don't *want* to keep her, that we wouldn't *love* to keep her with us if it were reasonably possible? But Jane had her for *ten months*. Not ten days. Not ten weeks. *Ten months*. To do anything else, to try to keep her, would just be too selfish."

Stephen Triplecorn looked at me.

"You can keep her, Jane," he finally said. "Of course, there will be formalities, but once it's known that this is what Emma's birth family wants…"

Sarah handed her to me, carefully avoiding looking at Emma, as if she were already taking steps into a different future, and I saw Dodo looking at Stephen Triplecorn and he back at her. Somehow I knew that, in time, things would work out for them.

Then I looked at this little person who had once been dependent on me, who would now be dependent on me again, and I realized that however far I'd come, however much better I ever became, I would never be good enough for the grace of her, and yet, whatever I was, it had to be enough.

I had one of the two things I wanted most in the world. It was time to reach for the second. It was time to ask for what I wanted straightforwardly.

I looked at Tolkien.

"Will you marry me?"